# "Taylor! W                    s

He felt the tears welling up in his eyes. "Come on now, buddy, wake up. Taylor, God damn you. You hear me? I ain't gonna let you die on me, now. Not now. Not after all we been through together. What am I gonna tell your folks?"

Clovis squatted, oblivious to the fact that he might be exposing himself to more fire. "Medic!" he screamed. "Oh, Jesus, somebody get me some help over here. Medic!"

Clovis glared at the impassive elephant grass, glared at the APC still retreating from the scene of the senseless killing.

"Oh, God damn you to hell, you murderin' bastards," he yelled helplessly after the track. "You gook, dink, ARVN cowards! Damn you and your whole stinkin' dink country! We oughtta let the goddamned gooks have it! You hear me? We oughtta give 'em the damned place, and let 'em kick the likes of you out of it!"

Clovis cradled Taylor's shattered head gently between his hands and softly rocked his friend in his lap.

"Come on, Taylor, don't die. Please, buddy. Please. Wake up, now. Come on, Taylor, wake up."

## VIETNAM: GROUND ZERO

# THE FALL OF CAMP A-555

## ERIC HELM

## A GOLD EAGLE BOOK FROM
# W✺RLDWIDE

TORONTO • NEW YORK • LONDON • PARIS
AMSTERDAM • STOCKHOLM • HAMBURG
ATHENS • MILAN • TOKYO • SYDNEY

First edition February 1987

ISBN 0-373-62704-1

Printed in Canada

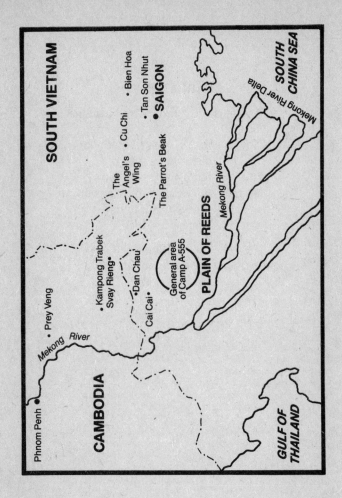

# VIETNAM: GROUND ZERO
# THE FALL OF CAMP A-555

# PROLOGUE

Major David Rittenour was not a happy man.

In the past half-dozen years that he'd been ferrying assorted Very Important People around the globe, he'd always been lucky enough to draw good air and ground crews and nice, fairly new aircraft that were outfitted more like commercial airliners than military cargo transports. On the whole, it had been good duty, with just enough layovers in interesting cities to make up for all the other times spent waiting for hours on some hot concrete runway at some out-of-the-way military air base, drinking undrinkable Army, Navy or Air Force coffee from paper cups too thin to prevent burning one's hand. During the past three years he'd been based in Maryland and had spent a lot of time flying the big boys from the Pentagon transatlantic to England, Germany and Holland. That had been plum duty. He'd even reached the point where he didn't mind the late-night phone calls that got him out of a nice warm bed with his nice warm wife and sent him hurrying off to the base, usually in bad weather, to haul some VIP over to Europe to deal with NATO's latest real or imagined crisis.

But nothing good lasts forever, and when the bad news came, it had been very bad indeed. Orders to a liaison outfit in Vietnam. It sounded like the kind of thing that could get a man killed.

So Rittenour had been pleasantly surprised when he'd found out that his duties would be flying VIPs around Southeast Asia, instead of serving as a forward air controller. The life expectancy of an FAC in combat was about two minutes. Rittenour knew that he was a lot less likely to get shot at chauffeuring some Saigon biggie. It could happen, but as a rule, generals and senior colonels getting ready to turn into generals didn't much like going out to play in the war. They had much more important work to do—shuffling papers and carrying their briefcases around and playing tennis with the distinguished members of the Saigon press corps.

All in all, Rittenour couldn't believe his luck. Until he saw the aircraft they'd assigned him. A beat-up old de Havilland Otter with a great radial-piston engine in the nose that you couldn't see over during takeoff and landing because the damned aircraft was a tail dragger. Christ! Nobody flew tail draggers anymore. Besides, it was noisy, and when it worked, the engine had an alarming tendency to miss at unexpected moments; the goddamned machine sat up much too high, was awkward to steer on the ground and handled in the air like a pregnant sow. And to top it all off, the cursed monster wasn't even made in America.

Rittenour nicknamed it The Antichrist.

And then they gave him this particular mission.

"Just a single passenger, old boy. Very important, very hush-hush. Better if you don't know who, exactly. We want you to fly him over to Phnom Penh for us. Some important business to conduct there. Very important. Very hush-hush. Better if you don't know what, exactly. Just be out at the airport ready to go at 2100 hours tonight. You'll be there two or three days. Think of it as a little R and R. We've booked a room for you at the Continental. You'll be called when he's ready to come back. Oh, one more thing, old boy. Be in the plane when he gets there—he doesn't like to be kept waiting. And just mind you, keep the cockpit curtain pulled, will you? Better if you don't actually *see* whom you're carrying. Safer all the way around that way."

Jesus! You'd have thought they were a goddamned bunch of British secret agents the way they'd carried on!

But Rittenour knew how to follow orders, so he'd gone out to Tan Son Nhut at the designated time and met his copilot, a captain called Jones. Jones, indeed. His captain's bars were just a little too new and shiny for Rittenour's liking, and his hair seemed a bit too long to meet military regulations. Besides, the man appeared a shade unconcerned about what was going on. But what really took the cake, as far as Rittenour was concerned, was Jones's apparent unfamiliarity with the Otter, especially when Rittenour learned that Jones was supposed to have been flying one for as long as he said he had.

Rittenour thought the whole thing smelled just a bit, but that was okay with him. They could play their damned spy games if they wanted to and carry on like a bunch of junior-grade James Bonds for all he cared. He was just an airplane jockey. Besides, it was a chance to see Phnom Penh, although what he'd do there for two or three days he couldn't imagine. Maybe the mysterious Captain Jones would know of a few good night spots there. He looked the type.

At any rate, right on time a jeepful of men in uniforms, with stark-white helmet liners and armbands that alleged they were MPs, pulled up and surrounded the airplane. One of them, wearing new lieutenant's bars, came aboard to make sure that they were ready to go and that the cockpit curtain was pulled.

"The general doesn't like to be disturbed," he told Rittenour. "Just stay in the cockpit and follow your orders. You'll be met at the other end." And then he left.

Five minutes later a closed Army van pulled onto the field, and a man carrying a briefcase and wearing an Army raincoat, in spite of the heat and the fact that there wasn't a sign of a cloud in the sky, got out of the back. He wore his hat low over his eyes, and Rittenour couldn't see his face clearly, although he could see the scrambled eggs on the bill of the hat.

The man shook hands briefly with another figure who remained in the van, invisible and with the MP lieutenant. Then the man in the raincoat climbed aboard. The lieutenant closed the door and made a cranking gesture with his hand. At this the MPs all got back into their jeep and drove away, followed by the van.

The flight to Phnom Penh was uneventful, and the enigmatic Captain Jones uninformative. Rittenour had to pry conversation out of the man, who exhibited an uncanny knack for answering everything in grunts and monosyllables.

When they landed, a carbon copy of the closed van and escort jeep was waiting for them, and their mysterious passenger was whisked away before Rittenour had completed the shutdown checklist.

As they exited the aircraft, Rittenour made one last attempt to crack Jones's cold shell.

"Well, Captain," said Rittenour, "I guess that's it for the next forty-eight hours or so. What say we check into the hotel and go have ourselves a couple of Scotches on the rocks?"

"Sorry, Major, but you'll have to excuse me," Jones replied. "I'm not billeted with you."

Jones turned and walked a short distance to where a yellow Toyota sedan was parked next to a hangar. There was a Cambodian dressed in civilian clothes behind the wheel. Jones got into the back, and the Cambodian drove off, leaving Rittenour standing beneath the wing of the aircraft holding his flight bag.

# 1

UNNAMED VILLAGE
NEAR AN KHE, REPUBLIC
OF VIETNAM
JANUARY 31, 1966

"Hey, Taylor! You got any idea where the fuck we are?" asked Clovis, shifting the heavy M-60 machine gun on its padded shoulder sling. The fifty-round short belt of disintegrating metal links and 7.62 mm cartridges, every fifth round a tracer, clinked slightly against the side of the machine gun's receiver. Clovis ignored the A-gunner and ammo bearer humping through the thick, tall elephant grass with him. They were green meat, less than a week and a half in-country. You couldn't expect a couple of FNGs to know anything.

Off to the left Taylor shrugged, breaking open his M-79 blooper and ramming a 40 mm high-explosive grenade into the chamber. He snapped the action of the grenade launcher shut, double-checked the safety, then fiddled momentarily with the sights. Like Clovis, he was a pro, having spent five weeks in-country. And he'd been involved in three firefights.

"Lookin' for gooks, Clovis, just like always. Lookin' for gooks and tryin' to find them before they find us."

"I meant geographically speaking," said Clovis.

Taylor flashed Clovis a smile and gestured expansively with his hand. "In the Nam, Clovis, in the Nam. Land of eternal summer. Land of eternal rain. Land of eternal steaming jungle and freezing mountaintop. Fragrant land of feces-fertilized rice paddy and endless reeded plain.''

''Shee-it! Man, there you go waxin' poetic on me again, when all I want is a simple answer to a simple question, like where the fuck are we. We're goin' into a ville what ain't got no name on the lootenant's map, and when I ask the only guy in the squad's got any sense of di-rection if he's got any idea where the fuck we are, you go to waxin' poetic on me.''

''The lieutenant letting you interpret his maps for him now, is he?'' asked Taylor, still grinning.

''Shee-it!'' said Clovis again, shrugging and spitting into the elephant grass over his right shoulder, barely missing the ammo bearer. Both the ammo bearer and the A-gunner looked at Clovis and Taylor as if they were dinky dau. They'd been in Vietnam long enough to know what that meant.

''Hell, Clovis,'' said Taylor, finally serious. ''What difference does it make? Don't matter if it's Moc Phuc or Bebop. It's a ville, just like all the other villes. It's got people in it, and we're gonna go see if they're friendly or hostile, just like we do with all the other people.'' He shrugged. ''Anyway, I reckon we're about ten klicks east of An Khe. I think that puts us in Binh Dinh Province, if I remember the map they showed us at Fort Polk right. Wherever we are, we're with the Twelfth of the First, and that puts us in a world of shit. Right?''

''Right!'' chuckled Clovis. ''The man is right. Hey, Taylor, if you was any more right, you'd be Barry Goldwater, I reckon.''

Taylor grinned back at the lanky machine gunner from the bluegrass hills of Kentucky. ''Now that, Clovis, is not a bad idea. Not at all. Because if I *was* Barry Goldwater, I sure as hell wouldn't be out here in the boonies with you.''

Clovis laughed. ''Barry, baby, take me with you when you go.''

''Back to that horse-breeding farm in Kentucky your folks got?''

''Nah, man. I wanna go to Iowa with ya, see one of them hog-and cattle-breedin' farms. Your folks got a farm, Taylor?''

''Sorry to disappoint you, Clovis. My folks live in town. Dad works for the post office.''

Clovis looked disappointed, then brightened. ''I'll go to Iowa with ya, anyway. Maybe there's some poon up there needs breedin'. Hey, Taylor, you got a sister?''

"Sure, Clovis. She'll be a year old in two days. Want to meet her?"

"Ugh! No, thanks. That's a bit too young for my taste. I like my women a bit more mature, say fifteen, sixteen. Fourteen, at the very least."

"Why fourteen?"

"Age of consent in Kentucky, man. Don't want to be messin' with no jailbait."

"Better set your sights on an older woman, Clovis. You try messing with that shit in Iowa, you'll wind up a jailbird or lying in some farmer's cornfield with a load of buckshot up your ass."

"All right, then, an older woman it is. How old they gotta be in Iowa to be legal game?"

"I don't know. Eighteen, maybe?"

"Eighteen. Shee-it! Man, that's almost as old as us."

"Clovis, just how old are you and Taylor?" asked the A-gunner.

"Nineteen. Nineteen and a half. Grandpappy Taylor over there's pushin' twenty-one."

The A-gunner looked blank, then stared at the ammo bearer, who scrunched up his shoulders and gave him an oh-well look. "Christ! I'm nineteen. Conrad's nearly nineteen. We figured you guys were a lot older than that."

Clovis wondered for a moment who Conrad was, then remembered that was the name of the new ammo bearer. "Give it a month and a half, uh, Malizuski." He'd had to search for the name of the A-gunner, as well. "After a month or two in the Nam, even green meat like you will start lookin' old."

Malizuski couldn't decide if he'd been complimented or insulted. He started to ask, but Clovis hushed him.

"You boys keep quiet now, and stay alert. We're gettin' close to the ville."

"You think there'll be VC in the village, Clovis?" It was a stupid thing to ask, but Malizuski couldn't help it. It was his first patrol, and he was scared.

"I don't know," answered the sixty gunner. "Maybe, maybe not. You and Conrad just stick close and keep your heads. Taylor and me will look out for ya."

They pushed on through the tall grass, feeling the sweat running down their bodies as the sun blazed high in the late-morning sky. The only sounds now were the clank and tinkle of equipment belts and weapons and the steady swish-swish of men pushing through the elephant grass.

There was a sharp metallic clank, and Clovis glanced over toward Taylor in time to see him stuffing a big, flat, black pistol back into the waistband of his fatigue trousers behind his equipment belt. Clovis knew it was a Star 9 mm, a copy of the Army-issue Colt 1911A1, but with a flatter grip because it took the smaller parabellum rounds instead of the big .45s.

Taylor had brought it with him when he came back from leave, Clovis remembered now, just before they shipped over together from the States. It was illegal under Army regulations, but Taylor had smuggled it over in a shaving kit. He'd taken the contents out of the kit, replacing them with the pistol, a couple of spare magazines and two fifty-round boxes of ammunition. Clovis had tried to talk him out of bringing it when they'd left Fort Ord, afraid his buddy would get caught with it and get into trouble. They'd been together since basic at Fort Leonard Wood.

"Hell, Clovis, what they going to do to me?" Taylor had asked him. "Send me to Vietnam?"

"Army's got plenty of guns. They'll give you one. You don't need another," Clovis had argued. But that first night in-country at the Long Binh Repo Depot when the Vietcong had mortared the transient barracks, Clovis had been mighty glad Taylor had brought the pistol, even if it did turn out they hadn't actually needed it. Because they were being mortared, and it was the only friggin' gun in the entire barracks because the friggin' Army hadn't seen fit to issue them rifles yet.

The next morning, as they stood in line waiting for their assignments, they heard the administrative specialist sitting behind the desk asking each man if he could type. The administrative specialist was getting a lot of noes and blank stares for answers.

"Hey, Taylor, you reckon we oughtta tell him we can type?" Clovis whispered.

"Can you?"

"Sure. I ain't fast, but I reckon thirty-five, forty, words a minute. You?"

"About the same, I guess."

"You reckon we oughtta tell him, then?"

"I don't know, Clovis. I don't think I'm going to. You do whatever you think is right."

"Not going to? Why not? Don't you want a cushy job? These puds probably get every other weekend off and go down to Saigon and chase poon."

"Yeah, I know. But do you really want to go back home to Kentucky and tell your girl and folks that all you did in the war was type out forms and chase poon around Saigon?"

"Can either of you guys type?" asked the administrative specialist as they stepped up to the desk.

"Not me," said Taylor. "What's a typewriter? All they taught us at AIT was weapons and tactics. Didn't say anything about needing to type."

"Yeah," echoed Clovis. He tapped the infantry badge pinned to his chest. "See, man, we're ground pounders. All we know how ta do is kill Commies and gooks."

The administrative specialist, a spec five with thick, Army-issue glasses and a bad case of acne, laid down his black plastic Army-issue pen and stared up at them.

"A couple of smart asses, huh?" said the spec five. "Well, smart asses, I'm going to fix your smart asses for you. I'm going to send you up to the First Air Cav at An Khe. What do you think of that?"

"What's An Khe?" asked Clovis.

The spec five looked at them. He smiled. "It's a meat grinder."

The spec five had been right.

When Clovis and Taylor arrived at An Khe Combat Base aboard the big CH-47 Chinook helicopter, First Air Cav's Third Brigade was still licking its wounds from the bloody battle for control of the Ia Drang Valley in late October and November and Second Brigade was picking up the slack. Something big was in the works. Second Brigade was being pumped up for it while Division did its best to rebuild the Third, and Clovis and Taylor both got posted to Bravo Company, Second Battalion, of Second Brigade's Twelfth Regiment, which was light because it had taken what Saigon and the Pentagon called moderate casualties the week before.

A first sergeant listened to their request to be assigned to the same platoon if possible. He said it didn't make a damned bit of difference to him and had no trouble finding a platoon that needed two replacements. There was just one catch. They didn't need riflemen—they needed a sixty gunner and a grenadier. Take it or leave it. Clovis and Taylor took it. They'd been together since basic. They weren't going to break up the partnership now.

That night they drew bunker duty on the berm line with Guffey and Erickson, a couple of pros who'd been there nearly four months already. About ten o'clock Charlie decided to probe the perimeter, but first he decided to soften things up a bit with a combination rocket and mortar attack. One of the 140 mm rockets landed directly on their bunker, collapsing it. Clovis and Taylor, who had been near the entrance, were eventually able to claw their way free of the ruptured sandbags and shattered timbers. Guffey and Erickson were not so lucky. It was Clovis and Taylor's second day in-country, and they had just been given a little Christmas present from the VC. It was December twenty-fifth.

"Man, I sure do wonder whatever happened to them typewriters," Clovis told Taylor after the shelling had stopped. He was sitting on the lip of the smoking, ruined bunker while a medic bandaged the cut on his forehead caused by a shrapnel graze.

"Cheer up, Clovis, it's bound to get better," Taylor told him. "Besides, look at it this way. You been here just two days, and already you earned yourself a Purple Heart. That ought to really impress those girls back in Kentucky."

"I hope you're right, man."

"Course I am. Women love a man in uniform, especially if he's got the Purple Heart pinned on it. Shows he was really there where the fighting was."

"I meant about it gettin' better," said Clovis. "Sure hope you're right about that."

But Taylor hadn't been. They'd been out on three patrols since that night, and each time the patrol had taken *moderate* casualties, which meant they'd got the shit kicked out of them.

And in between patrols they'd sweated during the day and frozen at night. They'd expected the sweating. After all, it was the Nam, but nobody had told them the place had mountains.

And then finally the big show got started. Operation Masher the brass called it. It had the Cav and the ARVN and the ROKs, and the Marines were supposed to be running a show of their own over in Qui Nhon Province, thousands of men in the field all at once. It was like an elephant looking to crush a rat. And like the elephant and the rat, you can't fix the enemy if you can't find him.

So today, like every day for the past week, they looked for gooks. Today it was in the high elephant grass choking the floor of a valley. Yesterday they had searched the jungle up on the slopes. The day before that they'd waded the grass sea of a different valley and the day before that some other mountain's slopes. It was all same-same. You looked for gooks, and you hoped you didn't find them because when you did, somebody you knew died.

Ahead, Clovis could barely make out the outline of a building through the elephant grass. It had to be a building of a pretty good size to stick up over the top of the grass like that, he thought. He wondered what such a large building was doing in a ville that didn't have any name on the map. He glanced left again, making sure Taylor was still there, then checked his position on line to the right. Conrad and Malizuski were muttering nervously to each other, and he had to shush them.

"Goddammit, ya dumb asses. Shut the fuck up. Want the gooks to hear us comin'?" Then, for some inexplicable reason, he softened it. "It'll be okay, Mal. Just hang in here tight and stay loose. If the shootin' starts, get down and put out rounds. Just like on the rifle range. Fire at the muzzle flashes if ya can see any. Nothin' to it."

The grass ahead was thinning, and he could see the building clearly now. It was a two-story structure that looked as if it might have been made out of poured concrete. The corrugated tin roof had rusted, and the rays from the sun high overhead glinted off the reddish-brown tin, giving the roof a golden look. There was a walled courtyard in front of the building, and through breaks in the wall he could see weeds growing in tangled profusion. It might have been an old Spanish mission in Arizona or an abandoned tourist hotel in Mexico if it hadn't been in the Nam. Clovis decided it had probably been a school or an administrative building of some kind left behind by the French. It didn't look as if anybody had lived there for a long time.

Somewhere far off the right Clovis could hear the low rumble of the M-113 APC engines as the ARVN Mechanized Infantry unit assigned to support them jockeyed their tracks into position. Clovis didn't like that. If he could hear the noise, the gooks in the village could, too, assuming there were any gooks in the village. In fact, Clovis wasn't too crazy about the whole idea of having the ARVN support them. After all, it was the ARVN's war. The Americans should be supporting the ARVN, not the other way around. Besides, you couldn't trust the ARVN.

A lot of their officers were corrupt cowards and you never knew if they'd stand and fight or run when the shooting started, and when the officers bugged out, the NCOs and grunts usually weren't far behind. It wasn't that the ARVN couldn't fight. If they had good leadership, some of the ranger units were really STRAC, and the South Viet Marines were supposed to be pretty good, too, but with the ARVN you just never knew for sure. If the leadership was good, which wasn't often, they'd fight; if not, they wouldn't. Worse yet, some of them might be, probably *were* Vietcong. The ARVN uniform meant nothing since the VC did its best to infiltrate all ARVN units and foment unrest among the troops, and there was no way you could tell the gooks from the dinks.

Maybe none of it would matter, though. Maybe the village would turn out to be abandoned, and it would be a skate, just a nice, easy walk-through. It sure *looked* abandoned. Or maybe the villagers would be friendly. Clovis didn't think so. There weren't many friendly villes around here. If there were, the unit wouldn't be out here looking for gooks.

Suddenly there was a great whoosh followed by a shattering explosion, and Clovis felt a wave of heat wash over him. B-40 rocket. He felt something sting his leg, but he ignored it, hosing down the building in front of him with the M-60 to give the others time to get down. Then the short belt ran out, and he dropped into the grass, hollering for Malizuski to bring him a belt of ammo, as he knocked open the cover on the M-60. Ahead he could hear the staccato bursts of RPDs and the ragged chugging of a heavy machine gun, while around him the pop and rattle of M-16s built slowly, punctuated by the bloop of Taylor's M-79.

"Malizuski! Where the hell is that ammo?" yelled Clovis.

Silently cursing the FNG, Clovis glanced over to see why Malizuski wasn't bringing the ammo. The A-gunner was lying very still in the grass, his uniform covered with blood. Conrad was sitting up next to him, staring dumbly at his own hands, which were dripping with Malizuski's blood.

"Conrad, you idiot, get down!" Clovis yelled at him, but it was too late. A long burst from an RPD caught Conrad across the chest, ripping him apart, and he tumbled backward into the elephant grass.

Swearing under his breath, Clovis shrugged out of the ammunition belt that was wrapped around his shoulders, fed it into the M-60 and got the machine gun back into action. Without an assistant gunner he couldn't use his left hand to hold the buttstock tight in against his shoulder. He had to manage the weapon as best he could with one hand, using the left to hold the belt and keep it from kinking so that the rounds would feed in smoothly.

He fired in short, controlled bursts, making it more difficult for the enemy to distinguish his muzzle flash from those of the M-16s firing around him. That way the VC wouldn't concentrate their fire on his position. Somewhere nearby another B-40 crashed into the company. Taylor blooped another round out of his grenade launcher in reply and crawled over to help Clovis, stopping long enough to check the new guys and dragging a couple of their ammo cans with him over to his friend.

"New guys have had it," said Taylor unnecessarily. He had to shout to make himself heard over the noise of the guns. He shoved the ammo cans up to where Clovis could get hold of them. "Your leg's bleeding. I'll have a look at it." He bent to check the injury while Clovis continued to engage the enemy.

Bullets popped and whined overhead as Taylor pulled out his old Case hunting knife and slit open Clovis's trouser leg. There was a ragged tear about an inch and a half deep across the back of the calf muscle but no sign of an embedded bullet or shrapnel. There was a fair amount of blood, but at least it wasn't spurting. Taylor pulled a field dressing from the first-aid pouch on his web gear and tied the compress tightly over the wound. Then he sheathed the knife and crawled forward to help Clovis with the M-60.

That was when they started taking fire from the bunkers hidden in the elephant grass on their flank.

They were caught in a cross fire. They knew that, if they tried to move forward and assault the village, they'd be cut to ribbons, and if they stayed put, that damned B-40 launcher would chew them up. They could hear Sergeant Stryker yelling for them to fall back, and they passed the word. Taylor loosed a final M-79 round at an open window of the two-story building, and he and Clovis began low-crawling toward the rear, dragging the machine gun between them.

They moved like this for nearly two hundred meters through the elephant grass, a task that should have taken them fifteen or twenty minutes at the most. Instead, it took them nearly two hours. Five times they were pinned down, unable to move forward or backward because of the cross fire from the bunkers and the village.

The VC had built the bunkers so low to the ground that it was almost impossible to see them, let alone bring effective fire on them. Calling in artillery or air support was out of the question. There was a whole series of bunkers scattered throughout the elephant grass, and the company, indeed, the whole second Battalion, was caught in among them.

To have called in shells or bombs would have caused more deaths among the Americans than among the Vietcong. Always assuming, of course, that there was still an officer or an NCO alive and with a working radio to adjust the arty or direct the air strike. The air was filled with the acrid smell of nitrocellulose, and a thick blue gunpowder haze clung to the top of the elephant grass like ground fog. Confusion reigned, and the men were alone.

"Goddamned motherfuckers," swore Clovis as a ragged burst from a twelve-seven tore holes in the air not more than three or four inches above their heads. If the sixty had been set up on its bipod, one of the rounds would have gotten it for sure. Both men had long since slipped the harness on their field packs and were dragging them.

"Easy, man," Taylor told him. "Just stay cool. We'll get out of this shit yet."

"It's these goddamned buttons on my uniform," Clovis answered. "The mothers are holdin' me up too high."

Taylor laughed, and Clovis risked a glance in his direction.

"What the hell's so funny, man? I don't see no humor in gettin' our asses shot off."

"I was just thinking," said Taylor. "I was just thinking that those typewriters sure would look good right now. Maybe we should have told that spec five we could type."

Clovis snorted. "I'll tell you what would look good right now. An ice-cold beer would look good. Man, I sure could use a beer."

"Forget that shit, Clovis. Damned gooks'd just shoot a hole in it before you could drink it."

"There it is," agreed Clovis. "I would like to know where the fuck those ARVN tracks are, though. We sure as hell could use a little armored support right now."

"Might as well forget that, too. Those pieces of junk are worthless against anything but shell fragments. Even an AK round will punch right through the side of one. Doesn't go all the way through, of course. Just punches into the troop compartment and rattles around the inside walls for a while until it's spent. Or hits somebody."

Clovis snorted again. "At least the fuckers could put out a little suppression. They got fifties on 'em, for Christ's sake."

The firing shifted as the twelve-seven gunner found somebody else whose life he could make interesting for a few moments, and Clovis and Taylor edged forward again. They made about another twenty-five yards, although Clovis couldn't have said which way they were crawling, down low in the elephant grass like that. He hoped Taylor's uncanny sense of direction was working. At any rate, nobody was shooting at them any longer, and they seemed to be moving away from the sound of most of the firing.

Clovis was just beginning to think they might actually get out of the mess alive when they unexpectedly pushed their way into a small elongated clearing. Before they could back away, two VC pushed their way into the open on the other side.

There wasn't time to shout a warning. Clovis made a desperate grab for the M-60, but his frame of reference seemed to have shifted into slow motion. He could see everything with a sudden crystal clarity. The two VC were both carrying SKS carbines, and one of them had his up to his shoulder and was swinging on them while the other enemy brought his weapon up. Clovis knew he was going to be too late getting the M-60 into action.

Two sharp reports, and it was time to die.

It took Clovis a moment to realize that it was the Vietcongs' time to die, not his and his buddy's. He watched both the enemy soldiers tumble backward and lie still in the elephant grass, their outstretched legs still sticking into the clearing. Gradually he became aware of the Star semiautomatic pistol in Taylor's hand. He'd beaten them all.

"Nice shootin'," said Clovis appreciatively.

Taylor stared at the two inert bodies for a second. "Yeah. Now let's get the hell out of here before somebody else starts shooting."

They backed off from the clearing, raised slightly to a high-crawl since it offered more speed and moved.

They crawled about another thirty yards before Taylor spotted something ahead of them in the grass and craned his neck for a better look. As he did so, Clovis heard the unmistakable double clang of a .50-caliber bolt slamming home, chambering a round and cocking the weapon.

"Don't shoot, ya stupid bastards!" yelled Clovis. "We're Americans!"

A short burst erupted from the fifty. One of the rounds caught Taylor, picked him up off the ground and dropped him like a sack of onions.

Clovis buried the side of his face in the dirt and screamed at the unseen gunner. "Don't shoot! Don't shoot! Americans! Don't shoot!"

The shooting stopped, and Clovis could hear the sound of an APC revving up.

"Don't shoot!" he yelled again, digging frantically in his rucksack for a smoke grenade. He found the grenade, popped it and watched it billow yellow smoke. "Don't shoot! We're Americans!" He heard the grinding of gears and the crushing sounds of the APC backing away from them in the elephant grass.

"Fucking ARVN shitheads!" he yelled futilely. He checked Taylor. A single round from the .50 caliber had caught him in the front of the helmet, making a big neat hole. It had made an even bigger not very neat hole coming out the back of his helmet.

"Taylor! Wake up!" cried Clovis, feeling the tears well up in his eyes. "Come on now, buddy, wake up. You hear me? I ain't gonna let you die on me, now. Not now. Not after all we been through together. What am I gonna tell your folks?"

Uselessly he shook his dead friend. "Taylor, you wake up now, goddammit!"

Clovis squatted, oblivious to the fact that he might be exposing himself to more fire. "Medic!" he screamed. "Oh, Jesus, somebody get me some help over here. Medic!"

Clovis stared at the impassive elephant grass, glared at the APC still retreating from the scene of the senseless killing.

"Oh, God damn you to hell, you murderin' bastards," he yelled helplessly after the track. "God damn you, you motherfuckin' gook, dink, ARVN cowards! Damn you and your whole stinkin' dink country! We oughtta let the goddamned gooks have it! You hear me? We oughtta give 'em the damned place and let 'em kick the likes of you out of it! Fuckin' bunch of dink ARVN shit-heads!"

Clovis cradled Taylor's shattered head gently between his hands and softly rocked his friend in his lap.

"Come on, Taylor, don't die. Please, buddy. Please. Wake up, now. Come on, Taylor, wake up."

# 2

"Wake up! Wake up!"

The images of Vietcong soldiers swam before his tired eyes. He could see it all so clearly, like a series of stop-action photographs. The soldier on the left, his carbine up and swinging toward them, the other one just beginning to raise his rifle, and then the two bright puffs of red, drilling each man neatly in the center of his chest.

"Captain Gerber, sir, I'm sorry to disturb you, but could you please wake up? General Crinshaw is on the radio, and he wants to talk to you. And he's not taking no for an answer."

U.S. Army Special Forces Captain MacKenzie K. Gerber sat up slowly on the Army-issue folding cot. He swung his feet over the side as he rubbed the grit from his eyes with the back of his hand.

"Who wants to talk to me?"

"General Crinshaw, sir."

"Crinshaw? Christ! Is he here?" Gerber managed to get one eye unglued and saw that he was being addressed by Staff Sergeant Galvin Bocker, the A-Detachment's senior communications specialist.

"No, sir," said Bocker patiently. "He's on the radio. I told him you'd been out with a patrol all night, asked if I could take a message. He was very nonplussed at my suggestion, sir. Mentioned something about breaking me all the way to civilian if I didn't get you on the horn most ricky tick."

Gerber waved his hand. "All right. Tell His Royal Highness I'm coming. I'll be there just as soon as I get my boots on. What time is it, anyway?"

"It's 0950 hours, sir."

"Christ!" Gerber glanced at his watch in disbelief. He'd been asleep less than an hour.

"Yes, sir. Christ. Want me to get you a cup of coffee, sir?"

Gerber shook his head. "Let's see what the general wants first. Maybe he just woke me up to tell me I should go back to sleep."

"Yes, sir. Maybe," said Bocker doubtfully. "I'll tell him you're coming, sir."

Bocker ducked out the door of the hootch in a hurry as Gerber began to struggle into a pair of sweat-stiffened socks. Then he pulled on his canvas and leather jungle boots but didn't bother to lace them up all the way. He simply snugged the bottom six eyelets and wrapped the laces around his ankles a couple of times before tying them. He zippered up the pants he'd been sleeping in, then rummaged through the mess of papers on his new improved desk, which was cobbled together out of shipping pallets and plywood, looking for his sunglasses. He finally gave up the search and put on his floppy boonie hat, pulling it as far down over his eyes as it would go. From the pegs above his bunk he picked up his M-14 rifle and inserted a magazine but didn't chamber a round. Then he slung the rifle.

On his way out Gerber cast a thoughtful look at the bottle of Beam's Choice bourbon perched precariously atop the upended ammo crate that served as his nightstand. Staring at the Beam's, he recalled the words of his old friend Bob Tucker, a former paratrooper turned science fiction writer.

"Always remember two things," Tucker had once told him. "First, never take a touch of the Beam's before five. Second, somewhere in the world it's always after five."

Gerber considered the early hour and the fact that he'd been drinking a bit heavily lately. And he knew precisely why. Recently everything seemed to be happening simultaneously around

Camp A-555. First, there'd been an increase in night patrols because the VC seemed less interested in daylight movement following the establishment of an ARVN fire support base in Dinh Dien Phuoc Xuyen. In addition to that, both the American A-Detachment and their LLDB counterpart team had found themselves shorthanded due to casualties. Finally, Lieutenant Bromhead had been promoted to captain and given his own team. So bombarded with all these occurrences, Gerber felt he had no choice but to rely on the Beam's a bit more than usual to keep himself going.

The stress of the long hours and hard work was not unlike that which he'd been under at this time just about a year ago when they'd been running the nighttime river ambushes, disrupting VC sampan traffic. Things had been complicated then by Karen Morrow, the flight nurse who had pretended she loved him but whose betrayal by running home to her husband had cut a deep wound. And now things were complicated by Robin, her sister, who was everything Karen was not and who loved him deeply and genuinely. Her intermittent presence at Camp A-555, however, served as a constant and often painful reminder of a love abused and trampled upon.

Gerber had started drinking heavily then but had eventually pulled himself out of it. Now here he was contemplating a snort at nine-fifty in the morning. His drinking wasn't a problem yet, but he could see its becoming one, and in that he recognized an inherited trait he didn't much like in himself. He was going to have to watch it.

In the end, though, he rationalized the thought that, when you've been up all night every night for the past week, nine-fifty in the morning isn't really morning—it's the middle of the night. And anyway, nine-fifty was sure as hell after five. Besides, if he was going to have to face Crinshaw at this hour, he was entitled to a little eye-opener.

"What the fuck," he muttered, shrugging.

He uncapped the bottle and took a pull of the bourbon.

"Smooth as a baby's bottom," he said softly, touching a finger to his lips. Then he recapped the Beam's and followed Bocker.

Outside his hootch the sun beat down unmercifully. Gerber squinted against the glare and held a hand in front of his forehead to help the boonie hat. He made a mental note to have Kepler, the team's Intel sergeant, bring back half a dozen pairs of sunglasses the next time he, or anyone else for that matter, went to Saigon. Then, realizing that it might look as if he was saluting and not wanting to identify himself or anyone else to some VC sniper, he let his hand drop and trudged across the compound to the communications bunker, his boots kicking up little clouds of red dust as he walked.

After the brilliance and heat outside, the commo bunker seemed pleasant by comparison. It was cool and dark with only a couple of dim red bulbs lighting its interior. He stood at the foot of the stairway for a moment, letting his eyes readjust to the darkness, then took the headset and microphone Bocker handed him. Gerber pressed one of the earphones against the side of his head and keyed the switch on the mike.

"Big Green, this is Zulu Six. Go ahead."

He recognized the Georgia cracker accent of Brigadier General Billy Joe Crinshaw.

"Zulu Six, this is Big Green. First, let me tell you right now, mister, don't you ever keep a brigadier general of the United States Army waiting again. Is that understood?"

Gerber held the headset away from him and stared at it for a moment as if it had just done something incredibly stupid. Then he grimaced at it and pressed it back against his ear.

"Yes, sir," he said carefully into the microphone. "That is clear."

"Good. Now listen. A U-1A aircraft went down last night in the jungle somewhere to the northwest of your camp near the Cambodian border. It was carrying a VIP back from an important meeting in Phnom Penh when it was forced to detour farther south because of bad weather near Prey Veng. They reported engine trouble southeast of Kampong Trabek, and then contact was lost. I want you to go out and find that airplane and bring those people in before the Vietcong find them."

"Yes, sir. I'll get a patrol right out there," Gerber answered.

"I don't think you're reading me, Captain. I don't want you to send a patrol. I want you to send an army. Strip the camp if you have to. I want you to do whatever it takes to find that airplane, wherever it is, and bring those people or their bodies in. Is that clear? Over."

"Sir, you can't be serious. About stripping the camp, I mean. With all due respect, sir."

"Captain Gerber, I am not only serious, I am giving you a direct order to take your team, every single one of them, and your Tai strikers and go out and find that airplane. Leave the camp in the hands of the Vietnamese and their PFs. After all, it's their country. Now do I make myself clear? Over."

Gerber couldn't believe what he was hearing. Crinshaw was talking about conducting a battalion-sized sweep.

"Big Green, may I respectfully remind you that MACV standing directives specifically state that there must be one American officer present on the camp at all times. Also, my counterpart was called to Saigon yesterday and is not expected back for another two days. Both his XO and mine are new at the job. I don't think it's wise to leave the defense of the entire camp in their hands until they've both had a bit more experience. Over."

"You may respectfully mind your own business and follow orders, Captain. I don't care how you solve your little problems, but I want that plane found and those people brought in. I don't care how many people it takes, where you have to get them from, what it costs or where you have to go. Just get your butt out in the field and do it. Now, Captain! Over."

Gerber glanced at Bocker, who was wearing a questioning expression.

"The general is really torqued up about some missing VIP whose plane supposedly went down near here last night. Anybody report hearing or seeing anything?"

Bocker shook his head.

Gerber keyed the mike again. "Big Green, do I understand that you are telling me to cross Stormy Weather, if necessary?"

"Captain, I am ordering you to do whatever it takes, to go wherever necessary, to find that airplane and to bring in the survivors, or their bodies for burial. Over."

"Sir, I can't do that without an order from Black Widow Six or, in his absence, Crystal Ball. You must know that, sir. Even then it would have to be a written order, and you are, sir, outside our direct chain of command. Over."

"Now you listen to me, Gerber. Neither Hull nor Bates is available right now. If they were, I wouldn't be talking to you. I am a general officer and I am giving you a direct order to go out and find that airplane, no matter where it is. Now are you refusing to obey the direct order of a general officer? Over.''

"No, sir, I am not," answered Gerber. "But I am requesting that the order be written, as I have a right to do under U.S. Army and MACV regulations. Why all this fuss over some VIP, anyway?''

"Captain, for the last time, you have your orders. Either carry them out or consider yourself under arrest and let me speak with your executive officer. Over."

"Big Green, I am not refusing to carry out your orders, but I am requesting, in fact I'm insisting, that I have them in writing. I will not cross Stormy Weather without a written order to do so."

Bocker's interest in the conversation, what he could hear of it, was perking up. The men of A-Detachment 555 had, in fact, crossed Stormy Weather, the border into Cambodia, on many occasions, but that had been before the sticky business of the attempted assassination of a Chinese military advisor who wasn't supposed to be working with the Vietcong. After that, crossing into Cambodian territory had been strictly verboten.

"All right, then, damn it," swore Crinshaw. "All right. You'll get your written order, Captain. But you damned well better not still be in camp when it arrives."

Then, incredibly, Crinshaw's voice softened. At least it softened as much as it could over the radio. In fact, it sounded tired.

"You'll get your written order, Captain," Crinshaw said quietly. "Now please get on with it. This isn't just any VIP that's missing. It's Regal Chops. Big Green, out."

Gerber slowly lowered the microphone and headset.

"Captain, what is it? What's wrong?" asked Bocker.

"It's Crinshaw. He said please."

"Crinshaw said please? Are you sure?"

"That's what the man said. He said please."

"I don't believe it. Not General Crinshaw. Do you think he's ill, sir? Or maybe up to something?"

Gerber gave Bocker a sharp look. It wasn't good to have the men speaking that way about generals, even if what they said might be true.

"I'll tell you what I think, Galvin. I think he's scared. Have you got any idea what Regal Chops is? I think that's what he said. Regal Chops."

Bocker shrugged. "Never heard of it. Supposed to be somebody's call sign?"

"I don't know. Could be. Check the SOI, will you?"

Bocker leafed through a thick ring binder, a perplexed look gradually growing on his face.

"Captain, are you sure General Crinshaw said Regal Chops?"

"Yes, that's right. What's the matter, isn't it in there?"

"Oh, yes, sir, it's in here, all right. It's just that, well, it must be a mistake or something. I mean, are you positive he said Regal Chops, sir?"

"Positive," said Gerber. "Who is it?"

"Well, sir, according to the SOI, Regal Chops decodes as General William C. Westmoreland, commander, U.S. Army Vietnam and MACV."

Gerber gave a low whistle. "Jesus! No wonder he's scared."

"Captain, are you going to tell me what this is all about, or just keep treating me like a mushroom?" asked Bocker.

"How's that?"

"Keep me in the dark and feed me bullshit."

Gerber grinned. "I promise to give you a bath and some sunlight, Galvin, but not just yet. You're going to have to stay a mushroom a little bit longer. This deal is so screwy that I want to make absolutely certain of my facts before we go stomping off into the jungle. Besides, it's the sort of thing that I really think all the men ought to be told about at the same time. Have you any idea where I can find Master Sergeant Fetterman?"

"Yes, sir. I saw him and the new XO over by the central command bunker with Sergeant Smith. I think Sully and the master sergeant are giving the lieutenant an orientation on the special defensive precautions."

"Fine. See if you can get hold of Colonel Bates or General Hull for me on some of that electronic wizardry of yours, will you? I'll either be at the command post or in my quarters."

"Right, sir. Colonel Bates first?"

Gerber nodded. "If you can't get either of them, I'll talk to one of their execs."

"Right."

Going outside was like walking into an oven. Gerber shielded his eyes until they became accustomed to the light, then walked back toward the command post located next to the fire control tower. Each of the camp's four outer walls of packed mud and sandbags had a forward command bunker located near its center from which to direct the defense of that section of the perimeter. But a fifth bunker, which served as the central command post, was located nearer the center of the camp. It contained the camp's backup long-range radio equipment and provided good fields of fire across the runway bisecting the camp in case the walls were breached during an attack. Its proximity to the FCT provided good observation of the terrain surrounding the camp, and the bunker itself was reinforced to withstand anything but a direct hit from fairly large artillery.

A covered trench with a sandbagged roof connected the command post to an inner defensive redoubt built around the American quarters, dispensary and main ammunition bunker. The trench was designed so that it could be intentionally collapsed by the detonation of hidden demolition charges, the location of which was known only to the Americans.

As he approached the command post, Gerber could see two men standing outside the sandbagged Z-shaped entrance. A more mismatched pair of soldiers would have been hard to find in all of Indochina, he thought amusedly.

First Lieutenant Greg Novak, A-555's new executive officer, who had arrived at the camp only yesterday, was built like a Sherman tank. He stood six feet two and a half inches, weighed two hundred and seventy-five pounds and affected a pistolero mustache that he had somehow managed to avoid losing during his processing in-country. He wore reading glasses when necessary, Gerber knew, and had an affinity for edged weapons that had already endeared him to the man standing next to him.

Master Sergeant Anthony B. Fetterman, on the other hand, stood a shade over five feet six and couldn't have weighed more than one hundred and fifty pounds sopping wet. He was in an advanced state of balding and looked more like a vacuum cleaner salesman than a hardened and much decorated veteran of three wars, assorted conflicts, police actions and special operations. In Gerber's opinion, Fetterman should have been sent back to the States, having recently been captured by the Vietcong and successfully escaped. He was usually an unfriendly fellow until he got to know you, but he'd taken an inexplicable immediate liking to the new lieutenant.

Fetterman had served as a paratrooper and ranger in the Second World War, worked with the United Nations Partisan Forces in Korea and been one of the first men to volunteer for Special Forces when it had been formed. Soft-spoken with blue-black, steellike eyes, he spoke seven languages fluently and had a good working knowledge of half a dozen more. As operations sergeant of the team, Fetterman had earned the respect and admiration of all who had served with him. Gerber was familiar with a side of the man—one who would go out of his way to be kind to small children and animals—that seemed to belie outwardly anything except what he actually was: probably the most dangerous man in Southeast Asia. In his long military career he had earned well over a hundred confirmed combat kills. No one, not even Fetterman, knew for sure how many unconfirmed enemy deaths he was responsible for.

"Good morning, Master Sergeant, Lieutenant Novak," said Gerber.

As Gerber walked up, a third member of the little group stuck his head out of the command post.

Gerber acknowledged him with a nod. "Good morning, Sully."

Francisco Giovanni Salvatore Smith, known universally as Sully, was the perfect complement to the other two men. Halfway between Fetterman and Novak in size, he was the product of a wartime union that resulted in marriage between an Air Force flyer stationed in Trieste, Italy, and one of the local maidens. Sully was the team's senior demolitions specialist. He had developed a liking for making things go bang when his father had bought him a junior chemistry set for his tenth birthday. The fascination with explosives had persisted and led him first into combat engineering and later into EOD. Sully was very good at making things go bang, but his father had never quite forgiven him for seeking a career in the Army rather than one in the Air Force.

"Good morning, sir," answered Smith cheerily. "I thought you went to bed."

"I did. Something's come up, though. I'd like to see all members of the team in the team house in fifteen minutes."

"We got a mission, sir?" Fetterman asked quickly.

"It looks that way, Master Sergeant. Find Lieutenant Bao for me, will you, and tell him that I'll want the First and Third Independent Tai Strike Companies ready to move out in half an hour with food and ammo for a three-day patrol, plus medical.''

"Big time, huh?"

Gerber nodded. "Sounds like it. There are a couple of details I need to check on first. Oh, and tell Lieutenant Bao he's to remain in camp with the Fifth Company as reserve."

"He's not going to like that," said Fetterman.

"I know. But tell him all the Americans are going to be off camp except for Lieutenant Novak, and he'll need a good man to help him run things until we get back. Besides, I don't want to trust the defense of the camp entirely to the PFs. Not with Captain Minh in Saigon."

"All the Americans except Lieutenant Novak, sir?" asked Fetterman, not entirely believing what he'd just heard.

"That's right."

Smith and Fetterman left to round up the rest of the team and inform the commander of the Tai strikers.

"Greg, did Sully and the master sergeant get through briefing you on all the special precautions?" asked Gerber when the others had left.

"Yes, sir, but we didn't cover all the E and E trails through the perimeter minefields yet."

"All right. Let's walk, then, and I'll fill you in on them before the briefing."

"Very good, sir." He hesitated. "Captain Gerber, I don't want to sound like an idiot or anything, but is it really a good idea to mine our own gun emplacements?"

"It's a necessity, Lieutenant. We've had to use a few of them before."

"You mean the VC were able to get inside the walls and take over some of the gun emplacements?"

"I mean the VC are inside the walls, Lieutenant. Although we can't prove it, we know we've got VC infiltrators in the PF strike companies. I wouldn't be too surprised to find out that one or two of the LLDB are VC, as well."

"Jesus! Who else knows about those hidden switch panels of Sergeant Smith's down there?"

"Only the team and Captain Minh, the camp commander, and even Minh doesn't know about all of them."

"You don't even trust the camp commander? That's pretty heavy, Captain."

"I didn't say I didn't trust Minh. He's one of the finest soldiers I've ever worked with, in any army. He's okay. We're just playing it safe, that's all. For that matter, so is Minh. Sully told me that, when he was laying the charges, he found several of the bunkers had already been wired. Since it might have been the work of the VC, I told Minh. He showed me his own control box. It's hidden beneath the sandbags on the west wall of the fire control tower."

"Jesus, what a way to fight a war."

"There it is, Lieutenant. This way to the minefields."

THE MILITARY PENCHANT for punctuality is well-known. Equally well-known to anyone who has ever worn a uniform is the corollary that nothing ever gets started on time, anyway. Half an hour had passed since Gerber finished briefing Novak on the safe routes through the perimeter minefields protecting the camp and checked again with Bocker on his calls to Bates and Hull. The Tai strikers were starting to collect near the south gate. One small group was standing a bit apart from the rest, and Gerber noticed that there seemed to be an argument of some kind. Seeing Fetterman approaching from that direction, the team captain queried him about it.

"It's Sergeant Krung expressing his displeasure with a command decision, sir," said Fetterman. "Lieutenant Bao noticed him limping and asked what the problem was. Krung said nothing, but Bao insisted on seeing the foot. Turns out Sergeant Krung stepped on a pungi stake on patrol last night but didn't tell anybody. Made the medic who treated him promise not to talk about it because he was afraid Lieutenant Bao would put him on light duty until it healed, which, of course, is exactly what Bao did when he found out about it."

"And the good sergeant would much prefer to be out killing Communists rather than taking it easy back here while we're out in the field."

"Yes, sir. You can't really blame him for wanting to go along, sir. The board isn't filled yet."

Gerber nodded. "Bocker is still in the commo bunker. Tell him to give it a rest and come on over to the team house so that we can get this show on the road."

"Yes, sir."

"Captain, what was all that about?" asked Novak when Fetterman had left. "About this Sergeant Krung, I mean."

"Krung is the senior Tai NCO," Gerber explained. "He's got a real hatred of the Vietcong. Most of the Tai have lost somebody, either family or friend, to the VC because the Vietnamese and the ethnic minorities have been at each other's throats for several centuries. Some of them don't like the South Viets much better than they do the VC, which makes our joint command here a bit tricky to keep a lid on sometimes. Krung just hates Communists, though. His father was head man in their village. A VC terror unit came one night and butchered his family. All except Krung's youngest sister. About a dozen VC were content with gang raping and sodomizing her. They left her alive as a living reminder to others in the village of what would happen if they supported the Saigon government. A few weeks later the girl killed herself. She was about twelve years old, I think."

Novak shook his head. "The man has reason to hate."

"I guess you could say that, all right. Krung escaped only because he wasn't at home when it happened. Ten days later he walked into a Special Forces camp in the highlands and asked to be allowed to help exterminate the Communists. I'm told he swore a blood oath on his family's graves not to rest until he'd killed ten VC for every member of his family. He keeps score by nailing the genitals of those he kills on a board in his hootch. Krung had a very large family."

"Man, that's some kind of hate."

"Like you said, right or wrong, the man's got reason to hate."

"Yes, sir."

Gerber changed the subject. "Greg, I'm going to leave you here when we go out. I want you to understand that my decision is not a reflection on you personally, it's just that—"

"I'm green meat, and you'd rather have somebody with you who knows his asshole from a hole in the ground."

Gerber grinned. "If that's all it was, I'd send you and stay here myself and drink all the beer. We've got to leave at least one American officer in the camp, and that means either you or me.

Also, for various political and security considerations, we're going to keep the Vietnamese out of this one.''

"Meaning you're afraid one of those VC infiltrators in the PFs you mentioned just might find a way to leak some information to his VC buddies outside the wire."

"Let's just say we're playing it safe again. Anyway, Captain Minh is in Saigon for a couple of days, which technically leaves Lieutenant Dung in command of the camp, so it would be more in keeping with our official position of an advisory role if I left someone of equal rank in control. If I left one of the sergeants, Dung might try to bully him around a bit. It's been known to happen. Not at my camp, but, well, Dung is new here. Less than a month. He's still an unknown factor. He might be just fine, and then again he might be . . ."

"VC?"

Gerber shrugged. "I hope not. It's happened before. The last LLDB executive officer we had here turned out to be a Vietcong agent."

"Jesus! It really is that bad?"

"It's probably worse. I'm going to leave Lieutenant Bao and one of the Tai strike companies here. Bao's a good man. Very good. You can trust him."

"With the picture you've been painting, I was beginning to wonder if I could trust myself."

"Don't worry about Bao." Gerber smiled. "I'd stake my life on him. In fact, I have, a number of times. The same goes for Sergeant Krung. You've got to restrain his bloodlust a little once in a while, but he's a damned fine soldier, and he really hates the VC. They both speak French and pretty good English, so you won't have any trouble communicating with them. Lieutenant Dung speaks English, too, of a sort. Things have been pretty quiet around here for a while, so just keep your cool, think before you act, don't get any big ideas and you'll do fine."

"Captain, what is it exactly that you expect me to do while you're gone?"

"Just run the camp. Our half of it, anyway. Don't go out on any patrols, don't leave the camp unguarded for any reason and don't pull any John Wayne stunts. That's all there is to it. We'll be back in two or three days, four at the most. We'll be in radio contact most of the time. I'll get Bao to assign you a good English-speaking commo man from among the strikers. Just remember, you can trust the Tai and most of the LLDB.''

"But not all of them?"

Gerber shrugged. "Out here nothing is ever one hundred percent certain."

Novak grunted. "I think maybe after the briefing I'll go sharpen my knife. Hey! What's that?"

Gerber followed the direction of Novak's gaze across the compound. A tall, compact blond woman wearing a boonie hat, a sleeveless OD undershirt and a pair of fatigue trousers cut off into shorts was approaching. The woman had several cameras and an assortment of lens cases hung about her neck.

"That," said Gerber, "is a reporter, as in magazine and newspaper. Opposed to a news reader, as in television."

"Yeah, but it's a girl."

"It's both. Although I think she qualifies for the title of woman. Robin Morrow, semiresident newshound and one of the principal reasons I'm turning prematurely gray. Also one of the other reasons I want you to stay here. Keep her out of trouble while we're in the field."

"Right," said Novak. "Out of trouble. Suddenly I don't think I'm going to mind being left behind at all."

"Try not to get too enamored of the young lady. I happen to know she's got a crush on one of the team members already."

"Rats! Still, you never know. It might not hurt to make a feasibility study of the situation. Maybe she'll change her mind."

"Maybe," said Gerber, laughing, "but I don't think right now is the time to find out. Unless I miss my guess, the young lady's nose for news is picking up a strong scent of something about to happen, and I don't think she's going to care much for what I have to tell her. You'd better go on ahead and protect your virgin ears."

"Spirited, huh? I like a woman with spirit."

"Just spirit yourself out of here, and tell the men I'll be along as soon as I've taken care of Miss Morrow. On second thought, make that as soon as I've talked with Miss Morrow."

"Right." Novak cast another appreciative glance at those long, tanned legs and went.

"Good morning, darling," said Morrow as soon as she was within earshot. "I thought you were in bed."

Gerber noticed that Novak's stride had skipped a step when Morrow called him darling.

"I was, but something came up," he answered her.

"Oh, really?" she said, dropping her voice and arching her eyebrows as she stepped up close to him. "Need any help making it go down again?"

"Robin, cut that out. And stop calling me darling in front of the men, damn it. It's hard enough on everyone just having you out here. What do you suppose it does to the rest of the men when you start cozying up to me?"

"Probably makes them envious as hell, if I'm any judge of my own looks. Oh, really, Kirky, stop being such a poop. It's not as if I were the only girl around here, you know. There are lots of them in the strikers' families. Some of them are kind of cute, too."

"That's different. You're the only round-eyed girl here. And stop calling me Kirky. I wish to hell I'd never told you my middle name was Kirk."

"I think it's cute. Kinky, Kirky. Fits you. Something's going on, isn't it?" she asked, skating away from what seemed about to become a touchy subject. "Who's going out?"

"We all are."

"All of you? My, my, it must be important."

"All of us except Lieutenant Novak. I'm taking the team and some of the Tai. The remainder of the Tai and the PFs will stay behind. Just a routine operation, that's all."

"Routine, huh? With all the team going except the new guy? Don't you bullshit me, Mack Gerber. I can smell bullshit coverage a mile away, and this one really reeks."

Gerber said nothing.

"Can I go along?"

"No."

"No? What do you mean, no?"

"I mean no. You can't go."

Morrow blew up. "Jesus H. Sebastian Christ on a crutch, how the hell do you expect me to do my job if you won't let me do it? I'm a reporter, remember? Assigned to cover the war, remember? How in hell am I supposed to cover the war if you won't let me see any of it? My credentials are in order, and I've got written authorizations from Colonel Bates and General Hull to be here. Even that asshole Crinshaw signed them."

"You've seen plenty of the war already," said Gerber. "Besides, your authorizations only obligate me to afford you all reasonable cooperation so long as it does not interfere with the performance of my military duties. In my opinion, your presence on this mission would interfere with those duties, so you're not going. That's it. That's final."

"Damn you, Mack, you're not being fair."

Gerber noticed that her cheeks beneath the freckles and tan were beginning to flush. He decided a little diplomacy might be in order.

"Robin, if I tell you some of what it's about, will you promise not to file a story or talk to anyone about it until we get back?"

"You know I can't do that. I'm a reporter, for Christ's sake. What kind of reporter would I be if I promised to sit on every story that comes along?"

"I'm not asking you to sit on every story. Just this one. And only for a little while."

"While somebody else with a pipeline to Saigon scoops me?"

"It's a possibility. I'll admit that. But believe me, it's important we keep this thing quiet for a little while. If we don't, it could cost some people their lives."

"Great! And if I do keep the story under wraps and get scooped and my editors find out about it, it could cost me my job. Some choice. My job, Mack, do you hear me? Not yours. Not ours. What is this *we* shit, anyway?"

"Mine's one of the lives it could cost if the VC get wind of what's up too soon," said Gerber quietly.

Morrow put her head in her hands. "Oh, hell. How long?"

"Forty-eight, maybe seventy-two, hours at the most."

"I get exclusive rights?"

"I can't promise that. But I'll give you everything I've got first. It's the best I can offer."

"It's no offer at all. Okay, give me a hint, so I can decide if it's worth it or not."

Gerber took a deep breath, wondering just how far he should go, if he'd already gone too far.

"An aircraft went down northeast of here last night, along the border. My orders are to locate the aircraft and attempt to recover the passengers and crew."

"That's it? That's the big story you won't let me come along to cover? Wait a minute here. Are you going into Cambodia with that army you're putting together down by the south gate? That's going to provoke one hell of a border incident, mister."

"We won't cross into Cambodian territory unless it becomes absolutely necessary to rescue the men. You know how touchy Saigon is about cross-border ops."

"Yeah. I do know. So how come suddenly they're willing to let you? Something just doesn't add up. Who was on that plane?"

"I can't tell you that. A VIP. That's all I can say."

"A VIP. I'll bet," said Morrow sourly. "So who was it, West-moreland?"

Gerber thought he was going to choke. He forced himself to speak calmly and to look her in the eye.

"That's exactly the sort of wild speculation that leads to irresponsible journalism."

"All right, then, so it wasn't Westmoreland. Who was it, the President of the United States?"

Gerber nearly did choke. He didn't know whether to laugh or cry, or both. Finally he snorted.

"That is without a doubt the most ridiculous notion I've ever heard," said Gerber.

"And you are without a doubt the worst liar I've ever known. It's Westmoreland, all right. Please don't insult my intelligence by denying it. Karen told me you were a rotten liar. I always thought she meant you made up things, but now I understand. You can't look a person in the face and lie to them convincingly, can you? You just don't know how to do it. Well, okay, fine, I'll sit on the story, even though it probably will cost me my job. But God damn you, Mack Gerber, don't you ever lie to me again. Just don't you do it, you hear me? I've never lied to you, and I won't. But so help me, if you ever lie to me again, we're finished."

Gerber nodded mutely. It wasn't exactly what he'd expected.

"Oh, damn you. I will get scooped on this. You know that, don't you? A story like this is too big to keep quiet. Somebody in Saigon will leak it to the media, and the story will be all over the five-thirty network newscasts back home."

"And twenty-four hours later the story will be in Hanoi, and twelve hours after that every local guerrilla with an old French rifle and a Party card will be out beating the bushes looking for him, and they'll find us and we'll probably take a beating. But that's thirty-six hours. It might just be enough. Besides, right now I get the impression that not too many people in Saigon know about it. We need the time, not just for the general but for the men with him, as well, and for ourselves. Thank you, Robin."

She waved a hand. "Forget it. So you owe me one, all right? Now then, I've promised to sit on the story. How about letting me come along and take some pictures of whatever you find? Give me at least that much of an exclusive. Besides, I was with you in a pretty tight spot on the wrong side of the border once before, remember?"

Gerber shook his head. "Not this time, Robin, it's just too dangerous. Weren't you listening? Before, when we went after the Chinese officer, we had a small team of experts with some chance of getting in and out undetected, and the enemy didn't expect us to be coming. This time we're going into the field with enough men to make more noise than a herd of water buffalo. Stealth will be out of the question.

"I don't like it, but it's the only way to conduct a ground search, and we can't get air assets right now because the First Air Cav is locked into some heavy contact up in Binh Dinh Province. We may not even be able to get medevac if we need it. And once the story does break, every Communist soldier in Southeast Asia is going to be after us because we'll be making more noise out there than anyone else."

"Mack, isn't it a little late to be talking about its being dangerous? Cambodia was dangerous when I went there to help you get the evidence you needed to get your men off that trumped-up court-martial. Hell, just my being here is dangerous. This place gets mortared every other night. And that vacation in Hong Kong wasn't exactly a picnic, you know."

"I know. That's why I can't let you go. Because of Hong Kong." Gerber found himself mildly surprised at what he had just said, but he realized belatedly that it was true. What had happened in Hong Kong was the real reason he couldn't let her go.

"I see," she said. "I'm not made of glass, you know. I didn't break then. I'm not going to break now or in the future."

"I know that. That's not the problem. The problem is whether I could live with myself if I let you be placed in that kind of position again."

Morrow's voice, when she spoke, had grown very cool.

"Mack, I understand your concern for my safety. I guess I'd be kind of disappointed if you weren't. How do you think I feel every time I watch you go out the gate with a rifle in your hands? But we both have our own job to do. I don't tell you how to do yours, but you seem to want to tell me how I ought to do mine."

"I'm sorry," said Gerber. "That's just the way it is right now. I know it's something we're going to have to talk about, but right now this isn't the place, and there just isn't time."

Morrow was silent.

"Well?" prodded Gerber. "What do you think?"

"I don't *know* what to think. Right now I think maybe I ought to go up to An Khe and see how the First Air Cavalry Division is doing. I think I need to get out of here for a while."

"I don't want you to do that."

"I know. But I don't want you running my life. I love you, Mack, but I'm not your property. I'm not just something you can put up safe on a shelf until you want to take it down and play with it. I'm not made that way."

"I never thought you were. I just don't want to lose you, that's all."

"Then don't strangle me," said Morrow, sighing.

Gerber nodded. Just the slightest movement of the head. He felt a tightness in his chest, a tightness that he hadn't thought possible.

"All right, Robin. You do what you have to do. I'll have Lieutenant Novak put in a request for transport. It'll probably take a couple of days to go through right now. I imagine you can get a lift on the supply chopper tomorrow morning when it brings in the mail if you don't want to wait. I just can't let you go with us. If I did, I'd spend all my time worrying about you instead of getting the job done. That wouldn't be fair to the men. It might even get some of them killed. I'm sorry. That's just the way it is."

"I'm sorry, too, Mack. For both of us."

Gerber watched her walk away across the dusty camp in the direction of the Vietnamese compound. He found he was having a hard time breathing, and his heart felt as if it wanted to rip itself from his chest and go running after her. He knew his eyes were moist, and somehow he felt curiously ashamed. She didn't look back.

GERBER BROKE THE NEWS to his men. They would proceed to the area of last known contact with the downed aircraft and split into four patrols of approximately fifty men each. Sully Smith and Staff Sergeant Thomas Jefferson Washington, the team's medical specialist, would advise one patrol. Sam Anderson, the team's junior demolitions specialist, and Derek Kepler, the Intelligence sergeant, would have the second. Master Sergeant Fetterman and Sergeant First Class Justin Tyme, the light weapons man, would have the third. Bocker and Gerber would take the fourth, which would serve as the command element. Each team would have a specific area of responsibility to search, yet each would be reasonably close to the other units to provide reinforcements in case of contact with the enemy.

Because of the First Air Cav's commitments with the major operation now under way in Binh Dinh Province, airlift support was not available, so they would have to walk. A single Cessna O-1 Bird Dog with a U.S. Air Force pilot had been scrounged from Bien Hoa to fly observation for them and direct fire support from the ARVN battery at Dinh Dien Phuoc Xuyen, and a gun team from the Hornets at Cu Chi would provide aerial fire support if not otherwise occupied.

It wasn't much in the way of help, but there was still a war going on out there in the countryside, and just now it had grown very big and very hot, especially in Binh Dinh Province, and it couldn't stop just to look for one airplane. Not even if that airplane contained one very important general. Gerber's troops, however, were available, unoccupied and in the appropriate area, so it was up to them.

Gerber did not tell his men that the initiating authority for the mission had come from Brigadier General Crinshaw or that he had been unable to reach Colonel Bates or Major General Hull for confirmation of the order. Even Major Pratt, Bates's executive officer, hadn't any idea what the hell Gerber was talking about when he'd called him, but the XO had promised to do what he could to clarify the situation and to arrange airlift support when they were ready to come back in. The men did not need to know any of this, Gerber decided, and it had no real bearing on the execution of the mission. He did, however, tell Novak to expect written confirmation of the order in tomorrow morning's mail pouch and to contact him immediately by radio in the event any additional information became available.

Gerber concluded the briefing with a few remarks to the men to remind the Tai of the need for noise discipline in the field. The Tai strikers were good fighters, but they did tend to get a bit loud at times.

"Captain, will our representative of the press be accompanying us?" Fetterman wanted to know.

"No," said Gerber stiffly. "I felt it best for a number of reasons not to permit Miss Morrow to accompany us."

"I understand, sir," said Fetterman. Which, being Fetterman, he did. Perfectly.

# 3

## EIGHTY-FIFTH EVACUATION HOSPITAL (SEMIMOBILE), QUI NHON, RVN

Lieutenant Colonel Alan Bates couldn't quite shake the feeling that the place somehow reminded him of a college campus. Not one of the Eastern Ivy League schools quietly crumbling with snobbery, but one of the big ten Midwestern universities, like the ones in Madison or Iowa City. In those places they were always tearing down some fine old building to erect a modern, sterile structure that in ten or twenty years' time would be converted into administrative offices because it had grown too small to handle all the students, and another more modern, more sterile structure would replace it.

The Eighty-Fifth Evac Hospital had that curious, half-finished air of any major institution still undergoing construction. It was a combination of concrete and brick buildings mixed with Quonset huts, containerized operating theaters and a sprinkling of big, open-sided canvas hospital tents scattered with raw two-by-four lumber and an occasional idle cement mixer. It might have been anything—a new shopping mall or a hotel complex and convention center—had it not been for the frenzied activity of all the people in combination uniforms of olive-drab fatigues and hospital whites.

And, of course, there were the wounded and the dead. Today there were a lot of wounded and a lot of dead. An awful lot of dead. They'd finally run out of body bags, something Bates didn't think was possible in the U.S. Army. Sheets were being used for the wounded, so the remaining dead lay wrapped in ponchos, just as they had come in from the field. There were a lot of bundled-up ponchos arrayed in neat rows along the far edge of the triage area. The bodies were turning ripe in the hot sun because the coolers in the morgue designed to hold them until they could be shipped to Saigon for embalming were full.

"This way, Bob," said Bates, skirting a group of medics and nurses clustered about a patient with a sucking chest wound. "That fellow seems to be in charge. At least he's giving the orders."

They crossed over to where the extended open-air morgue had been set up and consulted a haggard-looking young captain who barely seemed old enough to be a lieutenant.

"Captain Fischlander? I'm Lieutenant Colonel Bates. This is Sergeant Major Taylor."

"No, not those six. Those six over there," the captain shouted at a couple of orderlies attempting to load some of the poncho-wrapped corpses into the back of an ambulance which would take them out to the flight line for the trip to Saigon.

He turned then and faced the two men, having noticed them finally. One was a solidly built officer of medium height who looked as though he might have played running back at a small college once, the other was a tall, rawboned NCO. Both wore green berets and had jump wings and combat infantry badges pinned to their camouflaged jungle jackets.

"I'm Fischlander," he said, directing his answer to the colonel. "Is there something I can help you with? As you can see, we're kind of busy."

"We appreciate that, Captain," said Bates. "We'll take as little of your time as possible. We're looking for a body."

"Take your pick, sir. We've got plenty of them."

"We're looking for a particular one. Private First Class Eugene Michael Taylor. This is Private Taylor's uncle. He's to accompany the private home for burial."

The captain looked pained. "Colonel, I'm afraid you're a bit early. All bodies have to go through the mortuary at Tan Son Nhut for embalming before being sent back to the States. That normally takes three or four days, but right now I'd guess a week to ten days would be more like it. If the sergeant major wants to accompany the body home, you need to talk to Saigon, not me."

"I've already talked to Saigon and to your administrator here, and I've got the necessary authorizations," said Bates, handing the captain a thick sheaf of forms and typewritten orders. "We'll take Private Taylor's remains back to Saigon with us for burial preparation."

"I don't know about this, sir," said the captain hesitantly. "It's pretty irregular."

"We're aware of that. We'll be glad to wait while you find a phone and confirm those orders."

The captain looked at the papers, then at the rows of poncho-wrapped bodies, and shouted instructions to a second ambulance that had pulled up.

"Ah, what the hell," he said, scribbling his signature on one of the forms with his pen. "Sign here, sir, and he's all yours. Second row, over there."

It took them a few minutes to find the right one.

Sergeant Taylor read the identification tag carefully, then reached for the corner of the poncho. Bates gently laid a restraining hand on his shoulder.

"Are you sure you want to do that, Bob? It's not going to change anything, and it might not be something you really want to look at."

"I've seen dead men before, sir."

"Yes. I know that. But this one is family."

Taylor nodded. "I appreciate the concern. I have to, sir. His family will want to know."

Bates didn't remove his hand. He left it resting lightly on Taylor's shoulder while the sergeant major pulled back the poncho.

Someone had taped a large bandage to Private Taylor's forehead. It might have been covering a scratch. But there was a much larger bandage on the back of his head, and it had a funny shape. Otherwise, the boy looked calm, at rest. It wasn't at all the contorted death-face grimace Bates had feared. There was surprisingly little dried blood.

Sergeant Taylor stared at the young-old face for a long minute, fixing it in his mind, remembering. Abruptly he reached forward and extracted an object from his nephew's left breast pocket. It was a small copy of *The Holy Bible* with two foil gum wrappers marking places in it. Sergeant Taylor opened the book and read aloud short passages that had been circled in pencil.

"I have fought the good fight, I have finished my course. I have kept the faith. My times are in Thy hands."

Bates gripped Sergeant Taylor's shoulder. It was all he could think of to do under the circumstances.

"I reckon that'll give his family some comfort, sir, to know he read the Bible. He was a good boy but a bit on the wild side, if you understand me. Never mean or anything, but he liked a drink when he could get one, liked to raise a little hell now and then. Never was much of one for going to church."

"I guess it's true what they say. There aren't any atheists in foxholes," said Bates.

"No, sir. And I don't reckon there's any God in war."

Bates patted Sergeant Taylor's shoulders. "You going to be all right, Bob? I'll get the jeep. We can't keep that helicopter waiting all day."

"Yes, sir. I'll be fine. I'd like to stay here with him if you don't mind, sir."

"I understand," said Bates. "I'll get the jeep."

As Bates walked away, he glanced back. The big sergeant major knelt unmoving next to the body of his brother's son, holding one of the boy's lifeless hands in both his own, as a tear rolled slowly down his cheek. Bates felt mildly ashamed, as though he was intruding on a very private personal thing merely by his witnessing it.

Around them, the graves registration captain continued to shout orders at the orderlies loading bodies, and the medics, nurses and doctors continued to shout instructions back and forth over the wounded.

The two thousandth American serviceman to die in Vietnam was on his way home, watched over by his uncle, and the war bled on.

# 4

## THE JUNGLE
## NORTHWEST OF
## CAMP A-555

The heat rose off the jungle floor and clawed at the men like the hand of some insidious invisible monster. It was one of the hottest days Gerber could remember in the land of eternal summer, where all days were oppressively hot, but depending on your elevation, or proximity to the seacoast, the nights could leave you shivering.

They had crossed the reeded swamp that morning, struggling along beneath the weight of their equipment and trying desperately, at times vainly, to keep the radios dry, but their uniforms were soaked long before that by the combination of heat and humidity. When they had finally reached firm footing, they broke for rest and lunch but spent most of the time in a state of numbed exhaustion, burning off the swollen leeches from each other's bodies—when they could get a damp match and a limp cigarette lit, which wasn't often.

Now they were in a tangled mass of low jungle, where the possibility of booby traps and the thick, leafy shrubs pushing in close along both sides of the packed mud pathways, inviting ambush, made it dangerous to stay on the network of established trails. But the entangling creepers and vines made passage through the jungle itself an agonizingly slow process.

At 1400 hours Gerber decided to call a halt and ordered a ten-minute rest. He was dog tired from the route they'd had to take, covering some of the most difficult terrain in their AO, and from lack of sleep because of last night's unsuccessful ambush patrol. He collapsed on the trail and pulled out his map, trying to figure out how much farther they had to go to the search area. He silently cursed the Air Force pilot who was supposed to be flying aerial scout for them but who hadn't shown up yet. Without that observation plane, finding the downed Otter was going to be damned near an impossibility. In this kind of cover, they'd just about have to trip over it.

Gerber's mouth felt as if someone had stuffed it full of steel wool. He wanted a drink but didn't touch the canteen on his belt or the other three in his pack. They were going to be out for two or three days unless Crinshaw could kick loose some airlift support for them, which didn't seem very likely with the big operation going on up north. Crinshaw had never been generous with airlift support, anyway. He seemed to enjoy going out of his way to make life miserable for the troops in the field. Especially if they were Green Berets, and most especially if they were Gerber's Green Berets. The man just did not like soldiers who wore funny green hats.

Anyway, three days was a long time to go on four quarts of water. There was no guarantee of resupply: they were moving away from the river and canal network, and the swamp they'd had to cross notwithstanding, it was the middle of the dry season. True, the map showed a few small creeks and streams in the area they would be searching, but the map had been made by the French military cartographic service and was over twenty years old. It frequently didn't agree with the terrain, and the streams, if they could be found, were seasonal runoffs. This time of year they were likely to be as dry as the dusty, packed-mud trail beneath his feet.

While Gerber was vainly trying to make a small rocky outcropping on their left—the only reference point of any significance in sight—agree with where the map said it was supposed to be in relation to the trail, which was on their right, Fetterman came back from near the front of the column and squatted next to him.

"Captain, looks like we could have some trouble."

Gerber was instantly alert. "Such as?"

"Scouts report a big cross trail up ahead about half a klick. It's seen some heavy foot traffic late yesterday or last night."

Gerber glanced at the map. "There's not any cross trail indicated for some distance, and certainly not a big one."

Fetterman shrugged. "Well, there's one there now."

"You said heavy traffic. Could the scouts get any estimate of numbers?"

"All they'll say is beaucoup, beaucoup, many, many. There's something else, too. Carts. At least three of them. The scouts say they were heavily loaded, judging from the depth of the tracks."

"Damn. Supply wagons, you think?" asked Gerber.

"I think it's unlikely that three farmers picked last night to haul manure to their fields with the help of a few hundred of their closest friends along a trail that nobody knew was here."

"Wonderful. That's all we need, to run into a VC battalion that just happens to be passing through our area. Or have them stumble over that airplane before we do. Okay, pass the word to the strikers to be ready for anything, then send the scouts down the cross trail for five hundred meters in either direction. If they don't run into anything, we'll proceed with caution."

"We're not going to follow up?" Fetterman looked puzzled. "Just bypass and leave a large body of VC troops in our rear?"

"I know it stinks, but our first priority is to find that plane and Westmoreland, if he's still alive. We've no reason to suspect those VC were looking for us, any more than we're looking for them. Besides, if there's that many of them, chasing after them might not be the smartest thing we could do right now. We've no air support, at least none guaranteed. Anyway, if they were looking for us, they'd hardly burden themselves with a supply train."

"Yes, sir. Shouldn't we at least notify the camp so they can pass word on to Nha Trang?"

"We should. We can't. Radios are out. One of them's got a dead battery, and the rest are just plain wet or acting up. I've got Bocker working on them."

"Marvelous. We're out here bebopping around in Indian country, with a battalion of hostiles known to be in the area, looking for a lost general, without lines of communication. Great-great Granddad would have a fit."

"There it is," agreed Gerber.

"Yes, sir. I'll get right on it." Fetterman moved off to talk with the scouts.

Half an hour later the scouts had returned, reporting that the Vietcong column had passed well to the east of the Americans and strikers' lines of march and then angled southeast. There had been no indication of other traffic along that particular trail.

Gerber went to check with Bocker on the radio situation.

"How's it coming, Galvin?" he asked the lanky radioman. Gerber fully expected things to be in order. Staff Sergeant Bocker was the best communications man Gerber had ever known. He was certain that Bocker could improvise a radio out of seashells and C-ration tins if the situation called for it. This time he was disappointed.

"Not good, Captain. The humidity is so damned high that I can't get the wet sets to dry out properly. I thought this was supposed to be the dry season. The tuner is shot on one set, and the crystals have gone bad on that one there. These old PRC-10s have got a lot of miles on them—some of them are just plain worn out. The PRC-25s are more dependable, but we didn't have enough of them for this mission, and the Tai are more familiar with the PRC-10s. Anyway, I switched some of the batteries around and swapped a few parts, and I finally got one that *seems* to be working, but it's quirky. I can pick up some broken traffic, but I can't get anybody to talk to me. I think maybe the radio is okay, but we're sitting in a dead zone. About all I can suggest is that we press on and hope for a clear spot."

"That's not good enough, Galvin."

"Yes, sir, I know. It's the best I can do."

Gerber looked at Bocker and believed him. If the man said he'd done everything he could out here in the field, he'd done everything he could. Anything else would have to wait until they got back to camp where Bocker had set up a rudimentary maintenance shop.

"All right, Galvin. Get the rest of this mess back together, and we'll get out of here. If we're going to have to laager in for the night without adequate communications, I want to get as far as we can from that VC column and find a good defensible site before dark."

What Gerber wanted didn't seem to count for much. They walked until 1730 hours without finding any really good spot and were getting very close to the area where the Otter was supposed to have gone down. Gerber had finally decided he was going to have to settle for a shallow depression about halfway up a slight rise a hundred or so meters from the main north-south trail as their NDP. Suddenly the striker ahead of him, who was carrying one of the useless radios, spun around and dropped to the ground, blood spurting from the side of his chest. Immediately there was a single sharp report.

"Down!" yelled Gerber. "Everybody cover!"

The men dropped to the trail and sidled for the thick growth along the edges of it, but one man wasn't quite fast enough.

There was a second report, and another striker lay dead on the trail, shot through the face.

"Anybody see the sniper?" yelled Gerber.

"Working on it," called Fetterman, who was up ahead somewhere.

Another gunshot followed the second and dust kicked up on the trail a few inches in front of Gerber's face as the ricochet from the hard-packed surface went screaming past his head. He slid another few feet back into the brush, rolled quickly to one side and lay still.

"Somebody get that bastard's range. He sure as hell's got ours!"

The rifle cracked again, and Gerber saw a striker across the trail from him tumble out onto the pathway, clutching his thigh. The Tai immediately dragged himself back under cover.

"Fetterman! Can you see that son of a bitch?"

"Working on it, Captain," came the unruffled reply. The sniper wasn't shooting at Fetterman.

Another round whizzed over Gerber's head and plowed into a tree trunk behind him.

Almost immediately it was followed by a loud thunk and a shattering explosion a few moments later. There were two more explosions, and then the jungle got very quiet. The sniper did not fire again.

Several minutes later Fetterman returned. He had slung his rifle and was carrying an M-79 in one hand and a Mosin-Nagant M1891/30 sniper rifle with a 3.5-power PE telescopic sight in the other. As he approached, he handed the grenade launcher back to a striker following dutifully at his side and extended the Russian rifle for Gerber's inspection.

The captain nodded. "Was he alone?"

Fetterman shook his head and dug into one of the pockets of his fatigues with his free hand. "Found these."

The palm of his hand held several of the spent 7.62 x 53 mm rimmed cases for the Mosin-Nagant, and two 7.62 x 39 mm cases, one expended, the other a complete round. The shorter 7.62 x 39 mm round was used only in the SKS carbine and AK-47 assault rifle.

"The other man?"

"No sign."

"That really tears it." Gerber sighed. He'd half expected it but hoped against it. Snipers normally worked in pairs, one man doing the shooting while the other spotted targets through binoculars. Frequently they had a small, four- or five-man security detachment with them for protection, as well. Gerber looked at the dead and wounded strikers lying on the trail and wondered if a general, any general, was worth it. Washington and one of the Tai medics were working on the man who had been shot through the thigh. It didn't look good.

"Captain." Washington looked up. "This man's been hit in the femoral artery. I've got it clamped off, but there's only so much I can do for him out here. If we don't get him to a field hospital pretty soon..." He left the sentence unfinished.

Gerber nodded. "Do what you can for him, T.J."

"Captain Gerber!" called Bocker, coming up from the rear of the column. "I've got some good news, sir."

"I could use some," said Gerber sourly.

"Finally got somebody to talk to me on one of the radios."

"That's the best news I've had in the past forty-eight hours," said Gerber, reaching for the handset. "Who's on the other end?"

"That FAC who was supposed to spot for us. Hawkeye Two One."

Gerber's hand paused momentarily. "Did he happen to say where the hell he's been while our strikers were getting shot?"

Bocker nodded. "Said he couldn't find the RP and couldn't raise us on the radio. We can hardly blame him about the radios, sir."

"Where is he now?" asked Gerber, taking the handset.

"Unknown. He doesn't have a visual on us. His signal's a bit weak."

Gerber nodded and keyed the transmit button. "Hawkeye Two One, this is Zulu Six. We are approximately at Grid X Ray Yankee two six four four. We have wounded. Can you relay request for medevac, over?"

"Roger, Zulu Six," came the faint reply. "Say number of wounded, over."

Gerber looked at Washington.

"Three dead, two wounded, Captain. Both of them serious."

Gerber eyed the handset again. "Hawkeye, this is Zulu. We have five wounded. Two are immediate, over."

"Roger. Understand five, two immediate. Wait one for confirmation."

While they waited for the reply, Gerber looked at Fetterman and shrugged. "What the hell. Strictly speaking, it's only two, but we can't go carrying a bunch of bodies around the jungle with us. At least this way the poor bastards will get a decent burial."

A few moments later the voice of the Air Force pilot crackled over the earpiece of the handset again.

"Zulu Six, this is Hawkeye Two One. Be advised that Dust-Off Three Seven will be over your location in two zero minutes. Can you mark landing zone?"

"Top of the hill's got the least cover," Fetterman offered. "We'll have to do some clearing, and it's going to be awfully noisy."

Gerber looked at the two wounded strikers, considering. "Our hand's already been tipped, Tony, by that sniper's partner. Get them started on the LZ."

"Yes, sir. I'll go find Sergeant Smith."

Gerber keyed the mike again. "Hawkeye, this is Zulu. Advise Dust-Off that we will have to clear LZ. If he will contact us when in vicinity, we will mark with smoke."

"Roger. Will advise."

"Hawkeye, can you also contact Crystal Ball and ask them to relay a message to Zulu Five at Zulu Main? We have intelligence of a large VC force, possibly battalion strength, approximately nine klicks north by northwest of this position, moving in an east-southeasterly direction. Recommend maximum alertness. Over."

There was a significant pause.

"Uh, Zulu Six, this is Hawkeye. Are you in contact with the enemy? Over."

"Negative. We have taken sniper fire but have neutralized the source. We are not, repeat not, in contact with the enemy at this time. However, we have reason to believe there may be other enemy troops in the immediate area. Over."

"Roger, Zulu Six. Will relay. Stand by."

In the distance Gerber could hear Sully Smith shout, "Fire in the hole!" Men quickly sought available cover, and a few moments later a series of earsplitting concussions buffeted throughout the jungle and several trees located near the top of the rise toppled slowly to the jungle beneath. Finally the voice of the FAC came back over the radio.

"Zulu Six this is Hawkeye Two One with a message from Crystal Ball. Over."

"Zulu, go ahead."

"Crystal Ball Six wants to know if you will RON, or would you like a lift home?"

Gerber stared at the handset in disbelief. Apparently Bates had returned to B-Team Headquarters and was offering them airlift support back to camp.

"Hawkeye, this is Zulu. Do I understand that airlift is available?"

"That's a big rog, Zulu Six. Do you wish to utilize?"

Gerber considered the situation. They had spent most of the day walking to get to this spot and had lost three men doing it. Two others might not make it. And they were only now close to the area where the aircraft had reportedly gone down. He was loath to leave. On the other hand, they did not know precisely the location of the downed Otter, night was fast approaching and there was a large body of VC somewhere in the vicinity that would soon be alerted to the presence of the American and Tai patrol. They had no guarantee of close air support, and their communications were flaky. Bates, having returned to the B-Detachment TOC, was obviously fully aware of the situation and was offering them an out, a chance to get back to Camp A-555 before night set in and Charlie came looking for them.

"That's affirmative, Hawkeye Two One," Gerber told the FAC. "Is Crystal Ball aware that I have two companies out here and that the LZ has limited landing capacity?"

"I'll relay that information to Crystal Ball, Zulu Six. Please stand by."

While he waited for word from the FAC, Gerber couldn't help thinking how important the pilots of the tiny observation aircraft were to the job he was trying to do in Vietnam. True, he'd been pretty annoyed at this particular pilot to begin with, but as Bocker had rightly pointed out, the Air Force pilot wasn't to blame for the failure of the radios they were using. FACs were a tremendous help on almost any mission. They could scout ahead of an advancing column and warn of the enemy's presence. They could adjust artillery fires and coordinate air strikes and helicopter gunship support, even marking the target with smoke rockets for the fast movers. Often the most important work they performed was exactly what Hawkeye Two One was doing now—simply orbiting above or near an ongoing operation and serving as a radio link for the troops on the ground equipped with short-range FM radios. It frequently made the difference between success or failure, between life or death for the wounded.

"Zulu Six, this is Hawkeye Two One," came the call sign again. Gerber answered. "Zulu. Go ahead."

"Zulu, Dust-Off advises he should be over your position in zero five minutes. I'm getting low on fuel and will have to leave you, so I'll turn you over to him. Crystal Ball says to tell you that airlift will be there in three five minutes. That's cutting you a bit close for darkness, so if there are any snags, you may have to improvise lighting, but he says to tell you he has a plan to speed up the loading, whatever that means. Good luck to you boys. Have a nice ride home."

"Thanks for the assist, Hawkeye Two One. Zulu Six, out."

The medevac arrived on schedule, and the wounded and dead Tai were placed aboard. The helicopter rose above the splintered stumps that littered the tiny LZ, ran forward a very short distance and pulled up, barely clearing a treetop at the far end of the LZ.

Gerber pulled the perimeter in tighter about the hilltop, and they waited.

The airlift was early, and when Grasshopper One Seven made the call, Gerber's spirits lifted. He nodded to Bocker, who popped a green smoke and tossed it into the LZ. Then, as the first of the CH-47 Chinooks hovered into view over the clearing, Gerber's heart sank. There was no way one of the big helicopters could fit into the minuscule landing zone. Then, as Gerber watched, a naval-type landing net dropped from the tail of the first Chinook.

While the other helicopters orbited south of the clearing, the second ship maneuvered in close and also dropped a net.

"What in hell is that shit?" asked Anderson, who was kneeling next to Gerber.

"That, Cat, is the way home. You want to ride back to the camp, start climbing."

"Christ!" said Anderson. "I hate ladders."

"Cat?" said Gerber with some surprise. "What's the matter? You're airborne."

"That's different, Captain. I got two parachutes strapped on whenever I get foolish enough to step out of an airplane. Those are ladders. Chutes got nothing to do with ladders."

"Well, I'll be damned. Sergeant, I'm afraid you have a problem. You want to get back to camp, you've got to climb that rope ladder."

"Oh, I'll climb it, all right, sir," said Anderson. "No problem about that. But I don't have to like it."

"Fine," said Gerber. "I give you my permission to hate it as much as you want, but let's get moving. Shall we?"

"Yes, sir." Anderson started forward.

Gerber turned toward Fetterman. "Well, Master Sergeant, we don't want to hang around here all night. Move 'em out."

Two squads of strikers moved forward and began to climb the ladder with Anderson in the lead.

# 5

## SPECIAL FORCES
## CAMP A-555

Lieutenant Greg Novak was bored. Once all the details had been taken care of and Captain Gerber had left with the two-hundred-man Tai search party, things had gotten boring pretty fast. He'd walked the perimeter with Lieutenant Bao, checking the camp's defenses, while Sergeant Krung limped doggedly behind them, determined to prove that his injured foot shouldn't have kept him from going on the patrol. He'd invited Lieutenant Dung to accompany them, but the LLDB executive officer had begged off, pleading an excess of paperwork to do and saying he would leave the inspection in the competent hands of his allies.

Novak had then suggested that Dung have his team sergeant accompany them, but that notion, too, had been rebuffed, with Dung stating that Master Sergeant Hoai had accompanied Captain Minh to Saigon and that the rest of his men were all engaged in various important duties about the camp.

Novak had given up after that. It was, after all, the Vietnamese's camp, strictly speaking, and if the man didn't feel like checking the security arrangements, he didn't have to. Novak had heard that quite a few of the Vietnamese officers tended to be a bit on the lackadaisical side. But Gerber's cautionary statements about the possibility of VC infiltrators among the Vietnamese strike force and the political philosophy of the previous LLDB XO were still fresh in his mind. It made him doubly determined to make sure the camp's defenses were in an adequate state of readiness. It wasn't that he was actually suspicious of Dung. After all, the man had encouraged him to continue the inspection. It was just that he was trying to play it safe, as the captain had suggested.

They'd had no recent reports of significant VC activity in the area, according to Kepler, the Intel sergeant, who had briefed him before the men went out, but Novak didn't think the captain would appreciate having the camp damaged or overrun while he was out because his new XO wasn't on his toes.

After that he'd gone to the team house to get a bite of lunch and tried to make conversation with Miss Morrow, but the journalist hadn't seemed in the mood to talk to anyone. Mostly she sat packing, unpacking and repacking her gear and drinking barely cool cans of Carling Black Label and Point beer from the team's antique kerosene-powered refrigerator, which seemed incapable of getting anything really cold. That and snarling and snapping at anyone and everyone who tried to speak to her. Novak wasn't sure exactly what was eating her ass but got the general impression that she was irritated at being denied permission to accompany the search party, and pissed at the captain in particular. The safest course had seemed to be leaving her alone until she worked out whatever it was that was bugging her or until she got drunk and fell asleep.

After that he'd played pinochle with some of the PFs for a while but stopped when he'd lost forty-two dollars and begun to suspect that they were playing with a marked deck and that all the PFs were in on the gag. Then he'd cleaned his rifle and his pistol, rearranged his bunk and gear and written a letter to his mother for dispatch when the routine supply helicopter came in the morning with the mail pouch.

Finally, there being nothing much else to do, he'd found himself a miserable little spot of shade near the wall of the team house and sat down to sharpen his knife. But first he extracted a promise from both the Tai radioman and the LLDB communications sergeant on radio watch to notify him as soon as there was any word, either from the men in the field or from B-Detachment headquarters.

The knife didn't really need sharpening. You could use it to shave now if you were a bit on the suicidal side. It was just something Novak did when there was nothing else to do, the way some men smoked or twiddled their thumbs.

Novak was just putting the finishing strokes on the blade when a shadow fell over his shoulder and a slightly slurred voice asked, "What in hell's that thing?"

He glanced up to see Morrow, a can of Point in her hand, leaning against the entrance to the team house. As he watched, she drained the beer, set the can down on the edge of the sandbagged entrance and produced another beer from one of the pockets in her shorts.

"Hunting knife," grunted Novak uninterestedly. If she'd been too huffy to talk to him when she was sober, he didn't see any reason why he should talk to her while she was drunk. Or at least well on her way to being drunk.

"That's not a knife, that's a sword," said Morrow. "What would you hunt with a knife that big?"

"Whatever," Novak grunted again.

"Come on. Don't be such a snit. I'm trying to make up for being rude earlier. It's been a bad day."

"Boy, I hear that," said Novak, becoming more expansive. "I thought it was supposed to be cool this time of year. Cool and dry. I'm wringing wet." He was beginning to soften. It's hard to stay mad at a good-looking woman. Especially when you're not exactly sure what it is you're mad at her about.

"It is," said Morrow. "Supposed to be cooler and dryer, that is. The rainy season isn't due for a couple of months yet. Then it gets really miserable. I guess this must be the weatherman's idea of a joke. Look, how about a picture of you with the knife. Might appeal to my editors. If they don't like it, you can send a copy to your hometown newspaper."

"Mom would like that, a picture of me. Okay, I guess."

"Fine. Wait right there a minute. I'll get a camera." Morrow snarfed down the beer, set the empty next to the other one and ducked back inside. A moment later she reappeared with a black Canon 35 mm SLR in one hand, outfitted with a 28-80 mm zoom lens, and a can of Point in the other.

"You want a beer?" she asked.

Novak considered. "Better not. I'm on duty until the captain gets back, I guess. Sorta."

"Suit yourself."

Morrow took a big swig out of the can, but got a little too much. Some of it dribbled down her chin and ran along her neck to disappear in an interesting part of her olive-drab undershirt. She set the can down on a sandbag and wiped the back of her hand across her chin.

"Damned shame. Hate to waste it like that. Alcohol abuse." She fiddled momentarily with the camera. "First shot with you sharpening it, okay? Then I'll take a couple with you looking up. So your mother can see your face."

"Whatever you say."

The camera clicked. She advanced the film and took another.

"Okay, now look up as you hold the knife, but look serious. Okay?"

Novak did as requested.

"Now a big smile for Mom. Got it." She recapped the lens and carefully set the camera down next to the empty cans, picked up the nearly full one and drained it in two gulps. Instantly she produced another one from her shorts.

"Miss Morrow, I like the way you drink," observed Novak, "but what's your hurry? A beer that good ought to be savored, even if it is warm. How many of those things have you got in your shorts, anyway?"

Morrow gave a little burp and smiled giddily at him.

"Thanks for the compliment, Lieutenant. Not nearly enough, I'm afraid. Pretty soon I'm going to have to go back to drinking the Carling. Not quite on a par with this stuff, but there's more of it. With luck I think I can get the job done before I'm reduced to PBR and Schlitz."

"Miss Morrow, why are you so hell-bent on getting drunk this early in the day? If you don't mind my asking, ma'am. Want to talk about it?"

"No. I don't mind your asking, but no, I don't particularly care to talk about it."

Novak shrugged. "You know best, I guess. Sometimes it helps to talk things over with a neutral source. I just wanted to let you know I'm available to listen, if you feel like talking." He started to sheath the knife.

"Hey, how about letting me have a look at that thing before you put it away?"

"It's pretty sharp, ma'am. I wouldn't want you to hurt yourself." Novak wasn't sure that giving his knife to a drunk was such a hot idea.

Morrow exploded. "Men! Always worried you're going to hurt yourself. Or get hurt. Always overprotecting. Unless they need you or want to do the hurting themselves."

Novak sensed he'd touched a nerve, but for some reason rather than backing off, he pressed the point.

"Is that what this is all about?" he asked. "Some guy hurt you?"

Morrow finished her beer, fished out another and knelt beside Novak. She took a sip, leaned forward and rubbed one eye with the heel of her hand.

"Yes. No. Oh, hell. I don't know. It's both, I guess. A short time back, when the team extended their tour, Lieutenant Colonel Bates made everybody take an R and R. Everybody went back to the States except Mack, uh, I mean the captain, and Master Sergeant Fetterman. They went to Hong Kong. I went with them. While we were there, we ran into this Chinese officer who had been working out near here as an advisor to the Vietcong. I don't know what the hell he was doing in Hong Kong. Maybe he was on R and R, too. Anyway, things got a little rough. Now the captain treats me like I'm an egg and he's afraid I'll break. It's interfering with my job, and it kind of makes me mad."

"Uh-huh," said Novak, suddenly understanding the situation. "You kind of like the captain, don't you?"

"Well . . . kind of," admitted Morrow.

"And he kind of likes you, too?"

"I guess so. At least I thought he did. Now I'm not so sure. He knows how important my job is to me, but now he won't let me do it right. And the tighter he closes his grip, the more I resent it. It's almost like he was intentionally pushing me away from him."

"Sometimes people push people away from them because they're afraid of losing them," observed Novak.

"That doesn't make any sense," Morrow protested.

"Nevertheless. People frequently don't make sense. Maybe the captain is trying to protect you because he's afraid of losing you. Maybe he's subconsciously setting up a situation where he's sure to lose you because he expects to lose you. This way, the expected happens, and he can handle it. Otherwise, you get too close to him, and when he does lose you, it hurts too much.''

''That's ridiculous. You're saying he's afraid of losing me because he thinks he's going to lose me, so he's making sure he loses me. That's silly. It just doesn't make any sense at all. Why is he doing it? Because of Hong Kong?''

''That and because there's a certain amount of danger attached to your job. War correspondent. Unless,'' Novak prodded, ''you can think of some other reason?''

''Now you're really getting ridiculous. I've never given him any reason to . . . Oh, my.'' Morrow leaned forward suddenly and put her head in her hands, still holding the can of Point. A pained expression crossed her face. ''Oh, damn you, Karen. You sure did a number on both of us.''

''How's that?'' queried Novak.

''Karen. My sister. We're twins. She's about fifteen minutes older than I am. She's a flight nurse in the Air Force. She and the captain used to be a pretty hot item. Then she jilted him. Didn't really have much choice, I guess. She has a husband back in the States. Problem is, she didn't tell Mack about the husband.''

''That was thoughtful of her,'' Novak remarked sourly.

She shrugged. ''Kari's always been a bit flighty. One of those see-what-you-want-and-take-it-and-damn-the-consequences kind of people. Anyway, we met because we're so much alike. Or rather, I met Captain Gerber because my sister and I look so much alike. Except for the eyes. Hers are blue, mine green. I was at the officers' club in Tan Son Nhut having a drink with a couple of pilots I know when he spotted me at the bar and mistook me for Karen. I'm afraid I'm the one who let slip she had a husband. I thought they were just having one of those wartime flings, but Mack was serious about her.''

''Wonderful. This is better than a soap opera.''

''Look, do you want to hear this or not?''

''Take it easy,'' said Novak. ''I was just commenting on the convolutions of the plot. Continue. Please.''

''Well, anyway, at first I wasn't interested. But since Karen had gone back to the States and since I'd heard so much about the guy from her, I was kind of intrigued by him. It was strictly a professional interest, at first. I came out here to do a story on him and his team, but the more I got to know him, the better I liked him.

He's really dedicated to the job he's doing, but I don't think he hates the enemy. He respects the Vietcong. At times I think he even admires them. Not when they burn a village and kill civilians, of course. But when they show determination and fight. Then he sees them as soldiers like himself. And I don't think I've ever seen a man more caring or considerate of the troops under him. A lot of the officers are just here to get their tickets punched so it'll look good at promotion time. They don't give a rat's ass about their men. Mack Gerber isn't that way at all. He actually cares about his men and what happens to them.

"I'm getting wrapped up in my isn't-Mack-Gerber-a-swell-guy speech. Anyway, suffice it to say I felt like he was someone I'd known forever. I guess because Karen had told me so much about him. And when I finally fell, I fell pretty hard. Guess I made a bad choice, huh?"

"Not necessarily," Novak told her. "But I'd guess your timing could have been better."

"Okay, I get it," Morrow went on. "What you say makes sense. Mack was in love with Karen, who dumped him, so now he's making sure he won't get hurt like that again by forcing me to dump him under conditions he's in control of. It's twisted, all right. But it does make sense in light of everything else that's gone on. The question is, what do I do about it?"

Novak shrugged. "I listen to people's problems, I don't give advice. But it seems to me that running away from the problem is not the answer. For either of you. If you'll pardon my saying so, that's exactly what your sister did, and all it accomplished was to create more problems for everyone. If you and the captain are going to have any kind of relationship beyond friendship, you're both going to have to be willing to take risks."

"*I* am willing to take risks," Morrow protested.

"Are you? I suppose you're going to tell me you're not afraid of losing the captain every time he takes out a patrol. Who did you lose, Miss Morrow, that made you afraid to take risks?"

Morrow opened her mouth in denial, cheeks flushing, then drew a deep breath and closed it. She was silent for a few minutes, then spoke.

"Is it all that obvious?"

"No. But it shows, if you know what to look for."

"It was my father. He walked out on us when Karen and I were ten. It made some pretty hard years for Mom and us. I guess I never really understood why or forgave him for it. He was a newspaper reporter. I haven't seen him in fifteen years. Last I heard, he was in Wyoming someplace, managing a small weekly. He used to be a pretty big name with the *Chicago Times*."

"So you followed in Daddy's footsteps and became a reporter yourself, even though you never forgave him for leaving his wife and daughters. But because you loved him and he left you, you've been afraid to let yourself get close to a man ever since. My guess is your sister has, too, despite her marriage. Otherwise, she wouldn't have gone into a career that was going to keep her away from her husband for long periods of time, nor had an affair with the captain. I'll bet it wasn't her first affair, either. Was it?"

Morrow shook her head. "There were others. About every two or three years Karen would get restless and start seeing some guy on the sly. Always a married man, and she always broke it off after five or six months, so it never got really serious. That's why I didn't think her involvement with Mack was serious. Only this time she picked a man who was single and who really wanted to be in love with her, not just in her pants."

"Well, ma'am, I'd say you sure do have a problem. It looks to me like you and the captain, with the help of your sister and your father, have gotten yourselves locked into a nice little circle. You're so busy being in control of the situation so you won't get hurt that you keep hurting yourselves because feeling hurt is what you know how to do best."

"So how do we get out of it? Take a chance on being hurt?"

"That's not a chance. That's a certainty if you keep on going at things this way. What you've got to learn to do, you and the captain both, is take a chance on feeling good. About yourselves. About each other."

"You make it all sound so simple, Lieutenant."

"There's nothing simple about it. But it can be done. All you have to do is decide you're going to do it."

Morrow laughed nervously. "I can't believe it's that easy."

"There it is, ma'am. You can't believe. That's why you fail."

"You know, Lieutenant Novak," said Morrow thoughtfully, "I'm beginning to suspect that you make an awfully good psychiatrist for a first lieutenant."

"All I do is listen to people's problems. From the higher-ups down, and the down-belows up. That's what first lieutenants do best. Besides, I minored in counseling at UW-Milwaukee. Figured it was sort of a prerequisite for being a lieutenant. But I'm still just a listener. People make their own problems, and people have to solve their own problems. I'm not saying running away from a problem is never the answer, but usually it's not the best."

"Thanks for listening, then, Lieutenant. And please, call me Robin."

"All right, Robin. And you can call me Animal."

"Animal!" Morrow laughed. "Why on earth Animal?"

"You still got a beer in one of those pockets, Robin?"

Morrow fished out another can of Point and passed it over. Novak took the beer, but refused the offer of a can opener.

"Ever since I played football in high school, all my friends call me Animal. After a game the team would all get together for a few beers. More like a few dozen. We partied pretty furiously in those days. If we won, we partied to celebrate. If we lost, we partied to drown our sorrows. The guys called me Animal because I'd open my beers like this."

Novak bit down on the rim of the can with his teeth and tore the top off it. The beer fountained out in a geyser, and he lost about a fourth of it, but he spit out the lid, tilted his head back and swallowed the rest of it in a single gulp.

"I don't believe it," said Morrow.

"Must have cut my lip a hundred times before I perfected the technique. Sure used to impress the cheerleaders, though."

Morrow laughed again. "You really are an animal. Let me have a look at that knife, will you?"

Novak passed it over. "Be careful. It is sharp."

The knife had a ten-inch blade with a curved-up point and a short false edge. The rest of the back of the blade was covered with large saw teeth.

"It's heavy. What's this wrapped around the handle?"

"Fishing line."

"Is that for a better grip?"

"Partly. It's partly for survival, too. The handle is hollow. There's a small fishing kit, some snare wire, waterproof matches and a couple of water purification tablets inside. A cable saw and a few other odds and ends, too. The whole thing seals up water-tight because there's a rubber O-ring on the cap. The inside of the cap has a tiny compass set on a jeweled bearing in it.''

"I've never seen one like it before. What kind of knife is it?"

"It's a Parker Custom Hunter/Survivor. I got it from Iron-monger Jim."

"Who?"

"Ironmonger Jim and Lady Rose, Suppliers of Good Blades. They run a little shop in Anoka, Minnesota. Old Jim used to always tell me, 'When you're out of ammunition, nothing beats a good blade.' When I found out I was coming over here, I went to his shop and said, 'Jim, give me the best blade you've got.' That's it."

Morrow handed back the knife. "Thanks. I hope you don't get to use it."

"I hope I don't *have* to use it."

"That's what I meant. Thanks, Animal, you really have been a friend."

"No sweat. Let's go inside, and I'll buy you a beer. Maybe we can find one in there that isn't warm."

"Thanks, but I'll pass. I think I'll unpack my bags and take a nap."

"Sounds like a sensible notion. I believe I'll go catch a few winks myself. It's going to be a long night. Especially with the rest of the team out."

Morrow went back inside the team house, and Novak picked up his knife, his sharpening stone and his steel, and went off to his quarters.

IN HIS OFFICE Lieutenant Dung Cao Chiap signed the form he had been reading with a flourish of his fountain pen and placed it with the other forms and papers on his desk. He methodically stacked the pages and tapped their edges into alignment before placing them in the out basket. Then he checked his watch. It was nearly time.

With quiet deliberation he pushed back his chair, got up from the desk and walked over to the pegs on the wall that held his equipment. Carefully he buckled on his pistol belt and equipment harness and checked to make sure that his M1911A1 .45-caliber pistol was loaded and a round was in the chamber. Then he set the safety and holstered the weapon. From its peg he took

down his M-2 selective fire carbine with the two thirty-round ba-
nana magazines taped together end to end and opened the bolt to
make sure the breech and barrel were unobstructed. Then he
chambered a round, set the safety and slung the carbine, muzzle
downward, over his shoulder. Last, he buckled on his helmet and
picked up the pouch of hand grenades, slinging them over the
other shoulder. He returned to his desk and unlocked the bottom drawer, taking a second pistol from it and tucking it inside
his shirt. Then he walked calmly out the door and across the runway that bisected the camp.

Dung moved across the compound past the fire control tower
and the helipad to the communications bunker, reaching it in time
to nearly collide with Sergeant Duc, one of the LLDB communications specialists, who was coming up the steps of the bunker
in a great hurry, a scrap of paper in his hand.

"Slow down, Sergeant. What's the big rush?" Dung asked,
mildly curious.

"I was coming to find you, sir," said Duc. "We have just received a message from the patrol, relayed via B-Detachment
Headquarters. Captain Gerber reports finding evidence of a battalion-sized force of VC in the area, possibly heading in our
direction. The message is for Trung Uy Novak, but I thought you
would want to be informed, as well."

"Indeed I do. How very interesting. A battalion, you say. Is that
all?"

"That is the report," said Duc, puzzled. His lieutenant seemed
almost disappointed that there were not more VC.

"Very good, Sergeant," said Dung smoothly. "Give me the
message and I will give it to the American lieutenant and you can
get back to your duties."

Duc dutifully handed over the scrap of paper and turned to
reenter the bunker. He had taken two steps when Dung clapped
his hand over the man's mouth and drove his bayonet into Duc's
right kidney. Duc died without making a sound.

Dung lowered the ARVN Special Forces soldier's body quietly onto the steps below the top of the sandbagged entrance where
it would be out of sight. A stroke of the bayonet across the throat
ensured that the job was done. Placidly he wiped the bayonet's
blade on the dead man's uniform and replaced the weapon in its

sheath. Then he walked casually down the steps into the dimly lighted bunker.

The Tai radioman was bent forward over his tiny desk. He had one hand pressed against the left side of his head holding one of the large earphones in place while he scribbled another message on a small notepad. He was listening so intently that he did not hear Dung approach.

Lieutenant Dung moved to a position directly behind the radioman's chair and took something out of his pocket, which he held behind his back. He waited patiently until the Tai lowered his left hand, then quickly he brought the wooden-handled piano-wire garrote out from behind his back and snapped it down over the man's head, pulling it tight. The Tai kicked with his feet and tried to push his chair backward into Dung, but Dung held on tightly and stepped back with the man's thrust. The garrote bit in deep from bottom to top, nearly severing the radioman's head.

Moving purposefully, Dung tilted each of the radios forward until he could reach the power cables in back. Taking a pair of insulated wire cutters from one of the breast pockets of his jungle fatigues, he carefully cut through each of the cables and the antennae leads.

Dung checked his watch. It had taken fifteen seconds less than they had planned, a good omen.

He picked up the notepad, tore off the top sheet and read it. It was a second message from B-Detachment Headquarters, instructing Gerber to contact Lieutenant Colonel Bates immediately upon his arrival. Dung took the first message from his pocket and placed it with the second. He carefully tore the two messages into eight strips, then took out his Zippo lighter and burned them, letting the ashes fall to the floor of the communications bunker where he ground them into dust beneath his boot heel.

He checked his watch again. It was time.

Climbing the steps of the commo bunker, being careful to step over Duc's body so that he would not get any blood on his boots or uniform, Dung crossed the compound toward the command post, nodding almost imperceptibly to a few of the men as he passed. They in turn nodded to other men, who one by one detached themselves from whatever they were doing and began to take up positions about the camp.

At the base of the fire control tower, Dung hesitated briefly. He glanced around, checking the position of his men. Satisfied that most, if not all, were in their positions and armed and ready, he started leisurely up the ladder, taking care to grasp each rung, place each foot. He did nothing that might cause him to slip and fall. They had come too close, risked too much, to fail now because of some slipup during the final minutes. He would leave nothing to chance by rushing at the last minute.

At the top of the ladder, both Sergeant Duong, the LLDB heavy weapons specialist, and the PF striker on duty with him noticed Dung, but he merely nodded at them. They returned the nod and resumed glassing the surrounding terrain through their binoculars.

Dung clambered over the sandbags and onto the platform of the FCT. Nonchalantly he reached into his pocket and took out a package of cigarettes. He shook one out and placed it between his lips, cupping his hand over the end and turning away, as if to shield it from the wind while he lighted it. When he turned back, he had the silenced Tokarev pistol that he had been given in his hand. With utmost care he shot both men twice.

The gun was quiet but by no means silent. It made four small, sharp sounds, like hand claps. It was possible that someone directly below the fire control tower might have noticed the noise, but the only men below at that moment were expecting the noise, and they showed no outward signs of alarm.

Dung moved forward and checked that both men were dead, feeling for the carotid pulse at the side of each man's neck. Satisfied that neither would offer any resistance, he moved to the side of the tower and took a small metal mirror from one of his pockets. Sighting on a particular spot of the distant tree line, Dung gave the signal.

LIEUTENANT NOVAK SAT UP suddenly in his bunk. Heart pounding, sweat rolling down his bare upper torso, he strained his ears, trying to detect once again whatever sound it was that had awakened him. For a moment he could hear nothing. Then a series of shattering blasts rocked the camp and men began screaming.

Mortars.

Novak swung his legs over the side of the bunk, zipping up the trousers he still wore and buckling his belt. He paused long enough to pick each boot up by the toe and bang it a couple of times on the floor, out of respect for any scorpions, spiders or centipedes that might have decided to take up residence there while he was asleep, then jammed his feet into the boots. He didn't take time to lace them all the way, just wrapped the bootlaces around his ankles a couple of times and tied them.

Novak took time to slip into his jungle jacket, since he knew it could offer some protection against flash burns, but didn't wait to button it. He threw his web gear over one shoulder, picked up his helmet and reached for his rifle. Then he heard it. A low growl that built steadily into a high-pitched wail. It took him a moment to place it, but when he finally did, his worst fear was starkly realized.

Ground attack siren.

He jacked a round into the chamber of his rifle and ran out the door.

Outside, it was pandemonium. The air was filled with smoke and the crack, rattle and pop of small arms fire. Beyond the redoubt and across the runway, where the Vietnamese quarters were located, men were busy shooting each other.

Oh, my God, thought Novak. Oh, sweet mother's delight. They're inside the camp already. The motherfucking VC are inside the camp.

Novak glanced to the south, toward the Tai quarters. Two of the buildings were burning, and as he watched, another barrage of mortar bombs fell among the rest, sending forth great burning showers of embers that trailed dense clouds of thick white smoke behind them.

Willy Pete.

There seemed to be some kind of ground action going on over there, too. There was a lot of firing all along the section of the camp wall defended by the Tai. Most of it seemed to be directed inward, toward the Vietnamese positions across the runway and along the west wall. He could hear both the rapid chatter of .30-caliber Brownings and the slow, heavy booming of the fifties.

It was then that Novak realized the enemy mortars were falling only on the Tai quarters. No place else in camp was being shelled. A few of the Vietnamese hootches were burning, but if that had been done by mortars, the VC gunners manning the tubes outside the camp had lost interest in them as a target. Novak suddenly realized something else, too. The majority of the smoke wasn't coming from the burning structures or even from the white phosphorus mortar rounds the VC were dropping on the Tai. Most of it was billowing from HC smoke grenades that had been popped around the camp.

Then, from the west, beyond the walls of the camp and toward the tree line that marked the edge of the western perimeter, he heard a sound that made his body suddenly grow cold and clammy from the sweat covering it. The sound of bugles. Lots of bugles. Maybe half a dozen. As he watched the macabre spectacle in fascinated horror, all along the west and north walls of the camp, the gun emplacements there began firing. Into the center of the camp.

In a split second Novak made his decision. Crossing the open ground to the communications bunker would have been suicidal. Instead, he sprinted for Gerber's hootch. He shoved the captain's bunk out of the way and threw back the woven bamboo mat that covered the entrance to the tunnel that connected the hootch to the central command bunker. If he could get to Sully Smith's switch panels, he might be able to blow the bunkers on the west and north walls and get word out on the backup radio that the camp was being overrun.

He squeezed his massive frame through the tiny opening and dropped to the packed dirt floor below. He had no real plan except to blow the bunkers and get a message out. Then, if there was time, he would fall back and blow the tunnel to the command post and try to hold out for as long as he could in one of the machine gun bunkers inside the redoubt. If he could last until darkness, he might be able to slip through the perimeter, exfiltrate along one of the safe routes through the eastern minefield and E and E to Moc Hoa. It was a terrible plan, and he knew it, but it was all he could think of.

As he pushed along the narrow confines of the covered trench, feeling his way in the darkness, he thought of the reporter, Morrow, somewhere overhead. But there was nothing he could do for her now. His first responsibility was to the camp and to the men being slaughtered by the turncoat gunners along the west and north walls. He had to blow those bunkers and get word out on the radio. Afterward he might be able to find Morrow, if she had stayed inside the redoubt. A journalist, even a friendly female journalist, was too unimportant to worry about just now.

Novak reached the end of the tunnel and tore back the bamboo matting. He threw his massive weight against the single layer of sandbags that camouflaged the entrance on the other side. The walls collapsed, and he tumbled into the dimly lighted command post amid a shower of rubberized sandbags and sprawled on the floor. He looked up into the smiling face of Lieutenant Dung, who had his .45-caliber pistol trained directly on Novak's head. There were three other men with him, each of them covering Novak with a carbine. All four men wore a bright red strip of cloth tied about their left arms.

"Lieutenant Novak, no get up please," said Dung pleasantly. "Otherwise, I shoot. Permit please I introduce self. I no longer Lieutenant Dung. I now Major Dung of National Liberation Front. You my prisoner."

ROBIN MORROW STUCK HER HEAD out of the team house to see what all the noise was about and nearly had it shot off. As one bullet thunked into a sandbag in front of her face and a second whizzed past her ear, she ducked back inside. She'd seen enough.

At first she thought it must be some kind of crazy race riot and the Vietnamese were killing the Tai. Acting with journalistic instinct, she grabbed one of her cameras with a telephoto lens and crawled back out the door and up the short stairway. She couldn't see beyond the wall of the redoubt, but the American compound was filled with men wearing the tiger-striped camouflage fatigues of the strikers and the black pajamas of the Vietcong. Some of the strikers seemed to be helping the VC kill the other strikers. She got five photos before another burst of gunfire forced her back inside.

Morrow stood panting with her back pressed against the sandbagged entryway and tried to sort it all out. She wished her hangover would go away. Her temples throbbed maddeningly. Damn it! The camp was being overrun, and there were apparently VC infiltrators in the strike force that were helping from inside the camp. What a story it would make! If she could stay alive to write it.

Quickly she rewound the film and popped it out of the camera's back. If worse came to worst, at least she'd have a few shots of it. She wrapped the roll in her handkerchief and stuffed it into the bottom of one of the side pockets of her fatigue shorts. She scrambled crabwise across the floor for her camera bag, got a fresh roll and reloaded the camera, clicking the shutter and advancing the film until it was ready to shoot.

"Okay. Camera ready," she panted. "Fine. Now think. What next?"

Her gun. Where the hell had she put it?

Furiously she dug through the contents of her voluminous canvas suitcase until she found the pistol Bromhead had given her.

Bromhead, the former executive officer of Camp A-555, had insisted on giving her the weapon as a present, saying that no respectable young lady should be wandering about the jungle without one. Morrow had protested at the time that war correspondents, traditionally, were never armed. Bromhead had countered with the statement that it wasn't a traditional war. The Vietcong, he'd said, was an equal opportunity employer. And killer.

Morrow had taken the gun primarily because she didn't want to offend Bromhead. He was a nice young man, although perhaps a bit too serious at times.

Now Morrow studied the heavy black steel object in her hand, trying to remember how it worked. She opened the box of cartridges, shook out a handful and with some difficulty succeeded in loading the weapon. She poured the rest of the cartridges into a pocket of her shorts.

Keeping low to avoid any stray rounds that might happen to make it through the screened upper part of the wall of the team house, Morrow gathered her gear.

"Let's see now. Pistol belt with canteen, compass, first-aid kit and bowie knife. There's supposed to be a holster for this damned gun somewhere. Ah, here it is. My hat, wallet, sunglasses. Mosquito repellent. Definitely mosquito repellent."

She tied her poncho and blanket liner onto her rucksack and went over to the cupboards, filling the pack with canned goods and a couple of beers from the miserable refrigerator, then tightened it. She tested the pack.

It was heavy.

She eyed her collection of cameras and lenses, realized with disappointment that she'd have to leave most of them behind, along with her typewriter. It couldn't be helped. She picked up one, the Canon with the 28-80 mm lens, wrapped it in a kitchen towel and stuffed it into the top of the rucksack. She hoped it wouldn't get too beat up in there.

"Okay, fine. Ready to go. Now all I've got to do is find a way to get out of here without getting myself killed before somebody comes looking for me."

But it was too late. Two men, one in black pajamas, both of them armed with carbines, charged down the steps and burst into the room. Morrow spun to face them. She didn't hesitate.

Holding the pistol in both hands to steady it, thumbing back the hammer as Bromhead had showed her how to do, she fired steadily until the gun clicked empty. In the confined space of the team house, the roar was deafening.

Both men lay on the floor, each in his own little pool of slowly spreading blood. One of the men moved slightly, then was still.

"Ohhh shit!" moaned Morrow as she struggled to reload the weapon. Her hands were shaking, and she kept fumbling the cartridges and dropping them on the floor. "Robin, what have you done? You've really got yourself into a mess now," she muttered.

She slipped the straps of the rucksack over her shoulders, hung the camera with the big telephoto lens about her neck and started out the door.

A single pistol shot drove her back inside.

"Miss Morrow," called a voice from outside. "Please to throw out your weapon and surrender."

Morrow figured silence might be the best answer.

After a little while the voice spoke again.

"Miss Morrow, please. If you no throw out your weapon and surrender, I am forced to have my men use the hand grenades. I no wish that you must die, but I waste beaucoup time already now. Also you have make to die twos of my men. If you surrender now, I promise you will no be put to die. If you no surrender now, I am forced to order the hand grenades be used. Does this be clear to you?"

Then Morrow heard another voice.

"Robin? Miss Morrow? It's Lieutenant Novak, ma'am. I think you'd better do as he says. He means it. If you don't throw out your weapon and come out, he's got men ready to throw grenades in there. You won't have a chance if they do."

"Oh, hell, hell, hell," said Morrow, slowly banging her forehead against a sandbag. She had no intention of allowing herself to fall into enemy hands. Not after Hong Kong. She looked at the pistol in her hand and considered suicide. Where to put it? The mouth, the chest or the side of the head? Which would be quicker? Which the least painful?

She cocked the hammer and slowly raised the muzzle. Her hand shook only a little.

"Miss Morrow, you please to come out now. Otherwise, the grenades."

"*Mau!*"

"Robin, for God's sake, he means it!"

Morrow looked down the barrel. She could see the nose of the little bullet inside. Quiet, smooth, impassive, it waited for her to make up her mind.

It was no good. She just couldn't do it. The will to live was too strong. She lowered the muzzle and carefully let down the hammer.

"All right!" she called. "All right. I'm coming out. Don't shoot. Here comes the gun."

She emptied the cartridges from the pistol and tossed it up the stairway.

Morrow shrugged off the pack and let it drop to the floor of the team house. Hands raised high over her head, she walked slowly up the stairs into the late-afternoon sunlight.

There were two men waiting on either side at the top of the stairs with grenades in their hands. The little bastard had meant it, all right.

Morrow felt herself suddenly pushed forward from behind. Someone grabbed her arms and twisted them behind her back, holding them while someone else used a thin cord to tie her wrists and elbows together. It hurt like hell, and it gave her a funny, stiff posture. She felt hands at her waist, and someone took away the pistol belt with the canteen and bowie knife on it.

A few yards away she could see Novak. The young lieutenant's nose and mouth had been bloodied, but he seemed otherwise undamaged. He was tied in the same way as Morrow, except that a short hobble was tied between his ankles, permitting him to walk with a shuffling gait but not to run or kick out at anyone.

"So, Miss Morrow, you like the big knife, too. Yes?" said Dung. "The Lieutenant Novak, he like also the big knife, same-same as you. I like too the knife, but mine is so very smaller. Mine make little cuts, but you and Lieutenant Novak's knives, they make big cut. Yes? I think maybe later we see how big cuts. Yes?"

"Dung, you stinking pile of shit," growled Novak. "You promised you'd let her live if she gave up."

"Yes-yes. That true," said Major Dung. He walked forward and took hold of Morrow's chin, twisting her off balance so he could admire the line of her face.

He looked over at Novak.

"It very true I promise she no be put to die if surrender. But that all I promise. Miss Morrow kill twos of my men. For this she must be make to suffer. The Front's eyes no see her as journalist anymore. She enemy soldier now."

Without warning, he turned and punched Morrow hard in the stomach. When she doubled up, he kneed her in the teeth.

Novak lunged, even though his hands and feet were tied. It was a heroic gesture, a stupid, silly thing to do, but he did it, anyway. Then a rifle butt connected behind his ear, and the inside of his head exploded in fireworks. He slumped to the ground, dazed but not quite unconscious. He was dimly aware of his face pressing into the ocher dirt and the voices speaking around him. Their Vietnamese was too fast for him to follow, despite the short course he'd taken at the U.S. Army Language School, but he saw two of them pick Morrow up beneath the armpits and drag her off in the direction of the Vietnamese quarters.

Major Dung walked over and booted Novak in the ribs to get his attention.

"You will please to listen most carefully when it is that I am wish to speak with you, Lieutenant Novak," said Dung. "You are soldier no longer. You now prisoner of the Front. You must cooperate or you will be shoot to die. No more foolishness! Does this be clear to you?"

Novak remained silent, and Dung drew back his foot to kick the American again.

"All right," said Novak. "You've made your point. No more foolishness." Then he vowed to himself that, the next time he went for Dung, he'd make sure he could finish the job.

A VC soldier came up carrying the NLF flag. He spoke slowly enough so that this time Novak was able to follow the conversation.

"Comrade Major, I have the honor to report that all resistance has ceased. The camp is ours. The men are asking for permission to run up our glorious flag as a symbol of our victory."

"The men will have to be patient just a little bit longer," Dung replied. "I have received a message from the Americans' headquarters that the other Americans and their Tai mercenary soldiers are returning soon. They were not expected back for several days.

"It was a stroke of luck for us that so many of them were outside the camp when we were ready to put our plan into action. It made our victory much easier and much less costly. Now we will capitalize on that victory. Our many long months of planning enabled us to infiltrate key positions here. True, we were dealt a serious setback with the death of Major Vo, but the plan remained sound and we followed it to victory. Now, because of that, we find ourselves in the position of a unique opportunity.

"In half an hour six of the big American helicopters, the ones they call Chinook, will be bringing the others back into the camp. We must ensure that from the air they see only their camp, where work will appear to be going on normally. If they are curious about the damage, I will explain it was the result of a mortar attack, and they will believe this is so. When they land, we will turn the weapons of the camp upon them and destroy their valuable helicopters and kill all Americans and Tai inside. It will be a fitting tribute to our departed Comrade Vo," Dung concluded smilingly.

"It is a brilliant plan, Comrade Major. It will bring great honor to the Front and to you."

"Thank you, Comrade. I am merely utilizing my initiative, as the ARVN and Americans have so carefully taught me."

They all laughed at that. All of them except Novak, who kept his mouth shut and his ears open.

"After we have destroyed the American helicopters, Comrade Major, then may we hoist our flag in victory?"

"By all means. But hoist this with it. Beneath our flag, of course." Dung reached inside his jungle jacket and handed the man a large bundle.

"What is it?" asked the VC soldier.

"It is a Chinese flag."

"A Chinese flag, Comrade Major? I do not understand."

"It, too, is a kind of tribute. To the man who planned this operation. I promised him that it would one day fly over this camp."

The VC soldier looked puzzled. "As you wish, Comrade Major."

Novak had no idea what in hell they were talking about with the Chinese flag, then remembered that Morrow had told him about a Chinese officer who had served as an advisor to the VC in this area and who had given them such a hard time in Hong Kong. Suddenly it all began to make a twisted kind of sense.

"It is bigger than our flag, Comrade Major," the man protested.

"It does not matter, Comrade. Ours will be above it." He handed the man a key. "This is for the small storage shed near the helipad. Please assist Comrade Binh in taking this prisoner there. Then you may return to your platoon. Binh will remain to guard the prisoner. Everyone else must change into enemy uniforms or get out of sight. I will go now to make the necessary preparations. The rest of you men must come with me."

Novak's mind raced. In the E and E course they had always taught that you should make your escape attempt as soon as possible after capture. In the first twenty-four hours. It was said that your odds of a successful escape would diminish greatly after that because of the poor food and harsh living conditions a prisoner could expect. Unfortunately, the course hadn't covered what you were supposed to do when you were tied hand and foot.

This would likely be his best chance. There were only two men on him at the moment, and they weren't expecting any trouble because he'd been butt stroked and was tied up. Everyone else had temporarily cleared out of the American compound, except a couple of guys who were busy looting the dispensary of all its medical supplies, and they were preoccupied inside the building just now.

He thought of making another attempt to get to the demolition panels in either the command post or the fire control tower, if he could figure out a way to get free, but had to reject those ideas. Dung was sure to have someone on guard in the command bunker, and Novak would stick out like a sore thumb if he tried to get up the ladder.

Whatever he was going to do, he was going to have to do it pretty damned quick because Captain Gerber and the rest of them were about to fly into a lethal trap.

*"Di!"* said one of the guards. *"Di, mau!"* He prodded Novak with the toe of his boot to get him moving.

Then suddenly Novak saw it. It had been there all along. Just hanging right there in plain sight. The VC who had taken his web gear after they marched him out of the command post—what had Dung called him? Binh? Anyway, the one with the burp gun. He still had Novak's web gear slung over one shoulder. And on the web gear hung the knife. Now if he could just con one of the guards into using it . . .

*"Di!"* the guard insisted. *"Di! Di!"*

Novak struggled clumsily to his feet, shaking his head and stumbling, doing his best to give the impression of a man who had just been hit on the head with a rifle butt and is still a bit groggy. It wasn't very hard to give a convincing performance.

Carefully Novak took two shuffling steps, tangled his feet in the hobble and fell. The landing was a bit rougher than he would have liked because he couldn't use his hands to break his fall, but he'd been sacked enough times on the football field to know how to go limp and tuck his head in so he wouldn't injure anything seriously.

He let the air go out of himself when he hit, for effect, then lay there until Binh or the guy with the flags in his hands prodded him back up. This time he took three steps before falling.

The guards clearly were getting pissed. They shouted curses and kicked at him. Novak lay there and took it for a minute or so, then fought his way laboriously to his feet with a great deal of exaggerated gasping and wheezing. This time he only took one step.

The guards went absolutely ape. They cussed. They kicked. They threatened. They did everything but shoot him, which, Novak had to admit to himself, he'd been just a little afraid they might do after Dung's warning not to fool around.

Novak got obediently to his feet and went down after two steps.

The guards gave up and tried to drag him, but there was no way a couple of little VC were going to drag Novak's great mass. Especially while they were burdened with superfluous equipment, and most especially not while he was letting his whole body go slack so that he'd be nothing but deadweight.

Novak, ever the helpful prisoner, did his best to get up again. Walking very carefully, he took four small, shuffling steps before allowing the hobble to trip him.

Binh finally got the bright idea that Novak kept falling because he kept tripping over the hobble, and in a fit of disgust he yanked the big knife from its sheath. He had to transfer the PPSh-41 to his left hand in order to use the knife to cut through the hobble, and it was at that precise moment, when his legs were free, that Novak struck.

His first kick caught Binh in the groin and set him up for the second, a boot heel strike to the underside of the chin. It sounded as if the man's jaw broke with the kick. Novak hoped it had.

The burp gun, which Novak couldn't have used because of the way he was tied, went flying.

He rolled, drew his feet under him and launched himself directly at the VC with his hands full of flags, giving him a head butt to the bridge of the nose. There was a sickening crunch, and the man who had been holding the flags went down.

Both guards were now down and had completely lost interest in Novak. He knew it wouldn't last, but five or ten seconds was all he would need.

He looked around, spotted the knife where Binh had dropped it when Novak had tried to kick his head off and managed, with considerable effort and contortion to pick it up and stick the blade in the ground. Novak then scooted backward until he could reach the blade and, by rubbing his wrists parallel to the edge, succeeded in cutting through the cord around his wrists. He also succeeded in cutting himself, although the wound was not serious.

Having his wrists free gave Novak a little more flexibility, and he was able to pull the knife out of the ground and reverse it, holding the blade upward between his elbows. The massive blade was just barely long enough to reach that far up Novak's big arms, but he got the job done, thanks to the razor sharpness of the carefully honed edge. He only had to pause once to stomp on the trachea of the man who had been holding the flags. The guard had forgotten all about his flags and was busy holding his broken nose and complaining about it. His complaints were getting rather noisy, so Novak quieted him down. Permanently.

Not wanting to leave the job half finished, Novak took the knife and drew the blade across the throat of the inert Binh. Some, he supposed, might have called it murder to do that to an unconscious man. Novak preferred to think of it as fighting for his life. It made no sense at all to leave behind an unconscious enemy who might, at any moment, wake and give the alarm. Besides, Binh might well have been dead already, or at least dying. The kick had been intended to kill.

Novak slipped his own web gear over his shoulders and slung Binh's burp gun. Then he picked up both of the VC bodily, draping one over each shoulder like duffel bags, and hustled them down the steps into the team house, where they would be out of sight until someone came in and found them. He could expect that to be reasonably soon because there were already two bodies in the hootch, but with all the VC getting ready to ambush the helicopters, it might be an hour or better, and that would be time enough.

Novak checked the bodies of the men, looking for anything useful.

Binh had five spare magazines for the burp gun in his web gear, but only two of them were loaded. Novak took the loaded ones and checked the other guard whose weapon was an antiquated French 8 mm bolt action rifle that looked as though it might have been designed for shooting around corners, if you could judge anything from the condition of the sights. Novak decided he'd be better off with the burp gun and took the bolt out of the rifle, intending to throw it away when he got the chance. Without a bolt the rifle would be one less weapon for the Vietcong to use.

The other two bodies had already been stripped of their weapons and equipment, so there was nothing left to interest him.

It was time to move. Novak figured he had between five and fifteen minutes before somebody noticed he was gone and started a search. He aimed to put the time to good use.

He had to figure out some sort of signal to warn Captain Gerber and the others that they were flying into a trap and do it without giving himself away. The radios in the command post were out. Dung would have troops there, maybe even be there himself. Novak rejected the communications bunker, too. Dung was no fool. He would either have put the radios out of commission as soon as the VC attack started or posted a guard there.

But there was one very long shot that just might work. It was a pretty crazy idea, but so what? It was the only game in town.

Novak peeked cautiously out the doorway. The coast was clear. He sprinted into the open, snatched the NLF and Chinese flags from where they'd fallen and ran straight to the dispensary, knowing there were still a couple of VC inside. He figured the enemy was less likely to look for him in a building they already occupied. Or rather on top of a building they already occupied.

The dispensary was the second largest building in the American compound. Built of red brick with a green tiled roof, it was a distinctive structure easily spotted from the air. He'd noticed it coming into camp the day before.

There were some sandbags stacked around the walls and a few scattered about the roof in case of mortar rounds, but it was a halfhearted attempt at protection. Any patients within its walls would be removed to an underground bunker almost as soon as the first round dropped.

Novak slid to a halt and pressed himself against the five foot high barrier of sandbags that ran all around the dispensary and which was positioned a short distance from the walls to allow air circulation. He worked his way along it, listening to the sounds of the VC inside, who seemed to be having a great deal of fun breaking things. When he found an opening, he slipped through the sandbags and into the little space between them and the brick wall of the dispensary. He edged his way around to the back and pulled himself up on the roof.

Novak looked at the two flags. The Chinese one was the larger of the two. Quickly he unfolded it and spread it out on top of the dispensary, using a sandbag to anchor each of the four corners. It showed up very nicely against the green roof. And although it was possible someone in the fire control tower might notice it, it would be invisible from the ground.

Novak, however, was not. The exposed roof offered nothing in the way of cover, and he dropped to the ground, taking the NLF flag with him. There was no point putting it on the roof, as well. If anyone in an inbound helicopter looked at the roof of the dispensary, he could hardly help seeing the Chinese flag. And if no one looked, it wouldn't matter if there were two flags or two hundred.

The important thing now was to get away. As far away from the dispensary as possible so that, if he was discovered, no one would think to check what he'd been doing at the dispensary. He would have to get rid of the NLF flag, too. Both flags missing might be overlooked, but one flag missing and one flag on his person would be sure to attract a lot of awkward questions from Major Dung.

As he came out from between the sandbagged wall and the dispensary, Novak walked smack into a VC coming out of the building with his arms loaded with medical supplies. Novak couldn't shoot without bringing the whole camp down on his neck, and there was no time for the knife. Using his left hand, he swung the burp gun by the barrel. Hard.

The man's skull shattered, but so did the stock of the SMG. Novak was now left holding a worthless piece of junk. He reminded himself that guns are for shooting people, not hitting them over the head, and then he ran.

Behind him there was a cry of alarm.

Novak ignored it and made straight for one of the machine gun emplacements on the east wall of the redoubt. Nightfall was only about an hour away. If he could hold them at bay that long, he might be able to exfiltrate and E and E under cover of darkness. If not, he'd pile up as many of them as he could before they finally got him. Resistance to the end. Beyond that he had no plan.

He reached the nearest machine gun bunker and dived inside. The place was already occupied by two of the VC infiltrators who had been masquerading as PF strikers. They weren't expecting visitors, however. At least none in the form of a two-hundred-seventy-five-pound Green Beret lieutenant. Novak bludgeoned one of the men to death with the burp club and finished the other man off with his knife. Then he assessed his situation.

A pessimist would have noted that Novak was alone, without communication and inside a camp held by a battalion, give or take, of Main Force Vietcong, plus, say, the thirty or forty guerrillas who had infiltrated the strike force and who were now alert to the fact that he was running around loose and would very soon be coming to kill him.

Novak preferred to think of it another way. He was no longer a prisoner. He had a good, defensible position. He had a full canteen. And he had more weapons and ammunition than he was likely to ever get the chance to use. There were both a .50-caliber Browning and an M-60 mounted in the bunker, and he quickly repositioned the M-60 to cover the entrance to the bunker.

Both of the VC infiltrators had carried M-1 carbines, and he scrounged over a dozen magazines for those from the phony strikers' bodies, along with three hand grenades. He had done what he could to warn the others of the impending trap, and from his position he could deny the enemy access to the main ammunition bunker. At least until they were able to sneak a sapper team in close enough to blow him out of his bunker. And with the two Morrow had killed and the five he'd taken out, the enemy now had seven fewer men to try to kill him with. In Novak's opinion, things were looking up.

# 6

## SPECIAL FORCES
## DETACHMENT B-52 TOC,
## SAIGON

Lieutenant Colonel Alan Bates slammed the telephone handset down hard into the cradle and glared at the apparatus as if it was some evil monster he was about to crush. Bates was normally a no-nonsense, straightforward man but legendary among the Special Forces soldiers for his icy calmness under pressure. Right now he was anything but calm. It was the first time Bates's executive officer, Major Pratt, could ever recall seeing Bates look angry, and right now his commanding officer's face was positively florid. Bates shifted that terrible gaze to Pratt, and the executive officer felt his insides squirm uncontrollably.

"Just what the hell is this, Major? Some kind of plague? I go up to Qui Nhon for one day, just one single day, and when I get back, the entire war has gone to hell. Mack Gerber's got his whole damned A-Detachment and two companies of strikers out beating the bushes on the Cambodian border looking for a downed airplane with some hotshot VIP on board, and running into a battalion of Main Force VC who aren't supposed to be anywhere near the area. You say that he says he's out there on orders from General Crinshaw, who, I might add, has no authority to issue such orders, and when I try to find out what the hell is supposed to be going on—a reasonable enough thing for me to want to do as the commanding officer directly responsible for Gerber and his men—you don't know anything about it except what Gerber has told you.

"I try to call General Crinshaw, and nobody knows where he is. I try to call General Hull, and nobody knows where he is. I even try to call Westmoreland's office, and nobody knows where he is. I'd call the President of the United States, but I'm afraid nobody would know where he is, either. Everybody's missing. Nobody knows where they've gone, and nobody has any idea what in hell is happening out there. Now we can't even raise anybody at the camp. I don't suppose you have any additional light you'd like to shed on this subject?"

Pratt looked uncomfortable. "Sir, I've already told you everything I know. Captain Gerber contacted me early this morning, asking for confirmation of General Crinshaw's orders. I told him that you were unavailable. I didn't think I ought to be broadcasting over the radio that you'd gone to Qui Nhon with your sergeant major to pick up his nephew's body. I told him I'd check with you immediately upon your return and get back to him. I also told him I'd contact General Crinshaw's office and attempt to clarify the situation. I did that, but General Crinshaw had already left, and he didn't tell the admin sergeant where he was going. He just muttered something about having a mess to straighten out and said he'd contact the office later.

"I tried to get in touch with his executive officer, Colonel DuBois, but he had an early-morning tennis game at the racket club, and when I finally got hold of him, he didn't have any idea what was going on, either, as he hadn't been to the office yet. I called General Hull's office but was told he was out and not reachable. I asked to talk to his exec, but he's on R and R in Australia.

"By the time I got back in touch with the camp, Captain Gerber was already in the field. We did finally manage to establish radio link with him through an Air Force FAC—that's how we got the Intel about the VC unit whose trail he'd run across. I arranged airlift back to the camp for him and his men and left word with the camp radio watch to have him contact your office as soon as he returned, since I assumed you would be back by then and would know what it was all about. After that we lost radio contact with the camp. I was just about to try and contact him via the

choppers sent out for airlift when you returned. I can't tell you
any more because that's all I know."

"All right, all right," said Bates, waving his hand. He seemed
to be cooling down somewhat, and his color was beginning to return to normal. "I guess it's not your fault. Go ahead and get on
with it. Let me know as soon as you've established radio contact
with Gerber again."

Major Pratt got on with it.

Bates sat drumming his fingers on the duty officer's desk in the
tiny cubicle he'd commandeered for his conference with his executive officer. Bates realized he had been a little hard on Pratt.
It wasn't his fault. The whole mess was one of those situations that
result when nobody is doing his job because everybody wrongly
assumes that somebody is doing it for him. It was the kind of
mistake that shouldn't have happened because it was easily
avoidable, but it had. That was what had Bates doing a slow burn.
The situation had been avoidable.

That, and Crinshaw going outside the chain of command to order Gerber and his troops into the field, which clearly was wrong.
But how do you tell a general officer he fucked up without losing
your commission? Especially when you can't find him to tell him.

Bates tried to put himself in Gerber's position. What would he
have done if he'd gotten such an order out of the blue from a
brigadier general? Probably exactly what Gerber had done. So
what if Crinshaw wasn't directly in their chain of operational
command? He was still a general officer, and when a general tells
you to do something, as a general rule, by God, you'd better do
it and be quick about it.

Bates would have tried to confirm the order through proper
channels. That was exactly what Gerber had done, but he'd found
those channels closed because everybody had hung up the out sign
without telling anybody where he was going. In that situation
Bates probably would have requested a written order, and then if
the mission couldn't wait, he'd have got on with it. That, apparently, was what Gerber had done. Bates hoped for Gerber's sake
that the captain had requested a written order and that there were
witnesses to the request. This incident was the sort of thing that
could hurt a young officer's career. And Brigadier General Billy
Joe Crinshaw didn't exactly have a history of looking out for young

officers' careers. Especially Special Forces officers, and most especially Mack Gerber's.

Bates tried to figure out what it all meant. A transport plane down along the Cambodian border. What was it doing there? Supposedly carrying some VIP to or from somewhere. But where? And why? And just who was this VIP who was so important that Crinshaw would hit the panic button and order half of Camp A-555's personnel out to look for him? And if there was such a VIP missing, why didn't Bates or anyone else know who it was? Well, Crinshaw apparently knew; hence, he had given his orders to Gerber. But why hadn't anyone else heard about it? And just where in blazes was everybody?

It seemed as if everyone responsible for running the war had suddenly gone on holiday, just when the biggest operation of the war thus far was under way up north. And what in hell was that battalion of VC doing out there, anyway? Looking for the airplane with the missing VIP? Ridiculous. Who could be so important that the VC would put a whole battalion into the field to find him? For that matter, who could be so important that Crinshaw would go ape and order Gerber's team and two companies of the best strikers the Special Forces had at their disposal out to look for him? None of it made any sense at all.

And most important, why had they suddenly lost all communication with Camp A-555? There had been no hint of attack or other problems.

There was nothing that Bates could do until he heard from Gerber. Or Hull. Or even Crinshaw, for Christ's sake. It galled him to have to sit and wait without knowing what was happening. For a moment he had the irrational thought that he was being kept purposely in the dark, like a mushroom, and that galled him even more.

Bates became aware that he was drumming his fingers on the desk and stopped.

"Damn it," he sighed. "Whatever is going on, I've got a very bad feeling about this."

# 7

## SPECIAL FORCES
## CAMP A-555

Trung Si Nhat Krung lay in the stifling heat and darkness of the corrugated metal drainage culvert and watched the dim outline of the snake silhouetted against the open tube mouth two meters in front of his face.

It was impossible to clearly identify what kind of snake it was because of the choking smoke that hung like a shroud over the camp. The thick swirls threatened to rob Krung's tortured lungs of what little oxygen they were able to extract from the foul air normally present in the drainage tube. It did not appear to be a very large snake, though the way its body was bunched in coils could be deceiving in the poor light. It did not matter. Krung knew that the bite of a krait or cobra could be lethal no matter what the size.

Sergeant Krung had been supervising a work detail near the north end of the runway, filling some sandbags for a couple of new countermortar bunkers, when the VC had launched their surprise attack from both inside and outside the camp. The work party had immediately come under heavy fire from the treacherous Vietnamese strikers manning the northwest .50-caliber machine gun bunker. Most of the unarmed workers had been hit in the first burst. The big, full-metal-jacketed slugs had ripped apart the flimsy protection of the few sandbags that had been filled, leaving the survivors of the initial onslaught no place to hide. The remaining workers had fled across the open runway and been cut down by the murderous cross fire from positions along the north wall.

Krung alone had escaped.

Throwing himself behind a pile of sandbags when the northwest bunker had opened fire on the work detail, he had spied the open mouth of the drainage tube and immediately crawled inside, realizing it offered the best cover and concealment available. After that there had been nothing to do except continue to crawl through to the other side.

Krung had hoped that he might be able to reach the communications bunker once on the other side of the runway; the shallow drainage ditch that the tube fed into bent and ran along the edge of the helipad. It was just possible that it might provide enough concealment for him to be able to slip past the helipad beneath the line of fire of the guns on the north wall and make a dash for the communications bunker when he got close enough. If the communications bunker had not already fallen, it would provide a fairly good defensive position and the opportunity to call for help.

But all that had become problematic when he encountered the snake. The drainage tube was barely large enough for Krung to fit through. It was far too small a space to seriously annoy a snake in, especially since he didn't know whether the snake was venomous.

Of all the work party members, Krung alone had been armed. Soldiers assigned to perform hard manual labor generally did not prefer to do it with an extra six and a half to eleven pounds of carbine or rifle hanging about their necks. But Krung, because of his injured foot, had been supervising the filling of sandbags, not holding the bags or swinging one of the shovels, and like the American Green Berets who had taught him, Krung never went anywhere without being armed if he could help it. Not even in a supposedly safe camp. You never knew when the enemy might attack or from what direction, as today's events had so disastrously proven.

So although Krung had his carbine, he had wisely chosen the drainage tube rather than fighting, knowing that a man in the open, armed with a carbine, is no match for a group of men in a heavily fortified bunker armed with a .50-caliber machine gun.

At least it had seemed wise until he encountered the snake. Only a man interested in becoming suddenly, and perhaps permanently, deaf would consider shooting the snake in the confined space of the drainage tunnel. Besides, the noise might attract the Vietcong, who would probably get around to checking the drainage tube soon enough, anyway. And to challenge the snake with his knife in such a place was a thing no sane man could seriously contemplate.

So there was nothing else to do but wait and watch. Krung watched the snake, who in turn took a kind of bored interest in him. They watched each other, Krung wondering with his mind, and the snake with whatever mental capacity it possessed, just exactly what the other one was and which one of them would make a precipitous move first.

As it turned out, it was one of the Vietcong strikers that made the first move. He foolishly stuck his head into the mouth of the tube to see if anyone happened to be hiding inside, like Krung. The VC very nearly got a faceful of snake for his efforts. He obviously didn't appreciate it, either, as he rapidly used the bayonet on his M-1 Garand to drag the snake out into the open, then emptied an entire eight-round clip from the rifle into the snake.

From Krung's position the noise was considerable but not nearly as bad as it would have been if the weapon had been fired inside the tube.

When the VC had finished blowing the snake to bits, he reached down and flipped it over with his bayonet. The mangled reptile landed directly in front of the tube mouth, and Krung could clearly see it for the first time. The broad black-and-yellow horizontal striped pattern of the banded krait was clearly visible. Even with antivenin, a medical wonder of which Krung had never heard, the bite was usually deadly. Both the Vietnamese from the cities and towns and the Americans seemed to hold the krait in great fear because of this. But Krung, who had spent most of his life in the jungle or in small villages in the jungle, knew that the banded krait was an inoffensive creature, so mild mannered that the Tai peoples generally considered it harmless and a good meal. Yes, it could kill you, but it rarely bit anyone even if stepped on. This one had struck out at the VC only because Krung had been blocking its only avenue of escape.

The VC was apparently a city boy, however, as he lost all interest in exploring the drainage tube further after successfully killing the snake. Krung felt a curious sense of gratitude toward the snake. In a way it had sacrificed its life to save his. He promised himself that the next time he killed one for food, he would show it the proper respect and make an offering for its spirit.

Krung waited several minutes to make sure that no one else was going to investigate his hiding place, then edged cautiously forward for a look. The sound of firing had stopped, and some of the smoke was beginning to clear. Everywhere he could see men wearing the black pajama uniform of the Vietcong, some of them in black shorts. Sprinkled among them were a few men in the tiger-striped jungle fatigues of the strike force. These infiltrators had red bandannas tied about their left arms.

Several small groups of VC and striker impostors were herding bunches of PF strikers who had their hands over their heads. Krung realized that the camp had fallen. There was nothing else he could do until nightfall; perhaps it would be possible then for him to slip out of the camp and escape. Until then he could only do his best to remain undetected, and the best hiding place available seemed to be the one he already occupied. Reluctantly he slid back into the shadows inside the tube.

It could not have been more than five or ten minutes later, although Krung had not thought to check his watch, when he heard the sound of helicopters, suddenly very loud overhead.

Krung was confused. He did not know if the others had returned and were walking into a VC trap, or if the helicopters were gunships coming to attack the camp now that the VC held it. Krung did not think the VC had any helicopters. Yet, from the sound of it, the helicopters were landing. Krung slid forward again and risked a look.

He could see two Huey helicopters crowding the extreme opposite edges of the helipad. One of them had landed. The other was hovering and appeared to have a large metal box, camouflaged with green-and-brown paint, hung beneath it with cables. The box was set down at the edge of the helipad, and some of the men from the first helicopter came over to disconnect the cables. Then one of the men opened a door on the side of the box and stepped inside. He came back out in a minute and said something to another man who went back inside with him. As Krung watched, the two men carried something out of the box and set it up outside. Then they began running a heavy rubber cable from the thing to the box and started a small engine on the object. While they worked, two other men began fixing an assortment of antennae to the roof of the box.

In the meantime, the other helicopter had apparently landed at the extreme north end of the runway. The sound was above Krung's head, but he could not rise to see what was going on without exposing himself to the VC gunners on the north wall of the camp. Finally the sound of the helicopters' rotors died, and he heard a loud, angry voice demanding in English to know where everyone was.

After a minute or two there was the sound of many footsteps, and Krung heard a voice he recognized as belonging to Lieutenant Dung, the LLDB camp executive officer.

"Good afternoon, General. To what, please, owe us the honor of your visit?"

"Never mind that," said the loud, angry voice. "Just get me the American officer in charge here. And tell him I want him to get his butt down here right now."

"It is regrettable that I no can do that," said Dung. "Captain Gerber and some of the mens are not in camp now. I expect he return very soon. In meantime, I have my men escort you and your mens to the Americans' compound. You wait there. Yes?"

"Like hell I will. I'll wait right here. And as soon as Gerber gets here, you tell him I want to see him."

"Most regrettable, but I no can permit this," said Dung.

"You can't permit it!" sputtered the loud, angry voice. "Just who in the hell do you think you are, mister, to go telling a general of the United States Army what he can and can't do?"

"Please to excuse," said Dung. "I no remember to introduce self. Permit me. I am Major Dung Cao Chiap of the National Liberation Front, and you, General, you my prisoner."

For a moment, nothing. Then there was the sound of scuffling, and a single shot rang out. After that it got very quiet again. A few moments passed before Dung spoke.

"General, you will please to tell all your mens no to attempt any more foolishness. Already you get one of your mens shot. Maybe he die. Any more foolishness, my mens shoot them all. We control camp now, General. You all my prisoners. Take them to the

Americans' team house and guard them," said Dung. "We must make ready for the others. They'll be here soon."

There was the sound of men marching away.

In the drainage tube beneath the runway, Krung slid back into the shadows to await the approaching darkness and wondered what it could all mean.

# 8

## THE CAMBODIAN-VIETNAM BORDER REGION NORTHWEST OF CAMP A-555

Major David Rittenour painfully awoke amid the wreckage of his U-1A Otter aircraft. He was thirsty and his head hurt.

Before he had thought only his head hurt. Until he tried to move his leg. The leg convinced him otherwise. If it was pain he wanted, there was plenty of it in the leg. He touched it carefully. Broken. In two places, from the feel of it.

Just fucking wonderful, thought Rittenour.

He probed his back and neck gently. Both were stiff and tender to the touch, but he couldn't feel any deformities of the spine. Apparently the crash hadn't broken his back or neck, after all. At any rate, he was still breathing, and he had sensation in all his extremities. In fact, at that moment he would have been a lot happier with a little less sensation in one of his extremities. The broken right leg, for instance.

Belatedly he thought to look around for his copilot.

Jones was gone.

In fact, the entire right half of the cockpit was gone. Rittenour twisted his head slightly. About fifty yards away, wedged among the tree branches, he could see what looked like part of the aircraft's right wing. Nothing else was recognizable in that direction.

By twisting slightly in the seat, a movement that caused him considerable pain and took several minutes to accomplish, he was able to look behind him. The aircraft's fuselage seemed to have broken completely in half. He could see most of the mangled remains of the passenger's compartment, which was littered with papers. Apparently his one and only passenger's briefcase had either been open when they crashed or had been broken open by the impact. Of the passenger himself there was no sign.

Rittenour took a moment to assess his immediate surroundings and ascertain that The Antichrist wasn't in imminent danger of bursting into flames, then tried to recall the events of the crash.

They'd left Phnom Penh late last night but had to divert from their direct flight to Saigon because of a storm front that wasn't supposed to be there.

Last night? What time was it?

Rittenour checked his watch. He'd been unconscious for nearly sixteen hours. No that wasn't quite right. He had vague, indistinct memories of the long night and of awakening once during the heat of midday. Could a man be semiconscious for sixteen hours? Was that the right word for it?

He had dreamed. He remembered that much. Of his wife back in Maryland and of a girl he had dated in high school. Lydia was her name. He wondered why he'd dreamed of her. He hadn't seen her in fifteen years and probably hadn't even thought about her in the past ten. He wondered why he never had *those* kind of dreams about his wife.

Try as he might, he could not remember the crash itself. He could remember detouring around the storm front that shouldn't have been there since this was the dry season, except up in I Corps, where the northeast monsoon was still keeping things damp. It was the southwest monsoon that normally fouled up flying in this part of Southeast Asia, and that was usually from May through September.

He could remember the sudden, unexpected loss of power from the engine and the instantly impossibly heavy controls, a sudden downdraft, but no more. The actual impact had been blanked from his mind.

After that there had only been the dreams. First there was the strange conversation with his wife about the bizarre hat she had bought, made even more strange because Madge never wore hats. That dream merged into a different one with Lydia MacIntire's warm, wet, passionate lips touching his teenage body in places and ways he had only read about in the kinds of books and magazines his parents didn't approve of. He could still recall the excitement and feelings of lust and hunger for her firm young body that he had never before imagined possible and had experienced only seldom since that very special prom night.

And then had come that other dream. The unsettling one. Filled with gunfire and explosions and the screaming of men in pain and dying. And then a long awful, oppressive silence. Thank God that had only been a dream.

It had, *hadn't it*?

Yes. Of course it had. What other possible explanation was there? But not a dream. A nightmare. Only why then . . . why did it seem somehow more real than the others? More real even than the soft touch of those incredible lips he had experienced so long ago? Why did he imagine that after that long dreadful quiet he heard other explosions and a sound like that of great trees being uprooted and crashing to the ground amid shouts of "Fire in the hole!" And why would anyone shout "Fire in the hole!" anyway? You were supposed to shout "Timber!" when a tree fell. And why did he imagine that he had been awakened by the falling tree and that he could smell cordite and nitrocellulose and smoke in the air? Could you smell in dreams?

And then suddenly it dawned on him. He *could* smell something in the air. A faint hot smell, like woodsmoke, acrid and vaguely metallic. Was the aircraft burning after all? Not after sixteen hours surely.

Then he heard it. The soft, distant popping of rotor blades and the almost imperceptible whine of a turbine engine. A helicopter.

Rittenour tried to sit up straighter in the seat and nearly passed out again from the pain in his leg.

For several seconds he listened, straining his hearing, until he was sure the helicopter was drawing closer. He struggled with the closure on the pocket of his survival vest, and then he had it, the UHF emergency radio. Quickly he connected the antenna and switched it on, but to his dismay, the transceiver remained silent. Not so much as a crackle of static escaped the unit's tiny speaker. The damned thing wouldn't work. He didn't know if the battery was dead or if the radio had somehow been broken during the crash. It didn't matter. The thing was useless, and without it he had no way of contacting the helicopter.

The helicopter, although still some distance away by the sound of it, was clearly heading toward him. Frantic now lest it should veer off in another direction and miss seeing him, Rittenour dug through the various pockets of his survival vest for the tiny Penguin Industries flare launcher. Using it would entail a certain element of risk, of course. If there were any VC in the area, they were about as likely to see it as the aircrew. If they did, Rittenour probably wouldn't get the opportunity to find out whether the aircrew had seen it.

When Rittenour at last succeeded in finding the launcher, the sound of the helicopter was very close, perhaps a klick or less away. His fingers closed about the crosshatched surface of the fountain-pen-sized metal tube, and he pulled it from the pocket of the vest, the launcher's lanyard trailing out behind it. The tape bandolier, which was attached to the lanyard and held the ten small flares for the launcher, snagged on the zipper and caught. He tugged on it, but it held fast.

The noise of the turbine and rotor blades was very loud. Abruptly the sound decreased in pitch and volume. To a pilot with Rittenour's years of experience, there could be no mistaking the meaning. The helicopter was landing.

Whether it was dropping troops off or picking some up, Rittenour didn't know. He knew that sometimes Green Beret teams operating in remote areas ran patrols in the rugged country along the border, and there were rumors that they also sometimes sent small teams of trail watchers into Cambodia to keep track of Vietcong movements along the Ho Chi Minh Trail. There were even rumors that the Green Berets employed the Khmer Serei and KKK for such surveillance missions and perhaps other more secret operations against the VC inside Cambodia. Maybe the helicopter was deploying or recovering such a team.

The thought that the helicopter crew might actually be looking for him had occurred to him, given the apparently important nature of his mysterious passenger, but the fact that it was landing seemed to discount that theory. They wouldn't do that unless they had spotted wreckage, and at the moment he was sitting in the biggest piece of wreckage around.

Whatever the reason for the helicopter's presence in the area, it meant rescue. If he didn't manage to attract the crew's attention quickly, however, that rescue was going to slip away. Rittenour could hear the sound of the engine increasing in pitch and volume. The helicopter was taking off. He tugged again on the lanyard, but it was stuck fast. The helicopter's whine grew into a howl. Desperately he yanked on the lanyard.

The zipper ripped out and the flare bandolier suddenly popped free, whizzing through the air. It dinged Rittenour squarely in the temple, and he saw stars as his eyes filled with tears. From a combination of pain, surprise and frustration, he lost his grip on the launcher, and it fell.

Dumbfounded by the catastrophe, Rittenour could only watch in fascinated horror as the flare launcher and its little bandolier of bright red flare rounds slid across the angled deck of the shattered cockpit and dropped to the jungle floor with a small, rustling thump. He could still see them lying there, so close yet so far—impossible to reach five feet away. It might as well have been fifty. With the busted leg there was no way he could climb down and get them.

The sound of the helicopter built into a roar as it lifted and chattered away in whatever direction it had come from.

For a long time after that there was silence in the tiny jungle clearing containing the ruins of the Otter.

A silence that was broken only by the sound of Rittenour crying.

# 9

## OUTSIDE SPECIAL
## FORCES CAMP A-555

The air changed from cool to muggy to downright oppressive as the flight of CH-47 helicopters descended toward pattern altitude over the big mud, sandbag and barbed wire rectangle of U.S. Army Special Forces Camp A-555.

Gerber was leaning against the side of the cabin, his M-14 between his knees, helmet in his lap, eyes closed. He was beyond tired. He was exhausted. The lack of sleep had really taken its toll. Apart from that was the confusion and bitter disappointment over a screwball mission gone sour and the loss of the Tai strikers.

They had spent an entire day marching over difficult terrain to get to the search area only to have to break off the sweep because contact with an enemy sniper team had compromised their presence in the area to a probably numerically larger force of VC. The thing he'd feared most had happened, and without an adequate NDP and air support it had been too risky to remain in the area overnight. And, of course, there had been the fight—well, argument anyway—with Morrow.

Altogether it was just too much. He was beginning to wish he'd never agreed to the six-month extension of his tour. He'd be glad when it was over in a couple of months. His nerves were raw. He couldn't sleep nights even when he wasn't on patrol, and when he did manage to catch a rare few minutes' rest, his dreams were haunted by the images of dead men, both enemy and friend.

The first had been Master Sergeant Bill Schattschneider, killed during a VC rocket and mortar attack while Camp A-555 was being built. Then Miles Clarke, the young demolitions expert, had been shot to death during the raid on the VC Political Cadre at Ap Tan. After that it had been Schmidt, the commo specialist too weird to last anywhere in the U.S. Army except Special Forces. Only Vampire Schmidt, as the men had called him, hadn't lasted. He'd taken a crossbow bolt from a VC booby trap through the chest that had punctured both his lungs and heart. Steve Kittredge, the heavy weapons specialist, had been the next to go, calling artillery in on his own position when a VC company overran his patrol on a tiny hilltop in the swamp. And most recently Ian McMillan, the team's senior medical specialist, had been killed in a VC ambush while leading a patrol.

But the faces that haunted him most were still among the living. Sean Cavanaugh in a complete state of psychoneurotic paralysis in the mental ward of Third Field Hospital in Saigon, if you could call that living. Karen Morrow's face the last time he had seen her, like a very bad dream that just wouldn't end, no matter what logic told him about the situation. And Robin. After that Chinese bastard had finished playing telephone with her in Hong Kong. And the icy cool exterior she'd projected ever since, smooth, untroubled, but hiding what was underneath, like the shell of an egg ready to crack, despite the denials. Why wouldn't the damned woman go home to the States where it was safe, anyway? What was she trying to prove?

The touch of Fetterman's hand on his arm startled him, and he jerked back, banging his head on the side of the ship.

"Yes? What is it?"

"Sorry, Captain, didn't mean to startle you, but there's something funny going on down there," said Fetterman.

"What do you mean, something funny?"

"Looks like the place has been hit while we were out. There's a bunch of fresh craters on the runway, and a couple of the striker barracks have been burned. There're also a couple of Hueys and a big conex up at the north end of the runway."

"That *is* funny. I wonder what it's all about? I guess we'll find out soon enough. We'll be landing in a minute."

"That's just it, Captain. I'm not so sure we should. Land, I mean. At least not without checking things out with Lieutenant Novak on the radio first. I've got a bad feeling about this one."

Gerber sat up straight, instantly alert. In fifteen months he'd learned to put great faith in Master Sergeant Fetterman's bad feelings.

"Explain yourself," said Gerber.

"There's just not enough movement down there, sir. No one moving around at all. There ought to be some work parties, loafers, some of the strikers' families moving around, something. But nobody's moving down there. You'd think the commo watch would have popped smoke for the choppers by now. Also, the base has obviously taken some mortar damage, but we got no word of an attack. Seems a little strange Lieutenant Novak didn't relay word to us after we got a commo link with that FAC. I mean, what with the lieutenant being a new man and all, you'd think he might want to let you know about it ASAP. Also, there's a bright red rectangle on top of the dispensary."

"A big red rectangle?"

"Yes, sir. Can't really make it out from this altitude, but it sort of reminds me of an NVA or Chinese flag."

"Come on, Tony. Is that what's got you going? Some piece of red stuff that reminds you of a flag? You're letting your imagination run away with you, Master Sergeant. The Chinese guy is dead."

"Yes, sir. Only I didn't get to touch the body, sir. All I'm saying is I know trouble when I smell it, and something down there stinks, sir."

"All right, Master Sergeant. I'll speak with the pilot and have him check it out with Lieutenant Novak, if that'll make you feel better."

"Yes, sir. Thank you, sir. I'd feel a lot better."

But he didn't look it. Fetterman sat holding his rifle and staring out the tiny round window. He looked nervous.

And when Master Sergeant Fetterman looked nervous, that made Gerber very nervous indeed. He got up and went forward to the flight deck.

"What're the odds on me having a word with the camp before we land?" shouted Gerber over the roar of the turbines after he'd gotten the pilot's attention.

The nineteen-year-old warrant officer flying the big, twin-rotor helicopter shook his head inside his helmet and shouted back, "No can do, Captain. Can't raise anybody down there. Your boys must all be asleep or something."

"What? Veer off! Don't land!"

"Whaaa? Why? It's no big deal, Captain. We don't need radio to—"

"Just do it! Quick! I haven't time to explain."

The pilot looked at Gerber for a second, then shrugged. "It's your camp, Captain. You don't want to land there, it's fine with me." He keyed the microphone switch. "Flight, this is lead. We're going around. Break right, and we'll orbit east of the camp."

Fetterman pushed into the doorway of the crowded cockpit, a pair of binoculars in his hand. "Captain, it wasn't my imagination. There is a Chinese flag on top of the dispensary, sir. Communist Chinese. Something is very wrong down there."

Gerber nodded.

"Somebody want to tell me what this is all about?" asked the pilot, having completed his turn away from the camp.

"I know it's a pretty farfetched idea," shouted Gerber, "but my team sergeant thinks maybe the camp has fallen to the enemy."

The pilot looked astounded. "You can't be serious."

"I wish I wasn't," Gerber shouted back. "There's unreported battle damage down there, there's no sign of movement and there's a Red Chinese flag on top of the dispensary."

"Somebody's idea of a joke?"

"If it is, it's in damned poor taste. Besides, that camp down there is full of radios. We've always got two people on radio watch. But you tell me nobody answers when you call. With around three hundred and fifty men plus maybe another one hundred and twenty-five dependents down there, doesn't that strike you as being just a bit odd?"

"I see your point," answered the pilot. "What do you want to do about it?"

"There's an emergency landing zone about two klicks east-southeast of the camp, one of our E and E pickup points. Can you put us down there? We'll walk back and set up an NDP in that tree line down below. We can get artillery fire support from the

ARVN battery at Dinh Dien Phuoc Xuyen if we need it and ought to be able to patch a request for air through B-41 at Moc Hoa. After it gets dark, I'll send a recon team in to check it out. If everything's kosher, we'll all go in, and Master Sergeant Fetterman and I will feel very foolish, but nobody will have gotten hurt. If things are amiss, we'll punt."

"Like I said, Captain, it's your camp. If that's the way you want it."

"One more favor. When you get back to base, call Lieutenant Colonel Alan Bates at B-Detachment Five Two in Saigon and let him know what's going on, will you? No sense in letting the VC know our plans if something is wrong down there. You never can tell who might be listening to the radio."

"No problem. I'll give him your message."

Gerber and Fetterman started aft to get the men ready to disembark. Almost immediately the crew chief called them back.

"The AC says he's got the Vietnamese camp commander on the radio now. He wants to know if you want to talk to him."

Gerber took the headset the crew chief offered him.

"You push this button to talk, sir."

"Thanks." Gerber nodded and keyed the mike. "Zulu Six." He heard Dung's voice reply.

"Zulu Six, this White Wing Five. Do you intend to land? The runway has been the damage by VC mortars, but is still all okay for helicopters to land."

Gerber ignored the question. "May I speak with Zulu Five, please?"

"He not available."

"Why not? Where is he?" Gerber pressed.

"He make the wounded when mortars hit. He in dispensary."

Gerber thought for a moment. It was a plausible enough explanation. "Okay, let me talk to Suicide Six," said Gerber, using the call sign for Lieutenant Bao.

"He also not available. Do you intend to make the landing?"

"Why isn't Suicide available? Where is he?"

"He also make the wounded. We take beaucoup mortars. They hit barracks. We have beaucoup wounded."

Uh-huh, thought Gerber. How very convenient. He was beginning to think Fetterman was right. It seemed a bit odd that the VC mortars had done so much damage to the Tai barracks while from the air it was obvious that the Vietnamese quarters had hardly been touched. Further, it was stretching the limits of probability to believe that both Novak and Bao had been injured in the attack. And if they had so many wounded, where in the hell were they all? A couple of the buildings were still smoking. There ought to be wounded and soldiers all over the place down there, but the camp looked as empty from the air as a drive-in theater at high noon.

"Have you called for a medevac for the wounded?" asked Gerber.

"That negative," said Dung. "Have beaucoup wounded, but none too serious. We treat here in infirmary. Do you wish to make the landing?"

Gerber looked at Fetterman, who looked back and said, "Well, Captain?"

Unnecessarily Gerber unconsciously cupped his hand over the microphone. It wouldn't transmit unless he pressed the switch.

"It's Lieutenant Dung. He says Novak and Bao can't come to the radio because they were wounded in the mortar attack. He says they've got a lot of wounded, but he didn't evac anybody because the wounds weren't serious enough. He keeps asking if we're going to land, and he hasn't mentioned the helicopters or the conex sitting down there."

"It stinks, Captain. I'm telling you it smells like *kemchi* in *nouc mam*."

Gerber keyed the mike switch again. "Negative, White Wing Five. We are diverting to Moc Hoa. They have a problem there requiring our assistance. We will return in the morning. Zulu Six, out." Gerber peeled off the headset and looked at Fetterman again.

"You think he'll buy that, sir?" asked Fetterman.

"Let's hope so, Master Sergeant. I'm sure as hell not buying the line he's feeding us."

TWENTY MINUTES LATER the small landing zone east-southeast of Camp A-555 was crowded with soldiers. In the gathering darkness Gerber briefed his men.

"We'll leave the majority of the men here and establish an NDP around the LZ. That way we can either bring in reinforcements or get out in a hurry if we have to. Second Lieutenant Hung will be in charge, and Sergeant First Class Tyme will act as senior advisor to him.''

It was a diplomatic way of saying Tyme was in charge of the LZ. In fact, the Tai strikers worked directly for the Americans and took their orders, and money, directly from them. However, since Hung as a Strike Force lieutenant technically outranked Tyme and it wasn't a good idea to give the striker troops the impression that a sergeant should give an officer orders; Tyme would give the Nung Tai tribesman "advice" on the command of his men, which, naturally, it was expected Hung would follow.

"Sergeant First Class Kepler, Master Sergeant Fetterman and myself,'' continued Gerber, ''will take eight of the strikers and patrol to the tree line southeast of the camp, where we will establish an observation post and conduct a surveillance of the camp. If conditions warrant, we will then detach a one- or two-man patrol to conduct a reconnaissance of the camp itself and try to determine exactly what is going on in there. It may be that we'll find this is much ado about nothing and that we're chasing shadows. I hope so. But as I've already indicated, the evidence seems to indicate sufficient cause for us to proceed with extreme caution. Once we know exactly what we're up against, if anything, we'll be in a better position to decide what to do about it.''

Gerber looked at the men, their eyes large, like giant black buttons floating in a sea of white eyeballs. Their faces, masked with green-and-black camouflage face paint, were already indistinct shadowed outlines in the rapidly fading light.

"I guess I don't need to tell you guys what kind of treatment Lieutenant Novak, the LLDB and the strikers, especially the Tai, can expect if the VC have got the camp.'' He deliberately avoided mentioning Robin Morrow, as if not thinking about her might somehow prevent anything happening to her. ''Personally, I don't know how they could have taken the place without destroying it, unless they had heavily infiltrated the PFs and had outside help. That may explain the presence of that large VC force whose trail we cut earlier today. Anyway, the sooner we can act, the better the chance our people will have.

"We'll have to maintain strict radio security to avoid tipping our hand that we're in the area. The main group here will maintain a radio watch, but they're not to transmit for any reason unless under attack. The reconnaissance patrol will break squelch twice, every hour on the hour, to signal we're all right. Even if they pick that up in the camp and figure out it's some kind of signal, they won't know what it is or where it's coming from. At any rate, we'll be back not later than midmorning and figure out what we're going to do then. I guess that's it. Let's do it."

Because they moved with extreme caution, it took an hour and a half to cover the two kilometers to the tree line. When they had located a suitable spot from which to observe the camp, Gerber deployed the Tai in a U-shaped defensive position, then he crawled forward with Kepler and Fetterman for a closer look.

There were no lights to be seen, and that in itself was a bit unusual. Blackout regulations, though posted, were not rigidly enforced unless there was reason to expect trouble, and there were usually a few lights burning, especially this early in the evening. A few late cooking fires from the strikers' families, medical specialists checking patients in the infirmary, card games in the American or LLDB team houses, that sort of thing was routine and usually accounted for *some* light, but this evening there was nothing. The camp seemed almost preternaturally dark and silent. It gave Gerber the uneasy feeling that he was viewing a necropolis.

At long last he lowered the 7 x 50 mm Zeiss binoculars and rubbed his aching eyes. He knew that, if he could see them, they would look bloodshot. He was bone tired.

"Well, gentlemen, I guess that's about all we're going to see from out here," Gerber said softly.

"Right, sir," said Fetterman. "I'll be off, then. I'll try not to be gone more than about two hours."

"Nobody said anything about you going anywhere, Master Sergeant," said Gerber.

"Of course not," said Kepler. "I'm the logical one to do it. After all, I am the Intel sergeant."

"I appreciate the thought, guys, but it's my camp," said Gerber. "If anyone is going to sneak in there and have a look around, it's me."

"Captain, with all due respect, that's the dumbest idea I've heard of all day. Sir," said Fetterman, "just look at you. You're dead on your feet. I don't know how you've kept your eyelids open this long without tape. You go in there in the shape you're in, you'll likely stumble over your own feet and bring the whole camp out to see what the thud was when you fall down."

"Your concern is noted, Master Sergeant, but I'm perfectly capable of doing my job, thank you."

"No, sir, you're not. If you were, you'd look at this objectively and realize you can't go. You're not capable of going in there objectively, sir."

"Now just what in hell is that supposed to mean?"

"You know what I mean, sir."

Gerber knew, all right, but he didn't like it. Fetterman was reminding him that Morrow was in there. If you're a surgeon, you don't operate on your own wife. The same held true for soldiers' girlfriends.

"Master Sergeant Fetterman's right, sir," said Kepler. "We need an objective survey of what's going on in there. I know the camp, and I know what to look for. Let me go."

Fetterman interrupted. "I've the highest regard for Sergeant Kepler's ability to acquire things, sir. Whether it's Intelligence or motorboats. He's a very sneaky man. But he's not very quiet, sir. The men call him Wandering Buffalo when he's out in the bush."

"They do not," protested Kepler.

Fetterman continued without apparent notice. "Anyway, sir, I've had experience with this sort of thing before. You picked me for Nhu Ky when we had to go into the NVA camp, remember. Besides, I'm the only one small enough to pass for a striker if somebody spots me."

Gerber let out a sigh. "All right. I concede the logic of your argument. Don't get caught. If you do, there's nothing we can do to help you. And don't get yourself shot by some of our own guys, if we've guessed wrong about this."

"Not to worry, Captain. I got into and out of Nhu Ky, and I got out of that damned P.O.W. camp okay, didn't I? Besides, this time I know exactly where the defenses are—I helped build them. Piece of cake."

He shrugged out of his pack and web gear and piled his rifle and steel pot with them, taking a boonie hat from the side pocket of his fatigues.

"No rifle?" asked Gerber.

"It'll just get tangled up in the wire when I crawl through, sir, and cause problems. I've my knife and a couple of little extras. It'll be enough."

"What if you're spotted?"

"Then I'll look less dangerous if I'm not carrying a rifle. That can be a real advantage sometimes. Besides, sir, I'm sure as hell not going to fight my way out of a whole campful of VC with one lousy rifle."

"All right, Master Sergeant. It's your party. Take what you think best."

"Thank you, sir. If you'll just keep an eye on my things for me, I'll be back in about two hours."

Fetterman crawled into the darkness and disappeared.

"I wish you'd let me go, Captain," said Kepler. "Master Sergeant Fetterman's getting a little old for this sort of thing."

"Christ, Derek, he's only thirty-nine."

"That's what I mean, sir. It's a younger man's job."

Gerber almost laughed. "No, Derek. Fetterman's the right man for it. He's got the experience and he's got the killer instinct. I probably wouldn't have made it. You might have. Fetterman will. And he was right about one other thing. I'm exhausted. Wake me if anything interesting happens."

"You're going to sleep at a time like this?"

"I'm going to give it one hell of a try. You got a better idea?"

"Nope. Good night, sir."

Gerber closed his eyes and shut out the war.

# 10

## INSIDE SPECIAL FORCES
## CAMP A-555

It had taken Fetterman slightly less than an hour to cross the minefield between the inner and outer perimeters of the camp. He'd followed one of the hidden paths, secretly left clear of mines as an escape route for the American Special Forces team in case the camp was overrun, but he'd had to traverse it with caution, both in order to avoid detection in case anyone was watching from within the camp, as someone *should* have been, and in case the VC did, in fact, control the camp and had moved any of the mines or added to them. Ultimately, he'd found the pathway clear, which was good news. It would make getting out of the camp a lot simpler and faster than getting in.

Fetterman carefully snipped the barbed wire grillwork away from the mouth of the drainage tube in the packed mud and sandbagged wall. The jaws of the small pair of wire cutters, wrapped in strips of cloth to muffle the sound, made very little noise. Nevertheless, he paused after each soft *snick* to listen for any sound that might indicate his surreptitious entry had been overheard. He cut through only enough strands of wire to bend the bottom of the grillwork silently up out of the way, then tied a meter-long piece of black nylon cord to the grid. He slid into the tube headfirst, and used the cord to pull the grill back down into place behind his feet.

Fetterman considered himself lucky. His only companion inside the tube was a large rat, which hissed at him in protest of this brazen invasion of its territory, but the rodent retreated squeaking down the tube when Fetterman failed to buffalo and hissed back.

At the other end of the tube, Fetterman repeated his exercise with the wire cutters, waiting until he was sure the coast was clear before bending up the grillwork and slipping out of the tube.

As he turned to bend the wires back into place, he almost stepped into the body of a dead striker.

The man was very nearly killed twice. Fetterman already had his knife in motion before he noted that the striker's throat had been slashed from ear to ear. He checked his thrust aimed beneath the corpse's rib cage.

The striker's body had been propped against a pile of sandbags so that from a distance he appeared to be standing. Fetterman didn't recognize him, but then, he didn't know everyone in the strike force. He noted with interest that the cadaver bore two distinguishing elements: a strip of red cloth tied about the left arm and a slit in the trousers revealing a characteristic mutilation.

That bit of grisly trophy taking gave Fetterman more information than he might have gleaned from an entire night of roving about the camp. It told him that the camp was in the hands of the VC. That they had pulled off their coup by infiltrating the strike force. And that somewhere within the confines of the camp, Staff Sergeant Krung was still alive and loose, industriously engaged in the business of exacting his own peculiar brand of jungle justice.

In the darkness Fetterman's teeth flashed briefly in a smile.

Krung hadn't bothered to strip the body, probably figuring that its fully equipped but emasculated state would have a greater psychological impact on the VC who found it. Fetterman could appreciate the artistic nicety of it, but personally he would have taken the man's weapon rather than leaving it in a serviceable condition for the Vietcong, and he did so now, removing the man's cartridge belt and harness, as well. It would make a nice bit of additional camouflage if he had to walk openly about the compound, and despite what he'd told Gerber, he did feel a little bit naked without a rifle or, in this case, a carbine. Besides, he was loath to leave it for the enemy.

Knowing that a man with a carbine actually in his hands was likely to attract a few curious stares, Fetterman checked the safety, then slung it over his shoulder, muzzle downward in the Vietnamese manner. Quickly he checked the man's pockets for identification papers or anything else that looked interesting, pocketing a crumpled pack of American Camel cigarettes and a book of Army-issue damp-proof matches, as well. Except for an occasional pipe, or a rare cigar, Fetterman didn't smoke because of nicotine's detrimental effect on a soldier's night vision, but a burning cigarette could serve as a fuse, and it was possible to improvise a simple yet surprisingly effective incendiary device from a book of matches, so he took them. It wasn't that he had any plan for using them. It was just a question of not leaving anything of a weapon value behind for the VC. Then he took the band of red cloth from the striker's arm and tied it about his own. Pulling the boonie hat down low over his forehead to shadow his camouflage-painted face, he stepped away from the wall and walked boldly in the direction of the nearest Tai barracks.

DIAGONALLY ACROSS THE CAMP, in the Vietnamese compound near the north end of the runway, Major Dung Cao Chiap of the National Liberation Front reentered the quarters he had occupied for the past few weeks as Lieutenant Dung Cao Chiap of the ARVN LLDB. He removed his pistol belt and shoulder harness, hanging it on a peg on the wall of the hootch, then hung his carbine on the peg next to it. He unfastened the chin strap of his American-made, Saigon-issued helmet and hung it on the peg with the web gear and nodded to the two VC guards in the room. Finally he looked at his prize prisoner sitting on the bunk against the wall, her wrists and elbows still cruelly tied behind her back, dried blood showing at the corner of her mouth where he had kneed her.

She was not his most important prisoner. The American general in the Americans' team house was that, but to Dung she was the real prize. She was Gerber's girlfriend, and because of that he had something very special in mind for her.

"Excuse please I ignore you too very long," said Dung, smiling, "but I have much to do."

"Oh, that's quite all right, Major. Please don't trouble yourself on my account," said Morrow.

"Ah, you make with the joke, yes?" said Dung. "See, I laugh. Ho, ho. Very funny. But perhaps soon you not laugh too very much."

Dung walked over to the low sleeping platform with its woven mat upon which Morrow sat. He reached out one hand and ran it along her smooth cheek and over her split and bruised lip almost lovingly. Gently he stroked her silky fine blond hair. Then he knotted his fingers in it and pulled, lifting her excruciatingly into a half-sitting, half-standing position so that he could bend forward and put his face close to hers. His breath smelled like dead fish. For one awful moment Morrow thought he was going to kiss her, then abruptly he shoved her back down on the mat, banging her head against the side of the hootch.

"No," he said softly. "Soon I think you not laugh too very much at all. It perhaps interest you to know that your friend Lieutenant Novak has escaped his guards, killing five more of my mens," Dung continued matter-of-factly.

The news surprised Morrow and gave her hope, which Dung quickly dashed.

"Unfortunate for him, he not get too very far. He hide in bunker in American compound. Twos of my mens watch him now, so he no can escape. For the moment we leave him. He not in position to create bother at this time, and I no wish to lose more mens in try to capture him. We leave him there without food and water, and when time comes for us to leave, we will blow up his bunker with recoilless rifle. Big joke on him, yes? Perhaps you like to make the laugh at that one? No? Too bad. I thinks not."

Dung walked over to his desk and systematically began to clear everything from the top of it.

"Also, I have new guests. After your capture twos helicopters come into camp. My mens capture their crews and passengers. One of passengers is American general. I think this pleasing to my superiors very much. I only major for three months now, but I think maybe I make lieutenant colonel soon. Capturing an American general should be good for promotion, do not you think?"

Dung finished clearing the desk and turned back to face Morrow again.

"Ah, but I can see by expression on Miss Reporter's face that what she interested in is what happen to her American lover,

Captain Gerber." Dung almost spat Gerber's name. "Your captain was to have return this evening, and I have prepare big surprise for him and his mens, but at last moment they go to Moc Hoa to help with problem there. He not come back until tomorrow, so we must wait for him. I cannot leave without repaying debt I owe Captain Gerber."

Morrow wondered what in the world he could be talking about. She didn't have to wait long for an explanation.

"Your Captain Gerber and his Sergeant Fetterman cause much trouble for friends of mine. You remember Major Vo, my former commander whom Sergeant Fetterman kill? You remember also maybe a certain Chinese friend of mine you meet in Hong Kong?"

A sudden look of horrified comprehension crossed Morrow's face.

"Ah, excellent," continued Dung. "You remember. How very gratifying. They would be most pleased to know that their plan for destroying this camp succeed, although not quite as they envision it. Since they no can be here, I must collect the debt for them. Much of this I have done. The rest will undoubtedly be accomplished in the morning. However, I not, I think, be able to do it in so very entertaining manner as my friends would have desired it."

Dung sighed deeply, placidly, as if reconciled to an unpleasant situation that must nevertheless be seen through to the end. He rubbed imaginary dust from his hands and inspected his fingertips in a bored manner.

"Yes. It most unfortunate that your Captain Gerber not live long enough to provide the entertainment my friends would expect of him. You, Miss Morrow. You will be surrogate. You, alas, must provide the entertainment."

He addressed the guards. "Tie her to the desk."

With leering grins the two VC guards dragged Morrow across the room and threw her facedown across the desk. She tried to resist but lost interest in struggling when one of them struck her in the head with his carbine and a thousand tiny stars flickered into existence before her eyes.

Morrow felt hands at her feet, tearing her boots off and forcing her legs wide apart as her ankles were roped to the legs of the metal desk. Then suddenly the cords binding her wrists and elbows were severed and her arms yanked forward and down. She felt new ropes slipped around her wrists as the men secured them to the desk legs on the opposite side.

"No!" she yelled. She opened her mouth and tried to scream, but someone forced a rag into it.

"That not necessary," said Dung calmly. "Let Miss Morrow scream if she like. There is no one to help her. Now leave. And tell Commissar Dau and Major Ngoi that they may join me if they wish."

Looking clearly disappointed, the two guards left.

Dung walked slowly to the wall and took the bayonet from its scabbard on his web gear. He held it up so that Morrow could see the blade clearly.

"Yes, Miss Morrow, you may scream all you like. I think that you will want to scream a lot before we are done."

Dung walked forward to the desk and ripped Morrow's shirt and shorts down the middle with the bayonet, then cut through the legs and shoulders so that he could pull them off her, leaving her clad only in her panties. Those he pulled down to her knees, then ripped them apart with his hands.

Dung ran the point of the bayonet up Morrow's thigh and pricked her buttock with it, drawing blood. She jerked but did not cry out. Slowly he continued to run the blade up along her left side until he came to her breast. He pricked that, too, again drawing blood. She bit her lower lip to keep from screaming.

"I told you it is all right to scream if you like," said Dung.

Morrow bit her lip harder and tried to think of Gerber.

Unexpectedly Dung withdrew the bayonet.

"Good. You have spirit. I knew this when you killed my twos mens. A woman with your spirit will provide much entertainment," said Dung hoarsely.

He unbuckled his belt and folded it so that it was double.

"But now, I think, it is time for you to scream. You will scream for me, won't you, Miss Morrow!"

Holding the belt by the ends, Dung stepped forward and swung it hard.

Morrow screamed.

THE VC STRIKER DID NOT SCREAM as he came out of the latrine. In fact, he made only a few low grunts as Krung jabbed his knife repeatedly into the man's back below his rib cage. Then he made a small gurgling sound after the knife was drawn across his throat. He would have screamed had he been able to at what Krung did next, but by then the enemy soldier was beyond all feeling.

Krung dropped the bloody trophy into his pocket and dragged the man back inside the latrine, sitting him on the toilet seat with his pants around his ankles and his back against the wall, head leaning forward on his unmoving chest. It would make an interesting discovery for the next man using the latrine.

Krung eased his way outside, looking around casually, and strolled away from the latrine unconcernedly. He glanced at his watch and saw that it was fairly early yet. The VC soldier had provided the fifth trophy Krung had claimed that night. He thought perhaps he would take another one or two before attempting to find a way out of the camp. There was plenty of time, and these VC traitors were so easy to kill. Almost too easy. It lessened the satisfaction of adding to his trophy collection to kill Communists that died so easily. Still, it would do. After all, they were not only Communists, they were lowlander Vietnamese Communists. To a Nung Tai tribesman like Krung, that was two very good reasons to kill them.

Also, it would give him a little more time to reconnoiter the camp more thoroughly. He was almost certain that, when he reached American troops, they would want to know all he could tell them about the situation inside the camp.

Krung knew that, once he was clear of the camp, he would show himself only to American soldiers. He had never really trusted any Vietnamese except Captain Minh, the one lowlander he had known who had cared enough about the Nung Tai to try to understand their culture, who had fought the Saigon government for their rights and to get them better uniforms and equipment so that they could kill more Communists.

The Nung Tai strikers of Camp A-555 had appreciated this and had made Minh an honorary Tai, an honor Minh had accepted with great solemnity. A few others of the LLDB had tried to be friendly to the Tai, but for the most part they exhibited only a restrained tolerance toward them. The PF-RF strikers did not do even that, which Krung thought showed great arrogance for a race of people that had stolen his country. But for the most part the Vietnamese kept to their own side of the camp, and racial bloodshed was avoided. Besides, the Americans did not approve of the

Vietnamese and Tai killing each other, which puzzled Krung greatly since they approved heartily of killing Vietnamese Communists. There was no understanding the Western mind.

Yet Krung knew that he could trust Americans. So far, every one of them he had met had proven trustworthy. While the Vietnamese had once again proven themselves not to be trusted. Too easily they became Vietcong.

Krung moved with catlike precision, crossing open areas with the authoritative air of someone who belonged there and knew exactly where he was going, projecting the impression that he might have owned the camp. Yet in each patch of shadows he paused. To look. To listen. To smell. To make himself thoroughly aware and to remember the exact placement of each Vietcong soldier, each new automatic weapon emplacement or change in the camp's previously existing defense, anything that might be of a military value.

A company of Vietcong were scattered about the walls of the camp, occupying key machine gun and recoilless bunkers but leaving the individual weapon firing steps pretty thinly filled by bored, uninterested VC soldiers who were disgruntled at having to stand guard duty while the rest of their buddies got to sleep, pull easy duty guarding prisoners or have fun.

A lot of VC were having fun that night. They'd already drunk every can of beer and bottle of Coca-Cola in the camp, and in the strikers' family quarters some of the lines outside the hootches of better-looking *mama-sans* and *côs* were ten or fifteen men long. From some of those hootches a lot of crying could be heard; from others there was only an eerie silence, broken occasionally by grunts and groans of sweating men.

There were not many guards in the Tai barracks area. Most of the Fifth Independent Tai Strike Company had died defending the camp and their families when the VC had attacked. Afterward a team of Vietcong had walked among the shambles, dealing with the Tai wounded in the usual manner—bayoneting them. Krung did not know for certain how many of his countryman had survived. It was too risky to get really close and find out. But based on the number of Tai bodies he'd found stuffed into countermortar bunkers, he knew there couldn't have been more than thirty or forty left.

There were a lot more guards in the Vietnamese sector. Apparently most of the Vietnamese strikers had given up without putting up much of a fight. The VC seemed to be treating them reasonably well, although they were closely guarded. Perhaps the VC commander hoped to make good Vietcong out of them by showing leniency. Except toward the women, of course. The women were far too valuable a commodity to men who had been in the field for months without release not to be given the privilege of being allowed to make their own contribution to the morale of the Front. In this respect, no difference was shown between a Vietnamese or a Tai woman. Krung thought it a very egalitarian gesture on the part of the Vietcong.

As Krung approached the low dome shape of the POL bunker which was used to store fuel and lubricants for the camp's generator, two jeeps and four six-by trucks, he saw a figure in tiger-striped jungle fatigues with a strip of cloth tied about the left biceps. The figure was crouched near the wall of the dome, as though he might be tying his boot or trying to avoid being seen. As Krung drew closer, the man suddenly whirled and disappeared around the edge of the bunker. That, Krung knew, was a bad sign. Apparently the man had spotted him and realized that he was not one of the VC strikers.

Krung moved quickly across the open ground and came up short with his back against the dome of the bunker. He didn't know why the man had not shouted an alarm yet. He did know that his only chance was to kill the man before he could give an alarm. As silently as possible he drew his M-3 fighting knife from its self-sharpening sheath. Knowing the tendency of a man being followed to spend more time looking behind than ahead of himself, Krung edged quickly around the bunker in the opposite direction and ran smack into the man.

Two knives flashed simultaneously in the moonlight as both men struck, Krung aiming his thrust at the man's chest while the other slashed at the Tai's hands. He felt the two blades make contact, felt his own forced aside as the greater strength of the other man's attack carried Krung's knife away from the midline of the man's body.

Krung parried around his opponent's own block and stepped inside the blade, pressing the attack and grabbing the wrist of the man's knife hand with his free hand. As he did so, he felt his own wrist seized, and the man suddenly stepped back, using Krung's own momentum to pull him off balance and execute a perfect *tomoe nage*. Krung sailed over the man's head, did a passable *koho ukemi*, and rolled clear. As he came up into a ready crouch, he realized with some surprise that he was up against a man at least as good with a knife as he was. Probably better. And Krung only knew one person in all of Indochina he could say that of.

The other man had rolled and come up off the ground as quickly as Krung, and he launched himself at the Tai. Krung sidestepped and leaped back but not quite quickly enough—he felt the other man's blade slide along his hip in a glancing cut. Krung staggered but instantly lowered his own knife and held up his free hand in a gesture of surrender. The other man had lost his boonie hat while the two of them were rolling about on the ground, and the faint reflection of moonlight off the balding head had served to confirm what Krung already knew.

"Sergeant Tony," gasped Krung, winded, "you better stop now before we kill selfs."

"Krung? Is that you?" said Fetterman. "Jesus, man, why didn't you say something? One of us could have got hurt."

"One of us already get hurt," admitted Krung, sheathing his knife and pulling a field dressing out of the pouch of his LBE. "Although not serious, I think. How you expect Krung to fill trophy board if you cut leg out from under him?"

"What? Damn. Sorry," said Fetterman. "Here, let me take a look. What are you doing wandering around here?"

"VC control whole camp. They make big surprise attack. There many traitors among Vietnamese strikers. Lieutenant Dung, he VC, too. When attack come, Vietnamese not fight well because they have no one tell them what to do. Also VC hold too many key bunkers. Tai try to fight, but we surprised and there not enough of us. Fight maybe last only thirty minutes. Afterward I escape by hiding in metal tunnel under runway. VC not find because they find krait in tunnel first."

Fetterman gave Krung an appraising look at the mention of the deadly snake, then finished tying the compress in place.

"Dung, huh? It figures. They'd have to infiltrate somebody into the LLDB to find out where all the defenses are, and he's the newest on the team. Sorry about the leg. It doesn't look too bad, but it'll probably hurt for a few days. We'll get Washington to look at it when we get out of here."

"Understand. We not know selfs in dark so try to kill same-same. Besides, leg already hurt from pungi stake Krung stupidly step on. No hard feelings. Okay fine?"

"Right. No hard feelings. Now I think we'd better move, in case someone heard our little wrestling match."

"Where we go?" asked Krung.

"The American compound. I can't find Miss Morrow, and it's the only place I haven't checked yet."

"Sergeant Tony, Krung have bad news. Lieutenant Dung take *Cô* Morrow to his hootch. She there now, entertain Dung and two NVA officers. Krung no think she enjoy it much."

Fetterman felt his intestines turn involuntarily into cement and the muscles of his jaw tighten. For a second he said nothing.

"So that's what those bastards were doing. I could hear them working somebody over in there, but there were so fucking many guards around the place that I couldn't get close enough to see who it was."

Then it dawned on him what Krung had said.

"NVA? Did you say two NVA officers? Are there NVA troops here?"

"Krung no think so. See only two NVA uniforms. Mostly they Main Force VC and some local guerrillas. Think maybe NVA political cadre. One NVA keep trying make long boring speeches to prisoners."

"That sounds like a politician, all right," agreed Fetterman. "What about Lieutenant Novak? Is he alive? Have you seen him?"

Krung shook his head. "Krung no see new lieutenant. Not since fight. Not know if alive or dead."

"All right. I suppose we'd better go check the redoubt, see what the situation is in there, then get out of this place."

Krung laid a restraining hand on Fetterman's sleeve.

"Sergeant Tony, there more happen to tell you," said Krung. "Short time after attack all over, two helicopters land at camp. They bring big funny metal box with them."

"Yeah, I saw it. Up at the corner of the helipad. A conex out-fitted with its own generator, an air conditioner, and a radio setup big enough to talk to Mars."

Krung nodded. "Not get close enough to see all that. Also not see too good men who come with it, but hear Dung call one general."

"A general? Are you sure?"

Krung nodded again. "Him say general several times. Say 'Good afternoon, General.' Say 'General, you my prisoner.' And say 'General, tell your men no more foolishness.' Think maybe one of general's men try something and they shoot him. Hear one shot."

"Well, shit," said Fetterman. "That's just fucking marvelous. Did you see this general? Do you know who he is?"

Krung shook his head. "Not see, only hear."

"Did you recognize the voice?"

Krung shrugged. "Tai soldiers seldom see or hear any general. Besides, all generals sound alike to Krung."

"What did this general sound like?"

"Angry."

"I'll bet. Do you have any idea what they did with him?"

"Think maybe they take to American team house," said Krung. "Not positive, but think so."

Fetterman unsnapped the leather flap that covered the crystal and glanced at the luminous dial of his wristwatch. He'd told Gerber he'd try to be gone no more than about two hours. His time had been up seven minutes ago.

"All right," said Fetterman. "Looks like we'll have to go have a peek at the team house. The redoubt's only about five feet high. Maybe we can find a spot where we can get a look over the top without having to get inside. I'd hate to be trapped in there. Can you walk okay?"

Krung nodded, and the two men eased around the POL bunker and headed for the redoubt, Krung limping slightly.

AT THAT MOMENT Novak would have agreed with Fetterman that the redoubt was a lousy place to be trapped in.

Trapped seemed to be a pretty good description of his situation. The VC had finally figured out which bunker he was in, and although they'd made no move yet to root him out, there were at least a couple of Charlies outside to make sure he didn't go anywhere. He'd discovered that when he'd tried to slip out just after dark and they'd sent a couple of rifle bullets past his head, just to let him know they didn't appreciate his trying to leave without paying the bill. There was too much moonlight for him to squeeze out either through the narrow doorway or the low firing ports without being seen, and if it had been dark enough, it would also have been dark enough for them to slip somebody up next to the bunker and chuck a couple of grenades in on top of him.

Still, Novak rationalized, it beat hell out of sitting around with his hands and feet tied, waiting for that treacherous bastard Dung to come over and kick his teeth in.

Novak was a little surprised the VC hadn't made some sort of move by now. It wasn't easy for him to keep watch in all the different directions they could come at him from, and he couldn't figure out what they were waiting for.

The farfetched idea of putting the Chinese flag on top of the dispensary had obviously worked. He'd heard the flight of Chinooks veer off from their inbound course. A couple of Hueys had come in just before and apparently landed. He assumed the crews and passengers, whoever they were, had been captured, but the main group had got the signal and broken off their landing approach, so the VC had nothing more to gain by hanging around. He just couldn't see them trying to hold the camp. Not when Gerber could call on air and artillery fire to level the place. It made more sense for the VC to raze the camp themselves, then before morning scoot back across the border into Cambodia, where they could sit around safe in their sanctuaries and proclaim their glorious victory for the Front.

And then it dawned on Novak why the VC hadn't come to kill him and then run away, why they were so confident they had the time to wait him out, why Gerber *couldn't* bomb and shell the camp into a smoking ruin.

Hostages. Even taking into consideration all the strikers who had been killed during the attack, the VC had to be holding upward of three hundred prisoners. And something over a hundred of those would be women and children, dependents of the strikers. Plus an American journalist. A female one at that, who conveniently happened to be Gerber's girlfriend. The American and VNAF fighter bombers and gunships could make short work of the camp and the VC in it, all right. And then the Vietcong could turn it all into a great propaganda victory, the massacre of innocent civilians and a working member of the press by the imperialist warmongering American dogs and their Saigon puppet soldiers. The liberal Western press would love it, and no one would give a rat's ass that the Vietcong had been holding them all prisoner and would have executed them, anyway. Captain Gerber, wherever he was, was faced with a no-win scenario.

A flicker of movement over near the American quarters caught Novak's eye, and he eased the safety off the M-60. So far he'd avoided shooting at any of the occasional glimpses he'd got of the VC, figuring it was best to let sleeping dogs lie as long as they weren't making a move on him. Charlie, in turn, had reciprocated by not putting any pressure on him and by keeping clear the section of the camp's east wall that Novak could cover with the .50-caliber Browning. There'd been some movement over by the team house earlier, but he couldn't see what that was all about because the corner of Gerber's hootch screened his view of the entrance to the team house.

Anyway, that had been a couple of hours ago, and nobody had tried to rush him. Except for the couple of VC he knew were out there somewhere watching the bunker's exits, there'd been no other sign of activity inside the redoubt until now. Now it looked as if Major Dung had finally gotten tired of waiting and was making his play.

Novak laid the three hand grenades out in a row next to the machine gun, where he could reach them easily when the time came. They might have him boxed, but by Christ he'd take a few of them to hell with him.

There was another flicker of movement as someone darted across the open space between the dispensary and the ammo bunker. Novak almost fired, but it was only one man, and by the time he could swivel the M-60 to cover him, the guy was under cover again.

For a long time nothing happened. The deathly silence seemed to stretch on for hours, although Novak knew it was a matter of minutes. Then right outside the bunker door he heard a faint shuffling sound. Novak grabbed one of the grenades and pulled the pin. He hesitated, trying to decide which direction to throw it.

"Well, Lieutenant Novak," a familiar voice said in perfect English, "are you going to sit in there all night, or are you about ready to blow this pop stand?"

"Fetterman?" asked Novak. "Is that you?"

"You know anybody else who'd be dumb enough to sneak into a whole campful of VC? Coming in."

"Come ahead."

Fetterman slid into the bunker.

"Lieutenant, don't you think it might be a good idea to put the pin back in that thing before you forget and set it down somewhere?" asked Fetterman, eyeing the grenade.

"Huh? Oh, yeah. Lucky I didn't toss it."

"I'll say. People keep trying to kill me this evening for some reason."

"Uh, I meant the pin. If I'd thrown it away, I wouldn't have had anything to put back in the grenade, just have to sit here holding the thing and looking stupid. I'd never have found the pin in here."

"Can always use a bit of safety wire or a paper clip, Lieutenant."

"Master Sergeant, I realize this may come as a terrible shock to you, but I don't usually run around with a bit of safety wire or a paper clip in my pockets."

"Gee, that's funny," said Fetterman, "I always do. Now do you want to get out of here before the VC come and find us or not?"

"I'm sorry to break this to you, Master Sergeant, especially after you did such a fine job of slipping in here, but there's a couple of VC outside right now," Novak told him.

"Not anymore. Right now the only person out there alive is Staff Sergeant Krung. I'd sorta like to bug out of this place while things are still that way." Fetterman moved toward the .50-caliber.

"You found Krung? He's alive?"

"We sort of found each other by process of collision," said Fetterman. He checked the bolt and the bolt latch release lock, pushing down on the release and turning the buffer tube sleeve to the right.

"What are you doing?" asked Novak, stuffing his pockets full of magazines and slinging the two carbines.

Fetterman used the retracting slide handle to ease the bolt forward. He pulled out on the lock and up on the latch, and lifted the back plate up and clear of the receiver. "Pulling the bolt. No sense leaving the Cong a fifty in working order, and the damned thing's too heavy for us to take with us."

Novak snapped the grenades into the holders on his ammunition pouches, threw a couple of belts of 7.62 mm ammo over his shoulders and released the M-60 from its tripod mount. "Well, this thing isn't too heavy. Suppose we take it."

Fetterman glanced over his shoulder, the Browning's driving spring rod assembly in his hand. "Fine, Lieutenant. Just so long as you carry it. Try not to rattle too much when you walk." He put the assembly in his pocket and jerked the handle, freeing the bolt from the barrel extension, aligned the shoulder on the bolt stud with the clearance hole in the bolt slot on the right side plate and removed the bolt stud. He slid the bolt to the rear and out of the receiver, being careful not to drop the extractor, and stuffed the assembly into the side pocket of his fatigue pants. "Let's boogie."

They slipped out of the bunker, sprinted across the open area to the ammo bunker where they found Krung, sidled around the bunker and hopped over the wall of the redoubt on the other side.

They held there until a cloud crossed in front of the moon, partially obscuring it and reducing the light, then made their way toward the spot in the wall between the east command bunker and the Tai quarters where Fetterman had slipped through the drainage tube.

Novak had a bad moment when he spotted the striker Krung had killed and left near the tube. He swung the M-60 up, ready to fire, but Fetterman stayed his hand.

"He's dead. Don't worry about it."

Novak eyed the tube skeptically. "Christ, I'll never fit through that. It's too small."

"You better shrink, then, sir, because there's no other way out of here. Give me your web gear and jacket. I'll go feet first and pull them through behind me. Krung, you take the point."

Krung nodded, bent the grate up and disappeared into the tube.

"Wait a minute," said Novak as Fetterman slid into the opening. "What about Miss Morrow?"

Fetterman shook his head. "There's nothing we can do for her right now, sir. She's in Dung's quarters with half a dozen guys, and there must be another dozen guards standing around the place. We try to help her, all we're going to do is get ourselves killed."

Novak hesitated. Clearly he didn't like the idea.

"Really, sir. I know what you're thinking. I don't like it, either. But we'll help her a lot more by getting out of here and getting our information to Captain Gerber than by trying a three-man rescue in the middle of a camp chock-full of Charlies."

"All right. Go."

Fetterman vanished, pulling the lieutenant's gear with him.

Novak waited a minute to give the others time to clear the tube, then checked the safety on the M-60 and shoved it into the mouth ahead of him. He was right. It was a tight squeeze.

"Damn," said Novak when the others hauled him out the far side. "It's a good thing I don't have claustrophobia."

Fetterman held a finger to his lips and pointed down the wall to where a faint red-orange glow atop the sandbags marked the location of a bored VC sentry having a cigarette. He handed Novak his equipment, and the three men crawled down along the wall, beneath the VC sentry and out along the cleared path into the minefield.

# 11

Kepler touched Gerber's arm, and he instantly awoke. He didn't speak or move, nothing that might give their position away, but simply touched Kepler's hand in acknowledgment and waited for the Intel sergeant to fill him in on the situation.

"Movement out there in the grass, Captain," Kepler whispered. "About seventy meters off to the right, say two o'clock."

Gerber rolled into position, readying his rifle, and scanned the elephant grass. "You get a count?" he asked softly.

"Hard to tell. Could be one man or a dozen."

Gerber checked his watch. Nearly three hours had passed since he'd closed his eyes. "Fetterman's overdue. Why didn't you wake me?"

"These things take time, Captain. You can't run a recon into a hostile camp by the stopwatch. I'd have awakened you in a few more minutes. Besides, I figured you needed the rest."

"You were right about that." It gave Gerber a funny feeling to hear Kepler refer to the camp, his camp, as a hostile one, but the Intelligence sergeant was right about that. Or at least probably right. They wouldn't know for sure until Fetterman got back.

The silence stretched for several minutes, and then Gerber heard just about the last sound he had expected to hear coming from a sea of elephant grass in South Vietnam, the barking of a squirrel. He answered it at once with the call of an owl.

The familiar deep voice that always seemed too big to come from such a small body called softly from the grass. "Fetterman coming in. I've got Krung and the lieutenant with me."

"Come ahead." Gerber wondered where he'd found Krung and Novak.

The three men rose cautiously from the grass and moved forward. Gerber couldn't distinguish Krung from Fetterman by their silhouettes, but there was no mistaking the giant hulking outline of Novak.

"Lieutenant. Good to see you again." He noticed all the heavy hardware Novak was carrying. "Christ, Novak, I thought I told you not to pull any John Wayne stunts. What is all that shit?"

Novak started to protest, then realized Gerber was ribbing him. "Yes, sir. That's why I brought the machine gun, sir. I'm doing Audie Murphy instead."

"Murphy never lost an A-Camp," Gerber reminded him.

"Yes, sir. I am sorry about that, sir. I'm afraid I got caught napping, and by the time I woke up to what was going on, Major Dung had a .45 stuck in my face. It didn't seem like a good idea to argue at the time."

"Major Dung?"

"Yes, sir. He seems to prefer his NLF rank to the one Saigon gave him."

"Apparently you didn't enjoy his company, however."

"No, sir. I managed to give my guards the slip."

"That must have been a bit tricky."

"No trick at all, sir, once they were dead."

Gerber's opinion of his new executive officer immediately went up several notches. "Well done, Lieutenant."

"Sir, I did lose the camp," said Novak.

"Was there anything you could have done to prevent its loss?"

"No, sir," Novak answered immediately. "The Vietnamese strike force was heavily infiltrated. They hit us from inside and out simultaneously. I tried to get to the command post so I could blow the bunkers on the west wall and radio for help, but Dung was waiting for me."

"Does he know about the destruct charges?"

"I don't think so, sir. If he had, he wouldn't have infiltrated his people into all the key positions on the west wall. He'd just have taken the command post and blown the bunkers when the

VC stormed the wall. My guess is he put the commo bunker out of commission and seized the command post because the backup UHF was there. I'm glad you got my message, sir."

"You're responsible for the flag on the roof of the dispensary, then?"

"Yes, sir," said Novak, pulling out the NLF flag. "I was going to use this one, but the Chinese flag was bigger. I only had a couple of minutes before they found out I was missing, and it was all I could think of to try at the time."

"You get an A for inventiveness, Lieutenant. Where'd you get the flag?"

"Dung had it. I heard him tell one of the VC he'd promised a friend of his it would fly over our camp."

Gerber felt suddenly cold. It was like a monster from some Vincent Price horror movie that wouldn't die. Almost afraid to, he asked, "Are there any Chinese in the camp?"

"I didn't see any, sir. I got the impression that Dung was doing it as a sort of favor or honor for someone who wasn't there."

Gerber breathed a ragged sigh of relief.

"That checks with what Sergeant Krung observed," offered Fetterman. "He says he saw a couple of NVA officer types, maybe advisors or political cadre, but no NVA troops and no Chinese."

Gerber turned to Fetterman. "All right, Master Sergeant, make your report."

"Yes, sir. I crossed the minefield without incident using the E and E route and entered the camp through a drainage culvert south of the command bunker on the west wall. I then reconned the Tai compound and found heavy damage to several of the barracks and civilian quarters there. A thorough reconnaissance was impossible due to the presence of many VC troops in the area, mostly in the civilian quarters. Some of the enemy troops were dressed as strikers, but had a red armband about the left arm, presumably to identify them from the real strikers. The rest were mostly in green uniforms, indicating they were part of a Main Force unit, although some local guerrillas were present, as evidenced by their black pajamas or shorts. After that I crossed the runway and reconned the Vietnamese compound."

"How did you cross the runway?" Gerber interrupted.

"I took an armband from a dead striker and just walked across. Security is pretty lax in there, sir. The key crew-served weapons bunkers are manned, but there aren't many men on the walls. A lot of them are, uh, well, partying with the civilians, if you take my meaning, sir.''

"All right.'' Gerber nodded. "Continue.''

"Yes, sir. I searched the Vietnamese compound. Once again a thorough reconnaissance was impossible due to the large number of VC present. They seem to be holding prisoners in several of the Vietnamese barracks. After that I crossed back across the runway at the north end and checked out those two Hueys.''

"I was wondering about that. What's the scoop?''

"Both Krung and the lieutenant say the Hueys came in unannounced just before we flew over. One of them brought in a conex that's been outfitted as a mobile field command center. It's got its own generator, air conditioner and a radio big enough to talk to Mars. Krung says a general came with it.''

"Christ! They've got a general officer in there?'' asked Gerber. The situation seemed to be getting worse.

"Apparently so, sir. Sergeant Krung says he heard Dung tell some of his men to take the general and his men to the team house inside the redoubt. Evidently they're being held there, along with the chopper crews. I did see a couple of VC enter and leave the team house, but I was unable to positively ascertain the presence of any prisoners there.''

"Sergeant Krung, did you see this general? Do you know who he is?'' asked Gerber.

"Krung not able to see. But hear Dung call man general several times. Also man call self general. Later try get close team house and see, but too many VC like Sergeant Tony say. But hear voices there, American and Vietnamese.''

"I wonder who in hell it is,'' mused Gerber.

"Captain, I've been thinking,'' said Fetterman. "Do you suppose it could be our boy? After all, Westmoreland is supposed to be in the area.''

"No, Master Sergeant. It can't be. The report from Crinshaw said Westmoreland was in an Otter, remember? Not flying around in a couple of Hueys with his own private mobile command center.''

"The man is still a general, sir,'' Fetterman reminded him. "A four-star one at that. He could have called for the Hueys to pick him up, and we'd never have known about it. Besides, who else would be dumb enough to fly into the camp unannounced and get himself captured?''

"I hardly think that's an appropriate way for you to be talking about general officers, Master Sergeant, especially the commander of MACV."

"Yes, sir. I only meant that it's the sort of thing a general would do, sir. Not announce himself, I mean."

Gerber knew what Fetterman had meant, but he let it pass.

"After completing my reconnaissance of the helicopters and mobile field command center," Fetterman continued, "I proceeded to check the communications bunker, command post, and fire control tower. In each case, I found them occupied by anywhere from two to five enemy soldiers, precluding a detailed, close reconnaissance of the targets. I then proceeded in the direction of the redoubt, intending to recon that. While passing the POL bunker, I encountered Staff Sergeant Krung, who apprised me of his Intelligence, and the two of us proceeded on to the redoubt.

"While conducting our reconnaissance of the redoubt, we became aware that two VC were apparently sited so as to prevent someone's exit from the southeast machine gun bunker in the redoubt. Assuming that there were friendly forces in the bunker, we eliminated the enemy soldiers, thereby permitting Lieutenant Novak to egress from the bunker and join Sergeant Krung and myself. The three of us then proceeded to my original point of entry into the camp and exfiltrated through the drainage culvert and back across the minefield, again following the route left clear for E and E purposes."

"You left out one thing, didn't you, Tony?" Gerber asked quietly, needing to know the answer but afraid to come right out and ask the real question.

"She's alive, sir," said Fetterman. "At least she was half an hour ago. I'm afraid Dung and the NVA have got her over in his hootch. I don't think she's enjoying the visit much. They're not exactly holding a political discussion."

Gerber felt the bottom drop out of his stomach. It seemed as if the trees were suddenly pushing in on him, the whole jungle threatening to crush him. He'd insisted Morrow stay in camp because she'd be safe there. He'd been wrong, and because of that

Dung and his cronies were now doing God only knew what to her. Probably the very thing Gerber had tried to protect her against.

Gerber took a deep breath and tried vainly to push the thought from his mind. If Morrow, if any of the prisoners, were to have any chance at all, he had to keep a clear head and keep his mind on the immediate problem of how to get the camp back without getting all the prisoners killed in the process.

"All right," he said. "Let's go rejoin the others. Once we've filled them in, we'll try to route a call through Moc Hoa to Lieutenant Colonel Bates and see if he's got any ideas on how we're going to get those people out of there and get our camp back."

# 12

## SPECIAL FORCES CAMP
## B-41, MOC HOA, RVN

When Bocker put the call through to the camp at Moc Hoa, he was more than a little surprised that the radio operator at the other end answered him immediately and came through with such clarity.

Afraid that if there were VC in the camp they might monitor radio traffic, Gerber had asked the pilot of the CH-47 to forward a request through Bates that the Moc Hoa team monitor a different frequency and expect the call sign Captain Quigg. After all, he was dealing with a mutiny of sorts, and he'd figured it was unlikely that any of the VC would be familiar with the movie or that anyone else in Vietnam would be using that particular call sign.

What surprised Bocker was that such a roundabout method of communicating had apparently worked and that he was getting such good reception from one of the miserable radios he'd worked so hard to get back into operation. He'd managed to fix two of them now, and from what he could tell, they both seemed to be functioning fairly well. The rest of them were going to remain junk until he could get to the spare parts back in his tiny repair shop in the camp.

Gerber had gotten an even bigger surprise when Bocker had passed him the handset. Moc Hoa had advised him that Crystal Ball, meaning Bates, was en route to Camp B-41 and had requested that Captain Quigg meet him there and brief him personally, if feasible. Air asset was standing by for that purpose.

Gerber had acknowledged the request, and twenty minutes later, after a tricky nighttime pickup, he was aboard a Huey bound for Moc Hoa, along with Fetterman, Krung, Novak and Kepler, leaving the others at the LZ with Tyme in charge.

Bates was waiting for them when they landed, having arrived only minutes before. Captain Dave Henderson, the Mike Force commander, was with him. He was an old friend, and Gerber greeted him warmly.

"Colonel," said Gerber, shaking Bates's hand first, then Henderson's. "Dave, you old war-horse. I figured they'd have sent you home by now."

"Had to extend," said Henderson, smiling. "Can't go home until they give me my own camp. Problem is Nha Trang thinks I'm doing such a fine job of rebuilding other people's camps they wouldn't give me my own to play with. Colonel Bates managed to get me the Mike Force assignment just before your boys had that little trouble over the P.O.W. business, but I had to extend to keep it. SFHQ was going to put me back on fill-in duty."

"Just keep right on extending," joked Gerber, "and one of these days I'll go back to the States and leave you my camp."

"Ugh!" said Henderson. "No, thanks. Not if I'm going to have to rebuild it for you again. I'll stick with the Mike Force."

"Sergeant Major Taylor come out with you, sir?" asked Gerber, turning back to Bates. "I think we could probably use his advice on this one."

"Sergeant Major Taylor's on emergency leave," said Bates. "His nephew was killed up near An Khe. He's accompanying the body home for burial."

Gerber came to a dead stop. "I'm sorry to hear that, sir. I didn't know Sergeant Taylor had a nephew in Vietnam."

Bates nodded. "A nice-looking young kid from what I saw. He was a grenadier with the First Air Cavalry Division. I went up to the Eighty-Fifth Evac with him this morning to claim the remains. It sounds like you've been having a few problems while I was gone."

"Yes, sir," said Gerber grimly. "If you don't mind, I'd like to get a cup of coffee for my men and me before we tell you all about it. I brought Kepler along because he's the Intel specialist. The rest have firsthand knowledge of the situation in the camp."

When they were all seated in the team house with heavy china mugs of strong black coffee before them, Gerber began his briefing, recounting to Bates the details of the radio call from Brigadier General Crinshaw, informing him of the loss of the Otter with General Westmoreland aboard.

"That's the most preposterous story I ever heard in my life," exploded Bates. Then, seeing the look on Gerber's face, he quickly continued. "I meant Crinshaw's story, Mack, not yours. You acted in good faith and did the best you could to comply with stupid orders given you by a madman who needs close adult supervision."

Bates colored a little as the comment he'd just made sunk in. "Everybody please forget I said that. Even if it is true."

Kepler smiled.

"Forget what, sir?" said Fetterman.

Novak appeared to find something intensely interesting in his coffee cup.

Krung leaned back in his chair, took a whetstone out of his pocket and, apparently dissatisfied with the job done by the self-sharpening sheath, began working on the edge of his combat knife.

Henderson watched the show with mild amusement.

There was a long silent pause, then Bates said, "What I meant was, it seems hard to believe that Westmoreland's plane could have gone down without some official word coming through channels on it. At least by now."

"Are you saying you have no knowledge of the incident, sir?" asked Gerber.

"None whatsoever, except for what little Major Pratt was able to tell me, and he got all his information from you. Apparently General Crinshaw left his office shortly after talking with you, without telling anybody where he was going or discussing the situation with anyone. Both Pratt and myself attempted to contact Major General Hull and find out what this mess is all about, but he seems to have pulled a vanishing act, too, and his XO is out of the country on R and R. I can't find anyone who knows anything, and nobody seems to have heard anything about a missing general, Westmoreland or otherwise. I haven't even been able to confirm that we're missing an Otter. I contacted the Transportation Movement Control office, and some Air Force sergeant told me they couldn't give out that information. When I pressed the issue, a bird colonel came on the line and told me to mind my own business,'' Bates finished.

''Well, somebody's missing a general now,'' said Gerber, ''because he's in my camp, and the VC have got him.''

Novak and Krung each gave their account of the surprise assault on the camp and the betrayal of the VC infiltrators in the strike force, adding the bit about Dung being a VC Major and such particular details that they were aware of. When they had finished, Fetterman gave his account of his reconnaissance of the camp, including the linkup with Krung and Novak, and the additional details of the two Hueys and the mobile field command center modified conex.

When they had finished, Bates rubbed his face and looked tired.

''All right,'' he said, ''let's take a look at what we know. Number one, the VC are definitely in control of the camp. They've got how many troops in there?''

''Between three and four hundred,'' put in Fetterman. ''It was impossible to get an exact count, sir.''

''Okay, we'll assume the worst. Say four hundred. Number two, the VC show no inclination to leave the camp. In fact, it appears they're hoping we'll try to kick them out of there. That way they can slaughter their three hundred prisoners and claim they were all killed by us when we tried to retake the camp. Number three, one of those prisoners is a United States Army general, exact identity unknown but possibly the commander of MACV. Number four, another of those prisoners is a female member of the American press.

''As soon as the Saigon press corps finds out about that one, every newspaper in the Western hemisphere will be hollering for our scalps. Number five, we've still got two hundred men in the field outside the camp, twiddling their thumbs and wondering what to do. Number six, nobody in Saigon seems to know what in hell is going on out here, so whatever we do, we're going to have to do it with our own resources. And number seven, whatever we're going to do, we'd better do it pretty damn fast before the VC decide to hustle our mysterious general out of there. I don't think that they're going to be satisfied with just shooting him along with all the rest of their prisoners. Not when they can take him to Hanoi for a show trial. Sooner or later, and probably sooner, they're going to try and move him.''

"Excuse me, Colonel," said Novak, "but isn't there one more thing you're forgetting? What about the downed Otter?''

"Right now that's the least of our worries," said Bates. "We can't even prove for sure that there ever was a downed aircraft, let alone that Westmoreland was on board. We've only got General Crinshaw's word for that and no confirmation from any quarter. If there was a plane, we'll need an extensive air-and-ground search to locate it. In the meantime, we've definitely got a battalion of VC sitting in one of our A-Camps, holding an American general and a correspondent prisoner, along with a bunch of Vietnamese and Tai strikers and another bunch of local civilians. First we deal with that mess. Then we'll worry about looking for missing airplanes. Now then, do any of you have any idea how we're going to get our camp back without getting all those people killed? Because right now any idea is better than none, which is the sum total of what I've got.''

There was long, uncomfortable silence. It was so quiet Bates imagined he could hear his watch ticking. He could hear one, but it might have been anybody's in the room.

"Vertical envelopment.''

"What?" asked Bates.

"Vertical envelopment," Gerber repeated. "A combined air assault employing both heliborne and airborne troops, designed to strike the enemy with maximum surprise, stun him and then overwhelm him before he can carry out his plans to execute the prisoners or set up to properly defend the camp.''

"The enemy is already set up to defend the camp. We built the defenses for him. Your team once repelled an attack by an entire regiment on that camp, and the defenses have been improved and strengthened several times since then," Bates reminded him.

"But we lost it to a battalion," said Gerber. "We lost it because we weren't prepared sufficiently to deal with a surprise assault from within the camp. Everything out there is set up to defend against an assault from outside the camp. Nothing is set up to resist an internal attack. Even the redoubt is just a last line of defense in case the camp is overrun.''

"Granted, but the enemy had troops infiltrated into the camp. We don't. They hit the camp from both inside and outside at once."

"Suppose we did the same."

"The objection remains," said Bates. "They had agents inside the camp. We don't."

"But suppose there was a way we could put people inside the camp? Suppose… Damn it, it'll work," said Gerber. "It has to."

"Explain yourself," said Bates.

"Coast along with me on this for a minute, sir," said Gerber. "I haven't figured out all the details yet, but it runs something like this. We use the men we've already got in the field to create a big diversion, a feint attack, outside the camp, probably along the west wall. That'll draw the VC's attention both outside the camp and away from the open area east of the camp."

"Continue," said Bates.

"Then we'll put Hueys right into the camp. Each one will carry a squad-sized strike group tasked with a specific target. One to seize the command post, one to raid Dung's quarters where Miss Morrow is being held, one to take the commo bunker, another one, maybe two, to take the redoubt and rescue the prisoners in the team house."

"That's only thirty men. They won't be able to hold any of it for more than five minutes."

"They won't have to. As soon as they've got their targets secured, we'll air assault a company directly into the middle of the camp. We've got a twelve-hundred-foot runway cutting directly through the center of the damned place, and the VC will all be busy shooting at the diversion out west of the camp."

"Captain, mightn't the incoming fire hit our own birds?" asked Fetterman.

"The men outside the camp will have to lift their fire just before the helicopters go in. As soon as they're clear, the diversionary force can resume firing. While the VC are busy dealing with the threat from without, the air assault company can hit them from within."

"Which will still leave you outnumbered by only about three and a half to one," said Bates sourly.

Gerber shook his head. "Henderson's Mike Force is airborne qualified, right? So as soon as the air assault company is in, we'll parachute the Mike Force into the paddy area east of the camp."

"That's no good," said Henderson. "They'd have to land in the open, within range of the guns on the east wall, and assault across open ground and through a minefield before they could storm the wall."

"That," said Gerber, "is why we've got to take the command post."

"Sorry. I don't follow you."

"After that last bit of trouble we had with infiltrators in the strike force, I had Sully Smith and Sam Anderson mine all the bunkers, gun emplacements and mortar pits with demolition charges. They can be fired remotely from a control panel hidden in the command post. Once the strike team takes the command post, they can open a gap in the wall and neutralize any fire you take from there. One of my men can lead the Mike Force through the minefield by following the path left clear for E and E purposes."

Henderson and Bates stared at Gerber, stunned.

"You mined our own positions?" Bates asked slowly. "Is it that bad out there that you've got to do that sort of thing? Have you considered the political implications of such an action? What do you suppose our ARVN allies would say if they knew? Why, the camp commander would go absolutely ape."

Now it was Gerber's turn to look tired. "Yes, sir. It is that bad out there. The fact that the VC managed to sufficiently infiltrate the strike force to successfully take the camp proves it. And as for our ARVN allies, Captain Minh, the camp commander, is fully aware of the mines. In fact, he thought of it before I did. Sully Smith found the charges he'd laid while he was setting out the charges I'd ordered. At first I thought it might have been the VC, but when I presented the evidence to Captain Minh, he told me he'd mined all of the key bunkers because he knew he had VC infiltrators in the strike force but couldn't prove who they were. All I did was have Sergeant Smith improve on the situation a bit."

"Jesus!" said Bates. "Mack, you really do have a twisted mind. Either that or I really am getting too old for this shit. Maybe I'm just not unconventional enough in my thinking for this kind of outfit."

"Colonel," said Gerber, "unless I misunderstood everything they tried to teach us at Fort Bragg, being unconventional is what we're supposed to be all about. If it's wrong for me to take whatever steps are necessary to protect my men and safeguard my camp, maybe I'm the one who doesn't belong—in Special Forces or the Army."

"Take it easy, Mack," said Bates. "I didn't say you were wrong, exactly. Just a bit unorthodox. And you're right, they did teach us to be unconventional at Bragg. I haven't forgotten the lessons we learned there. It's just that I need to be reminded of them once in a while."

"You know, Colonel," said Henderson slowly, "the idea just might be screwy enough to work."

"There's too much riding on being able to breach the east wall. You don't know that those firing circuits are still intact."

"We don't know that they aren't, either," said Gerber. "Besides, there are other ways to open a breach. We can take in demolition charges with us. The Mike Force can bring in a 90 mm recoilless. Hell, sir, we can have the Air Force bomb a stretch of the wall big enough for Henderson's people to get through, if necessary."

"Henderson?"

He shrugged. "Life is full of uncertainties, Colonel. If he's willing to try it, I am. Besides, what choice have we got?"

"None," Bates admitted. "Do you really think you can do it? Go in there and get those people out without getting them killed, *and* take the camp back?"

"We can try," said Gerber. "I'm not saying there won't be casualties. We're going to lose some. But if everything clicks, I think we've got a good chance of rescuing Miss Morrow and the men in the team house. I'm hoping that when the VC suddenly find they've got a campful of Mike Force strikers and a force of unknown size outside the camp, they'll be more concerned with saving their own skins than killing prisoners."

Bates looked at his watch. It was nearly 0500 hours.

"All right," he said. "Start putting it together. I'm going to go wake up my chopper pilot and get back to Saigon. You'll undoubtedly need some coordination from that end, and in the meantime, maybe I can find somebody who can tell us just exactly who in the hell it is they've got captured out there. If it is

Westmoreland, the shit's going to start hitting the fan pretty soon now. I'll leave the details up to you two. When will you want to go in?"

"About dawn tomorrow," said Gerber. "We'll need a day to get it set up and coordinate everything with the Air Force and the men we've got in the field. Also, sir, I'm going to need airlift to bring Bocker, Anderson and Washington in from the field. They know the camp, and I'll need them to lead part of the strike teams. They'll need to be here for the briefing phase as well. I'll leave Sergeant First Class Tyme and Staff Sergeant Smith with Lieutenant Hung and his strikers."

"All right. We'll send my chopper out for them first. Anything else?"

"We could use a few more radios. We're having a lot of trouble with the ones we've got in the field."

"I'll speak with the camp commander and see what can be arranged. Anything else?"

"Just one thing," said Gerber. "I'd better stroll over to the commo bunker and give Lieutenant Dung a call."

"Call the VC?" said Bates. "Why, for Christ's sake?"

"When we spotted Lieutenant Novak's signal and veered off, Dung radioed the choppers to ask if we were landing. I told him we had to divert here to help with a problem that had arisen and that we'd be back in the morning. Now I'm going to have to tell him the problem got worse, and we'll be delayed a couple of days. Just as soon as I think of a plausible problem."

Krung, who had remained silent until now, spoke up. "Captain Mack, why you no tell him Tai and Vietnam strikers get into big fight here and try kill each other. If Dung like most Vietnamese, he think very funny."

Gerber looked at the others. "It could work. At least it's a plausible reason for our having to stay here a few days until things cool down, dealing with a racial dispute."

One by one they considered it and nodded.

"Good!" said Krung, drawing the blade of his knife across the sharpening stone a final time. "Then we go back and kill all VC. Big surprise for Major Dung." He sheathed the knife. "Very good indeed."

# 13

## THE CAMBODIAN-VIETNAM BORDER REGION NORTHWEST OF CAMP A-555

With the approach of dawn Rittenour came slowly awake. It would have been impossible for him to sleep unless he'd been in a coma. The morning air was filled with the screeching and gibbering of monkeys, the call of birds and the sounds of animals crashing or slithering through the brush. Distantly he heard the roar of a tiger, or at least what he assumed was a tiger, and was glad of the caliber .38 special revolver in the holster sewn to his survival vest, although he mentally questioned whether the anemic, full copper-jacketed bullets with their low muzzle velocity would actually do the job if needed.

Rittenour was lying beneath what was left of the forward half of the fuselage, his leg bent and twisted at a curious angle. The five-foot fall from the cockpit floor hadn't helped it any, even though he'd been able to take most of the weight on his good leg. Releasing the seat belt and allowing himself to drop out of the shattered aircraft with a leg broken in two different places had seemed like a lousy idea even when he'd done it, but there'd been no real choice in the matter. He'd heard a flight of helicopters come in from the south shortly after the single chopper had flown out. They were big ones from the sound of it, a whole bunch of them, and he'd needed the flare launcher to signal them. And the only way to get it was to let go of the seat and drop.

The only problem with that idea was that, when he had hit the ground, the pain was so bad he fainted. By the time he had come to, the jungle was dark and the helicopters were long gone.

Rittenour had spent an uneasy night where he fell. He'd thought of trying to build a fire, but that hadn't seemed like a really good idea since he didn't know who might see it. Besides, he'd have to splint his leg before he looked for firewood and that meant finding something to use for splints. Not an easy trick when he could barely see his hand in front of his face and had to crawl, dragging a busted leg behind him. The tiny first-aid kit in his survival vest held a few bandages, some tape and a bottle of water-purification tablets. There was no way it could hold anything usable as a splint.

So he'd spent a restless, pain-filled night in the darkness beneath the wreckage of the Otter, awakening twice to chase the rats off himself and getting back to sleep only when exhaustion overcame him.

And now it was morning. Time to fix the leg as best he could, see if he could find the big survival package with its canned water and tinned food that had been stored in the aft fuselage of the aircraft, assess his surroundings and try to find out what had happened to Jones and the passenger. They had to be around here somewhere, whatever was left of them.

Rittenour looked around for the flare launcher. There it was. He had to shift his position slightly to get hold of it, but he reached it, finished unraveling the lanyard and looped it about his neck. There'd be no more losing that particular piece of equipment.

It took Rittenour about two hours to find a couple of fallen dead branches suitable for a crude splint. Even crawling about, it wouldn't have taken that long if he hadn't kept passing out.

There were all kinds of dead branches lying about, but most of them were the wrong size or the wrong shape or too rotted or riddled with termites to be useful. He finally found a couple long enough and solid enough to do the job, although he had to cut them to fit with the little cable saw from his vest. When he finally had them sized right, he used his nylon flight jacket to pad the leg and tied the splints on with his handkerchief, neck scarf and a couple of field dressings, immobilizing the injured leg below the ankle and above the knee.

If he'd had help, he could have cut the branches extra long and lashed a crosspiece below his boot to make a rudimentary sort of traction splint and take some of the pressure off the fractures. He remembered how to do that from Boy Scouts, but he couldn't do it without help. Still, when he'd finished, the splint worked fairly well, and without the broken bone ends grating together every time he moved, he found he could crawl about without fainting, provided he took things slowly. By the time he'd finished the splint and crawled back to the broken aircraft, it was nearly noon and hotter than the inside of a napalm strike.

The big zippered survival case was right where it was supposed to be, inside the aft cargo door. Rittenour almost wept with joy when he found it. He rooted in it until he found the military-issue pocketknife with the can opener on it, then guzzled down two of the dull gray cans of flat-tasting distilled water before tearing open the ration packets. He scarfed down two tropical chocolate bars, a handful of cardboard-tasting crackers and part of a tin of dehydrated beef, washing the meal down with most of another can of water.

Afterward Rittenour got sick. When he finished puking, he sipped the rest of the can of water very slowly and gnawed on a couple of crackers. It took a while, but by late afternoon he began to feel a bit better. He improvised a crutch from a forked branch, gathered some dry wood for a signal fire and stuffed a couple of day-night distress marker flares from the big kit into his pockets. Then he set out to explore his immediate surroundings.

About forty-five yards away, a short distance on the near side of where the right wing was hanging in the trees, he found Jones. The faintly pungent, sweet odor and the buzzing of flies gave away the location before he spotted the body.

It wasn't a pretty sight. Jones's head and upper body were almost black with flies. When Rittenour managed to shoo enough of them away long enough for a look, he instantly regretted it. The copilot's right arm and about half of his head were missing.

Rittenour backed off a couple of feet and got sick again. After a while he pulled himself together and relieved the dead man of his survival vest, knife and pistol. He tried to take one of the man's dog tags because he seemed to remember you were supposed to do that, but Jones wasn't wearing any. Finally, because he had no shovel, he used the knife, the crutch and at last his bare hands to scoop out a shallow depression and cover the copilot with dirt. The grave might not be deep enough to keep the animals from digging him up, but at least it would keep the flies away and cut down on the smell as the body continued to decay.

Clumsily carrying Jones's survival gear, Rittenour hobbled back to the aircraft and dropped the vest inside the door. He sat in the open doorway until he caught his breath, then picked up the crutch and worked his way around to the other side of the aircraft. A short distance away he found his passenger.

He didn't smell quite as bad as Jones had, and there were fewer flies. Perhaps because there were no open, external injuries. The neck lolled to one side, grotesquely twisted, obviously broken.

An army-green, baseball-type cap with four white stars sewn to it, made familiar by the press and television news, lay nearby.

Rittenour rolled the body over and stared at the name tag above the right pocket of the jungle fatigues. It said Westmoreland.

Rittenour stared at the cap, the name tag and the face of the man. He had a real problem with that name tag, unless Westmoreland had suddenly become a thirty-year-old with close-cropped red hair and green eyes. Rittenour had seen Westmoreland's picture plenty of times in the newspapers and on TV. He'd even flown him to Europe once.

He'd never seen this guy before in his life.

# 14

## OUTSIDE SPECIAL
## FORCES CAMP A-555

After Bates's helicopter had taken Bocker, Anderson and Washington back to Moc Hoa, Tyme and Smith had little to do.

Kepler had ridden out with the chopper to give Tyme and Smith a brief outline of the plan of action being formed. He'd promised them more detailed information later by radio and given them a sheet of code words and phrases he'd worked out, designed to help convey information to them while confusing any VC who might happen to be listening on the radio.

Once the actual operation began, there would be little need for continued radio security of such an extreme nature, and most of the code words would be dispensed with. They would then use normal operating codes and call signs. It wouldn't matter, for instance, if Gerber was referred to as Captain Quigg or Zulu Six, his normal call sign, once he was inside the camp. By that time the assault would be well under way, and knowing that Gerber was in the area would provide no useful information to Dung and the other VC.

Kepler also brought them two sets of fresh batteries and an extra PRC-10, along with a bagful of the spare parts that Bocker had requested. The necessity for the repairs meant that the helicopter pilot had to drop Kepler off, then swing south and orbit outside the area for twenty minutes before coming back in for the pickup, but Kepler needed the time to brief them and get the latest Intelligence on movement in the camp, anyway. By the time he'd finished, Bocker had put three more of the PRC-10s back in operation, giving the two companies of strikers a total of six working radios.

When he was sure he'd wrung every drop of information he possibly could out of Smith and Tyme and made the proposed rescue operation as clear to them as he could with the data available at that stage of planning, Kepler called the Huey back in. He boarded with the other three, and the four men flew off to Moc Hoa, leaving the two Green Beret sergeants and two companies of strikers to watch the camp and ready their part of the operation.

There wasn't much getting ready to do. The men were already in the target area and quite well enough armed to create the required diversion. Tyme noted that they were a bit light in the area of automatic weapons and ammunition for an actual assault on a fortified position, but since their role was primarily to create a diversion, what they had would do. Once all the assault elements were inside the camp, the men with Tyme and Smith would function as a blocking force to keep the enemy from escaping to the west, toward the Mekong River and Cambodia.

At least that was how it was supposed to work. Providing things didn't suddenly go to shit on the strike teams and assault troops. Both Tyme and Smith knew from bitter personal experience that even the best-planned operations had a tendency to change once things got under way. Primarily because no amount of planning could eliminate the two variables that were always in effect—the human factor and a certain amount of plain dumb luck.

Tyme and Smith spent a quiet, boring morning taking turns observing the camp once Kepler and the others were gone. They would not move into position for the feint attack until after dark in order to preclude detection by the enemy, but they had shifted around a bit to be closer to the objective.

A platoon of strikers had been left behind to secure the LZ, in case it should be needed to fly in more equipment or supplies or for evacuation. Second Lieutenant Hung, on Tyme's advice, had moved the rest of the strikers into a shallow ravine some distance behind the observation post. The ravine and its approach were screened from observation from the camp by the tree line where Tyme and Smith had established their OP, and having the strikers there meant that they would have a lot less farther to walk when it came time to set up the diversion.

It was just past noon when Smith, who had been observing the camp through binoculars, touched Tyme's arm. "Wake up, Boom-Boom, we've got troubles."

"What sort of troubles?" asked Tyme, sitting up and rubbing the sleep from one eye.

"Something going on down by the south gate," answered Smith, handing him the binoculars. "Take a peek. Looks to me like they're getting ready to move some of the prisoners out."

"Shit!" said Tyme. "That we don't need. Let me see."

He took the binoculars and scanned the area along the south wall until he came to the gate, then lifted them until he could see inside. The sandbags and machine gun emplacements surrounding the gate made it impossible to pick out any real detail, but he could make out a knot of men just inside the gate. Some of them were obviously carrying weapons while others didn't seem to have any arms and exhibited strange, stiff postures, suggesting that perhaps their hands were tied behind them. As Tyme watched, one of the men walked over to one of the armless men and struck him with a rifle, knocking him to the ground. He lay there for a few moments, then struggled awkwardly back to his feet.

Tyme lowered the binoculars and turned to one of the two Tai strikers with them. "Go tell Lieutenant Hung I need twenty men with rifles, ready to move fast. Hurry."

The striker slithered back into the trees until he couldn't be seen from the camp, then got up and ran.

"What're we going to do, Boom-Boom?" asked Smith.

"As soon as we see which direction they take, we're going to try to get in front of them and hit 'em," said Tyme.

"You think that's a good idea? It's liable to blow the captain's plans for the assault. We hit 'em, it's going to be noisy."

"I don't see that we have any choice, Sully. If we don't do something, they're going to take those guys out of here. What if one of them's Westmoreland? We'll just have to let them get out from the camp a ways and pray for the best. Our only chance is to take out the guards before they realize what's happening, and hope that not too many of the prisoners get in the way."

"That sounds like a pretty lousy plan to me."

"You got any better ideas?" snapped Tyme, annoyed.

"Nope. I'm just saying they're sure to hear the shooting."

"Not much we can do about that."

"How about calling Dinh Dien Phuoc Xuyen and getting the ARVN battery there to drop a few rounds between the ambush and the camp? It might help mask the firing when we spring the ambush."

Tyme considered the idea, then rejected it. "No. They might hear a few rifle shots, and they might not. If we go to chucking artillery shells around, the VC in the camp are going to wonder why they're shooting and who's directing the fire, not to mention what's being shot at."

He scanned the camp again. "They're moving out. Looks like they're heading for Cai Cai. They'll probably cross the border north of Dan Chau where the swamp narrows. That'll be our best bet to hit them. It'll be far enough they probably won't hear the shooting in the camp. Especially if we can catch them in the swamp where the trees will have a chance to deaden the sound somewhat."

"That's a long way, Boom-Boom. Three and a half, maybe four, klicks. It'll seem a lot longer going through the swamps."

"If we move now, we can get ahead of them, take the road to just south of Cai Cai, then strike straight north cross-country, bypass the abandoned village east of Cai Cai and set up along the main trail just where it enters the swamp again."

"What if they don't take the main trail? What if they veer off someplace before they get to Cai Cai and strike straight north themselves, through the main swamp?"

"Then we'll miss them. There's no way we can catch up to them from Dan Chau if they take the trail through the main swamp. Even if we crossed the border ourselves and moved along the edge of the swamp, I don't think we could get ahead of them in time."

Tyme turned to the other striker. "Listen. I'm going to send your friend back here. I want the two of you to take this radio and follow the VC with the prisoners. If for any reason they change direction before they get to Cai Cai, you call me and let me know. Okay?"

The striker nodded and grinned, showing his filed teeth. "Understand," he said. "We follow VC. Call if they no go to Cai Cai."

"Right. Don't let them see you following them."

The striker looked offended. "They no see. They Vietnamese."

"Right."

He turned to Smith. "Let's move."

In the ravine Tyme quickly explained the situation to Hung. He advised him to remain in the ravine with the majority of his force but to send four men forward to reoccupy the OP and keep the camp under surveillance.

Then Tyme and Smith each took one of the other PRC-10s, putting the radios in rucksacks and bending the antennae down at an angle of about one hundred and thirty-five degrees to the rear. In that position the antennae would avoid snagging, still give good reception and, combined with the rucksacks, would make them much less tempting targets for any VC sniper wishing to ding himself a radioman. Smith's and Tyme's size, which marked them clearly as American advisors, would provide plenty of temptation without the additional attraction of carrying a radio. They then joined the patrol waiting for them under Sergeant Harai.

Tyme looked at the short tribesmen, bowed under the weight of their equipment and giant Second World War vintage Garand M-1 rifles. Everything was too big for them. They looked almost like little boys who had been given their fathers' real rifles to go hunting with. That was one of the reasons the Special Forces tried to issue as many M-1 and M-2 carbines as possible. They were striker-sized weapons, and generally the troops could handle them a lot better. But there weren't enough carbines to go around. The military assistance planners back in the States still hadn't caught on to the size differential in Indochina and insisted that you needed a *full-sized* rifle to fight a war with, so they kept sending Garands. The Garand was a good weapon, reliable and accurate, proven in any number of combats. It was just too damned big for Vietnamese or Tai hands.

Still, Tyme had asked for riflemen, not men armed with carbines. He'd done it because the straight-shooting Garand, with its big heavy bullet, could do what a carbine wouldn't. Routinely deliver one-shot kills. The carbine would incapacitate ninety-nine times out of one hundred at close range—and the ambush would have to be sprung at very close range—but sometimes a follow-up shot with a carbine was needed to finish the job. Tyme wanted to make sure the job got done right the first time before the VC could kill any of the prisoners and with the minimum number of shots being fired. The Garands would give an extra edge.

"Sergeant Harai," said Tyme, "I sure hope your men know how to shoot. They'll only get one shot apiece."

Harai nodded. "The worst can shoot fly off water buffalo's ass at hundred meters."

Tyme gave him a look that said he wasn't buying any of that crap.

"Serious, Sergeant Boom-Boom," said Harai, "they all number one shots. I pick them myself."

Tyme nodded. He knew Harai could shoot. He'd trained him. "All right, then, let's go. We've got to get to Cai Cai before the Vietcong do."

They moved out on the double, following the ravine until it met a larger one running to the northwest, with a small creek flowing through the center of it.

Tyme knew that, if it had been the rainy season, the creek would have been a raging torrent, filling the ravine. At this time of the year it provided fairly decent walking. The bottom of the ravine, though rocky, contained little in the way of scrub or vines to hinder them.

They followed the ravine until it petered out into a field, then followed the tree line on the other side until it cut the road to Cai Cai. After that they ran.

It was a calculated risk to move in the open along the road. Tyme was banking on all the VC in the area being in the camp, except for the patrol with the prisoners. If he was wrong and they got ambushed along the open road, they'd probably be wiped out.

They ran for twenty minutes, walked for ten and then ran again. By the time they turned off the road toward the abandoned village, both Tyme and Smith were wheezing like asthmatics. The diminutive strikers with their heavy equipment and eleven-and-a-quarter-pound rifles weren't even breathing hard.

They crossed the open ground, a combination of mostly rice paddies with an occasional vegetable garden occupying the rare spot of high ground, still moving fast. At the entrance to the swamp, Tyme had Harai drop off one of the strikers to watch for the VC, and they proceeded down the trail to set up their ambush.

Tyme selected a fairly long, straight stretch of trail with good cover on both sides, just before the pathway rounded a slight bend.

He deployed the men along both sides of the trail in an alternating pattern, making sure that each man understood to shoot only at targets within his own particular field of fire. The light weapons sergeant emphasized the need to kill the guards instantly without injuring any of the prisoners, and stressed that each man would have to carefully select and track his target and shoot without hesitation when the time came.

Tyme said he knew that this would be difficult because prisoners might get in the way but that they must do the best they could. He made it clear to each of them that the only hope of rescuing the prisoners was to kill all the guards at as close to the same instant as possible. Anything less could allow one guard with an automatic weapon to slaughter all the prisoners before he was killed. Even a dying man, Tyme pointed out, could reflexively pull the trigger in his death spasm and kill someone, even though he himself was technically already dead.

The best way to prevent that, said Tyme, was with a zero reflex kill shot. If possible, the men should shoot the VC guards between the eyes, through the mouth, immediately below and behind the ear or where the back of the neck met the base of the skull. Any of those shots would cut the brain stem connection to the spinal column and kill the enemy soldier with no chance that he could pull the trigger. The signal to fire would be when Tyme did.

Tyme had barely finished positioning the men when the striker left to guard the trail ran up. He was panting. For a Tai to be out of breath meant he had run very hard indeed.

"Sergeant Boom-Boom, Sergeant Sully, VC come."

"How far?" asked Tyme.

"Four, maybe five, minutes. No more."

"How many prisoners?"

"Look like eighteen, maybe twenty."

"How many guards?"

"Count eight rifles, two SMG."

"Was there any officer with them?"

"If officer, no see. Count no pistol. If officer carry pistol, no can tell from prisoner."

Tyme appreciated the deductive reasoning. "How were they dressed? Could you see that?"

"Think all prisoners wear tiger suits. VC wear black or green."

"Both guerrillas and Main Force, then. How were they dispersed?"

"One VC walk point, maybe fifty meters. Him carry SMG. Other SMG walk behind prisoners. Rifles walk four each side."

"Fine. You did well. Go with Sergeant Smith. He'll tell you what to do."

Tyme turned to Smith. "Sully, you two will have to take out the point man and deal with anyone who manages to slip past us. I'll take the last man in line. I'll break squelch twice on the radio when the point passes me. When you hear me shoot the last man in line, take the point out."

"Got it." Smith and the striker hurried down the trail.

Tyme checked his men's positions one last time, making sure he couldn't spot any of them from the trail. Then he took his own place at the end of the firing line.

It couldn't have been more than three or four minutes before the point man walked past him. Tyme let him go. He pressed the transmit button on the handset of the PRC-10 twice, then switched the unit off. The last thing he wanted was to have Gerber or somebody else try to contact him and tip off the ambush. He raised the M-14 and eased the safety off.

As he waited motionless in the grass looking down the barrel, he could see the heat shimmering up from the front sight and flash suppressor, and for a moment he worried that the VC might see it, too. Then he remembered that it was a mirage effect, a property as much of the viewing angle as the temperature and atmospheric conditions. When he squinted through the rear peep sight, the illusion disappeared.

He felt an involuntary twinge in his shoulder, a reminder of a wound only recently healed, and it brought back painful memories of his own capture and brutal treatment at the hands of a sadistic Main Force Vietcong major named Vo. No matter what happened in the next few minutes, he would not permit these men to be taken away to suffer as he had. If something went wrong and the ambush went awry, if all the prisoners were killed, it would still be better for them than their winding up in a VC prison camp where they would be tortured and dehumanized, reduced to animals dependent upon their captors for survival, which would remain a daily uncertainty. Right or wrong, Tyme believed that with all his heart and soul. That was why his group had to try their best.

The first of the prisoners came into view, and Tyme saw that it was First Lieutenant Bao, the Tai Strike Force commander. It made him feel curiously relieved. He had not dared to hope that his friend, a man he had helped train and had fought alongside on many occasions, had survived the attack on the camp. Beyond Bao he could see two of the LLDB team members, Tran, the Intelligence sergeant, and Tam, one of the medical specialists. He scanned the line of faces briefly but couldn't spot any that looked American. Then it was time to stop sightseeing and concentrate on his target.

As the last man came into view, Tyme noted his weapon, an old French MAT-49. Not the best submachine gun in the world by any means, but it had a certain romantic Foreign Legion flair to it and was still a deadly weapon at close range. Tyme sighted carefully on the man's head, and as the enemy soldier came abreast of his position, the Green Beret sergeant shot him directly through the left ear.

The VC soldier's head exploded in a geyser of red-and-gray chunks, as if it had been a watermelon suddenly dropped from a great height. As he toppled, Tyme put an insurance round into his throat, then swung the M-14 to cover the next closest guard.

The report of Tyme's second shot was lost in a ragged roar as the peaceful jungle trail suddenly erupted in a tempest of muzzle flashes and copper-jacketed bullets. Tyme saw his second target go down before he could fire, the back of the man's skull blown out, leaking pinkish-gray brains onto the trail like some disgusting mass of tapioca pudding. There were a couple of other shots and then silence once more.

"Cease fire!" yelled Tyme. He rose slowly to his feet and went forward, weapon ready, to make sure of the kills and check that the prisoners were okay. A few minutes later Sully Smith and the striker who had gone with him reappeared from around the bend. Smith was carrying a Chicom Type 50.

They freed the prisoners and treated the one wounded, an RF platoon sergeant who had been too close to one of the guards—his shoulder blade had been grazed by a stray round. A couple of the others had wounds, as well, but they had been received defending the camp. Tam took charge of them and changed their dressings, using bandages supplied by Smith and Tyme.

The battle had lasted less than seven seconds. A total of twenty-eight rounds had been fired, all of them by the strikers and the two Americans. There were no VC prisoners.

Tyme stared for a moment at the carnage. Ten men, VC to be sure, but still soldiers like himself, each with part of his head missing. There was a terrible, hellish beauty to the precision of it. He felt both exhilarated and ashamed. No. Not quite ashamed. Embarrassed, perhaps. A little self-consciously he glanced up at Smith, who flashed him a giddy grin.

"Well, Boom-Boom, that's what I call a smashing success," said Smith.

Tyme let out a sigh and shook his head. "No, Sully, only a partial success. No Miss Morrow and no American general. Come on. Let's get back. We've still got a camp to help recapture."

They stripped the bodies of their rifles and ammunition to provide weapons for some of the freed prisoners, then formed the men and moved out. Sergeant Harai walked near the head of the column with Sergeant Tran, who was carrying the MAT-49. If there was any racial prejudice between the two men, they showed no sign of it now. Smith and Tyme walked near the center of the group with Bao and Tam.

They left the VC with the shattered heads where they had fallen.

# 15

## MACV HEADQUARTERS,
## SAIGON

While Gerber was planning the raid and Tyme was performing the rescue of Bao and the others, Lieutenant Colonel Alan Bates was vainly trying to find someone, anyone, who could tell him what in hell was going on.

He'd tried General Crinshaw's office first, but the brigadier was still doing his Judge Crater impersonation. Nobody had seen or heard from him since he'd left his office the morning before.

A visit to General Hull's office hadn't produced any better results. His executive officer was still on R and R, and Hull was still unavailable. The administrative aide assured Bates that the general would be back tomorrow morning. He was very sorry, but he couldn't tell Bates where General Hull could be reached. Bates got the impression that the confounded man knew where Hull was but was under orders not to divulge the information.

Finally, in desperation, he contacted Lieutenant General John A. Heinteges's office. He was informed that General Heinteges was currently up-country observing the direction of Operation Masher but Colonel Bradlow, the general's chief of staff, would be pleased to see Bates at 1400 hours that afternoon.

Bates wasn't sure the colonel would be pleased to see him after he'd heard what Bates had to say. As it turned out, it was Bates who wasn't pleased.

The meeting went fine until Bates tried to explain the purpose of his visit. Then the conversation took on a decidedly icy chill.

"I can assure you, Colonel," Bradlow was saying, "that General Westmoreland is not missing. I spoke with him myself on the telephone not twenty minutes ago."

"He's here in Saigon, then?" asked Bates.

"I didn't say that. I said I had spoken with him on the tele phone. He's quite well and perfectly safe, I assure you."

"Well, where is he, then?" Bates wanted to know.

"I'm sorry, Colonel Bates, but I am not authorized to give out that information."

"Well, then, perhaps you can tell me who is."

"Certainly. No one."

"Christ!" said Bates. "The man is the commander of MACV Somebody's got to know where he is."

"I do know," said Bradlow. "I'm just not authorized to tell you, or anyone else."

"Fine. If General Westmoreland isn't missing, then perhaps you can tell me who is because the VC who are in possession of Camp A-555 right now are holding a general officer as their pris- oner."

"So you said. Do you mind telling me just where this report came from?"

"From Captain MacKenzie K. Gerber, senior advisor at the camp."

"I see. Did you speak with Captain Gerber before the camp fell. or is he still in the camp now?"

"Captain Gerber was not in the camp at the time of the at- tack," said Bates tiredly. "The information was reported to him by Master Sergeant Anthony B. Fetterman after he had con- ducted a reconnaissance of the camp."

"So actually it was this Master Sergeant Fetterman who saw the captured general officer."

"No. He only saw the two helicopters the general flew in with and the mobile field command center he brought along, a mod- ified conex with a lot of communication gear crammed into it."

"It is against MACV regulations to utilize a conex for such purposes," said Bradlow.

"Maybe the general it belongs to didn't realize that," said Bates sourly.

Bradlow ignored the remark. "So, then, this master sergeant did not actually see any general officer, he merely saw the co-nex."

"That's right. But the presence on the camp of a general officer was confirmed by Lieutenant Novak and Sergeant Krung."

"Oh. I see. They're the ones who actually saw the general in the camp being taken prisoner by the Vietcong?"

"Well, not exactly. Neither of them actually saw the man. Lieutenant Novak saw the general's helicopters come in and land shortly after the VC had taken the base, but he didn't personally see the general. Sergeant Krung had escaped the VC dragnet in the camp and was hiding near the helipad when the helicopters landed."

"So it's this Krung who saw him?"

"He couldn't see him because he was hiding in a drainage tube beneath the runway, but he heard him speak, and he heard Major Dung address him as General."

"Dung? Who's he?"

"He's the LLDB executive officer who turned out to be a Vietcong infiltrator."

"Lieutenant Colonel Bates," said Bradlow heavily, "just who in hell are these people? You come to me with some fantastic story about a Special Forces camp being captured by the Vietcong, a mysterious American general whom nobody has seen swooping into the camp like some demented bird of prey and getting himself captured by an ARVN Special Forces lieutenant who turns out to be a Vietcong spy, and a major at that. When I ask you where this Intelligence comes from, you tell me that you got it from a master sergeant, who got it from a lieutenant who was there when the capture occurred, but presumably escaped afterward somehow, who got the information from an indigenous sergeant something or other."

Colonel Bradlow looked as though he was seriously considering throwing Bates bodily from his office. "Do you really expect me to put any credence in such a fabulous story, Colonel?"

"Sir, I know Sergeant Krung, Master Sergeant Fetterman and Captain Gerber personally. I've known Mack Gerber ever since Korea. If they tell me the VC are holding an American general out there, they've got one."

''Colonel, don't you think if we were missing a general officer, we'd know about it?''

''I'm beginning to wonder.''

Bradlow glared at him but said nothing.

''What about the report of the downed Otter with General Westmoreland on board that Brigadier General Crinshaw sent to Captain Gerber.''

''Ah, yes, that. As it turns out, I do have some word for you on that. You can forget about it.''

''What do you mean, I can forget about it?''

''Just that, Colonel Bates. I mean forget it. The missing aircraft is no longer your concern or Captain Gerber's.''

''It's been found, then?''

''Not yet. We expect that it will be shortly. Responsibility for its recovery has been turned over to another agency.''

''What other agency?''

''I'm sorry. I'm not authorized to give you that information.''

''Jesus H. Christ. I don't believe this crap,'' Bates finally exploded.

''Lieutenant Colonel Bates, you would do well to control yourself. Such outbursts of profanity are not appropriate for a United States Army officer and will not be tolerated in this office.''

Bates threw up his hands. ''All right, Colonel. You sit there and tell me my story is fantastic? Well, let me tell you another one. I get a report of an American general being captured by the Vietcong, and I believe it because it comes from men I know and trust. This report says the highest ranking officer in Southeast Asia is now in enemy hands, so I go first to the man who originally initiated the report of such a possibility—General Crinshaw. Only he's gone somewhere and nobody seems to know where. So I check with his XO, who doesn't know anything, including where he's gone. So then I go to my commander, Major General Hull, only he's gone, too, and his XO is supposedly on R and R in Australia. So then I try to check with General Westmoreland himself, the man who's supposed to be missing, and sure enough, he's gone somewhere and nobody can tell me how to get in touch with him. So I ask to speak with his deputy commander, and I get told he's not available, either, but I can talk to you if I like.''

Bates drew a breath but continued before Bradlow could stop him. ''So I'm asking you, Colonel Bradlow, what the hell is this, some kind of plague that affects general officers only? If that isn't Westmoreland out there, just who in the hell have the VC got?"

Bradlow rose and leaned over the desk. "Colonel Bates, for the last time, I'm telling you that I spoke with General Westmoreland only minutes before you entered this office. He is not missing, and to the best of my knowledge, no other general officer is, either. If you want to know who this mystery man is that so many people seem so concerned about but nobody seems to have actually seen, I suggest you go ask the VC since they seem to be in possession of him now, and of one of your camps, I might add."

Bates returned Bradlow's glare.

"Thank you for your advice, Colonel Bradlow. If you'll excuse me, I believe I'll go have Captain Gerber do exactly that."

By the grace of God, Bates somehow remembered to salute before he stomped out of Bradlow's office.

# 16

## THE CAMBODIAN-
## VIETNAM BORDER
## REGION NORTHWEST OF
## CAMP A-555

It was nearly dusk of his second day in the jungle when Major David Rittenour heard the sound of the big helicopter beating the air into submission and began firing flares.

In fact, it was almost exactly twenty-four hours since he'd first heard the lighter helicopter, probably a Huey, come in and land somewhere nearby, then take off again. Later, while still trapped in the wrecked cockpit of the Otter, he'd heard a second helicopter, a flight of several helicopters, in fact. They'd been big ones, probably Chinooks, but they hadn't landed, although they'd stayed in the area for quite a while. It had almost sounded as if they were hovering over the same spot, one after the other, but it didn't really make sense to Rittenour that they'd do that.

This helicopter sounded big, too, but it was a little different somehow from the ones yesterday. As it drew closer, it dawned on him what the difference was. No turbine whine. This one was powered by an internal combustion engine, a big radial from the sound of it.

Just at that moment it wouldn't have mattered to Rittenour if it was powered by a large windup key or a giant rubber band. It was a way of getting out of the jungle, and that was all that mattered to him. He fired flare after flare to attract its attention. As fast as he could reload the tiny launcher, he sent brilliant red balls of fire streaking upward through the trees.

Rittenour knew the day-night flare markers would be useless. The bright orange smoke of the distress markers would be more visible during the daylight than the tiny red flares from the launcher, but the overhead canopy of the trees would tend to trap the smoke and diffuse it close to the ground. Well, close from a helicopter pilot's point of view, anyway. So he stuck with the flares from the Penguin launcher. They were designed to penetrate jungle canopy, provided they didn't encounter a substantial branch on the way up, and they rose several hundred feet, had a brightness in excess of twenty thousand candlepower and didn't burn out until they had almost reached the ground. As fast as he could screw fresh flares into the launcher he fired them until he had exhausted the ten-round bandolier. He was about to start using the flares from Jones's vest when he belatedly remembered that the vest had contained an emergency radio transceiver like his own useless one, and he dug that out instead.

He connected the antenna and battery, switched it on and was stunned to find someone trying to talk to him. They had seen his flares and were coming to get him. If he would stop shooting them off, they'd be overhead in a minute and would appreciate it if he would mark his position with smoke, if possible.

Joyfully Rittenour acknowledged the call. Unwrapping one of the six-inch-long green distress signals from its plastic bag, he pulled the tape over the cap marked Day, 45 Sec. Orange Smoke. Holding the cardboard tube away from his body, he used the coated surface of the end cap to strike the igniter button. The smoke signal popped noisily to life, billowing a thick orange cloud, and he tossed it a short distance away from the aircraft, watching the smoke climb toward the underside of the branches overhead.

When the Piasecki/Vertol HH-21B Shawnee finally hovered above him, Rittenour was so pleased to see it that he didn't even care that it was painted the wrong color. In fact, when the Air Commando pararescue man came down in the sling on the hoist, Rittenour was so delighted to see him that he didn't even pay any attention to the man's Sears and Roebuck camouflage hunting coverall or the Beretta Model 12 submachine gun he was carrying.

The man slipped out of the sling and, holding the Beretta loosely in his hands, walked over to where Rittenour sat in the open doorway of the Otter.

"Are you Captain Jones?" the man called as he approached.

Rittenour shook his head. "Major David Rittenour. Damn, am I glad to see you guys."

"Where is Captain Jones?" the man asked.

Rittenour nodded his head in the direction of the shallow grave beneath the right wing still hanging in the trees.

"He's dead. I buried him over there."

"Where is your passenger?"

"Other side of the aircraft. He's dead, too."

The man walked around the broken fuselage and disappeared. Rittenour could hear him digging up the shallow grave there. After a few minutes he came back around the tail section and walked off toward the detached right wing.

"Hey!" called Rittenour. "How about getting me out of here?"

The man ignored him. Rittenour could see him digging up Jones's body. The thought was nauseating. When the Air Commando had finished uncovering the corpse, he took a walkie-talkie out of his pocket and said something into it.

The rescue sling on the end of the hoist vanished back up among the trees. A minute later it came down again with two five-gallon jerricans tied to it.

The Air Commando untied the cans and took one of them behind the aircraft. A minute later there was a loud whoosh, followed by a crackling sound and the smell of burning flesh.

"Hey! What's going on over there? Just what in hell do you think you're doing?" yelled Rittenour when the man came back into view.

"Following orders, Major," the Air Commando told him. "Just sit tight. I'll be with you in a minute." He walked over to where Jones lay, soaked his body with the rest of the contents of the can and set the corpse on fire.

The man in the camouflage suit stood there for a few minutes, making sure that Jones was burning satisfactorily, then walked back and picked up the other jerrican. He tossed the empty into the plane past Rittenour, then opened the other can and climbed into the wreckage. Methodically he began dousing the interior of the aircraft with kerosene.

"Hey, now!" yelled Rittenour. "Just a goddamned minute here. What the hell do you think you're doing, mister?" Hopping up from the doorway, he struggled to draw the .38 from its holster. "I want some answers, and you're going to tell me what this is all—"

He stopped. The Air Commando had swung up the Beretta to cover him and snapped off the push-button safety.

"Just take it easy, Major. I got no orders to burn you, too. Unless you cause trouble. Now, then, I'll just have that revolver of yours. Nice and slow like. Two fingers only, on the butt. Just put it on the deck there, and step away."

Rittenour looked at the submachine gun, looked at the expression on the man's face and did as he was told.

"All right now, why don't you just pick up your crutch there and hobble out away from the aircraft. Once I've finished what I've got to do here, I'll come back outside and have them send the sling back down again. If you're a good little major, I might even take you with me. Now move."

When it was finished and the Otter, the mystery copilot and the general impersonator were in flames, the Air Commando helped Rittenour into the sling.

"You're not going to tell me what it was all about, are you," said Rittenour as the man slipped the sling around Rittenour's arms. It wasn't really a question. "I'm never going to know what this was all about, or who that man was impersonating General Westmoreland, or why."

The man in the Sears and Roebuck camouflage suit did something amazing. He looked sympathetic.

"I can't tell you, Major. I don't know. My guess is that somebody wanted somebody else to think Westmoreland was somewhere that he wasn't, and now they're covering their tracks. All I know is that my case officer told me to come out here and find whatever was left and make sure nobody else ever found it. The orders didn't cover what to do with survivors because they didn't expect us to find any. You're somebody else's problem now, not mine. Listen, Major, you take my advice. You forget this whole thing ever happened. You forget about those men and that plane. You forget your flight ever took place. Somebody with a lot of juice wants this whole incident forgotten. If you're smart, you will, too. Now up you go. Watch your head getting in."

Above, the hoist whirled away, and Rittenour was lifted slowly from the jungle floor. For a moment he watched the three fires burning below him and the Air Commando standing there in a six-foot clearing, waiting to be picked up. Then he looked up at the doorway of the helicopter.

The man who helped him aboard the Shawnee was dressed in the same civilian camouflage suit and Jones-style hunter's cap as the man below, but there the similarity ended. He wore a revolver in a Western-style holster on a belt with all the cartridge loops showing, and he had an Uzi slung over his back. Quite unlike the man on the ground, he was friendly and talkative.

"Welcome aboard, Major. Careful of the head. How's that leg of yours doing? Looks like you busted it up pretty good. We'll see if we can improve on that splint of yours once I get John up."

He leaned out the doorway to look down as he ran the hoist back out, then glanced back over his shoulder at Rittenour. "How long you been down there, Major?"

"Two days," answered Rittenour.

"Oh. You won't have heard the news, then."

"What news is that?"

"About the Aussies. They're upping the stakes. Going to send a whole bunch more guys over here to help us out."

"The Australians are coming into the war?"

"They've been in. Had a battalion, a logistics company and support troops here since last year. They're going to send a lot more, though. Bunch of battalions, some armored cavalry units, a field artillery unit, the works. Big buildup for the Aussies. They announced it this morning over AFVN. I guess somebody must have finally convinced 'em to quit straddling the fence and give us a real hand."

"That's nice," said Rittenour distractedly. His leg was hurting again.

"How's that again, sir?"

"Nothing," said Rittenour. "I just said that's good news. I'm very tired, that's all." He leaned back and closed his eyes and tried hard to forget.

# 17

## MOC HOA, SPECIAL
## FORCES CAMP B-41 RVN

Gerber stood at the front of the room and looked at the men. They were seated behind the long tables that were used for meals when the briefing room was turned into a mess hall. Normally the premission briefing was scheduled far enough in advance of a mission that a few cans of beer could be passed around, but not this time. As near as Gerber could figure, he had, at the most, five hours before the first of the assault troops landed at his camp.

Gerber glanced at his agenda, notes scribbled on random scraps of paper so that he wouldn't forget anything he needed to mention. He looked up at Fetterman, who sat flanked by Kepler and Henderson. Most of both A-Teams were there, the exception being Sully Smith and Justin Tyme, who were still in the field but now moving toward the west side of the camp. In the back of the room were several helicopter pilots who would be flying the first lift in.

"Okay, let's get started. This is the latest information we have. It's based on some personal observations and various reports. If there are any questions, please hold them till the end."

He turned to where a rough map of the camp had been tacked to the wall. "According to Sergeant Fetterman, the majority of the American prisoners are being held here, in the team house. The reporter, Miss Robin Morrow, is being held in the northeastern corner hootch in the Vietnamese section." Gerber held up a hand to stop the protest. "No, we were not able to ascertain the identity of the men being held, although we do know that one of them is a general officer.''

Gerber moved away from the map on the wall and consulted his notes. ''I'll give you a general view of the mission, and then we'll hit the specifics. First, just prior to dawn, Sully Smith and Justin Tyme and their force will launch a diversionary attack on the west wall designed to freeze the enemy troops in place and draw their attention. Two minutes after that they will cease firing as Huey helicopters land strike teams in various locations. One each to take the command post, the commo bunker, the redoubt and Dung's hootch where Morrow is being held.

''As soon as the helicopters break ground and vacate the area, Sully and Justin will hit the west wall again. This will keep the VC from stripping the wall.

''Now, as the teams hit their targets, taking them out, Smith and Tyme will stop the attack a second time, and a force will land on the runway in CH-47s.'' Gerber glanced at Henderson.

''Coordination has been completed,'' said Henderson. ''We've got three Chinooks coming from Saigon, slated to land here in about thirty minutes. They're ours until noon tomorrow. Colonel Bates arranged for the C-130s for the Mike Force to stand by at Cu Chi.''

''All right,'' said Gerber. ''The assault company will rally on the eastern side of the runway and assault the Vietnamese quarters. Normally, the tactic to clear buildings would be to toss in a grenade and follow it in, but we don't know where all the Vietnamese prisoners are being held. We do know that a large number of them were taken off the camp and have joined Sergeants Smith and Tyme. We'll need to use discretion with the grenades.''

One of Henderson's men asked, ''Didn't Sergeant Fetterman make a recon of that?''

''Tony?'' said Gerber.

Fetterman got to his feet and turned to look at the men behind him. ''Time constraints and a heavy enemy presence restricted my movements. I was lucky to learn where the general and Miss Morrow are being held.''

As Fetterman sat down, Gerber added, ''Not to mention there are quite a few striker hootches on the compound. We have a similar problem with the Tai area. We just don't know where they are being held with any degree of certainty. That complicates the mission.''

Gerber waited, and when no one asked anything else, he continued. ''Again, as soon as the helicopters are out, Tyme and Smith will begin firing again. Now if everything has worked as planned, Sergeant Fetterman will hold the command post and that will allow him to take out the command bunker and the flanking bunkers on the east wall. As Smith and Tyme again break the attack, we'll want the Mike Force to parachute onto the east side of the camp. As the bunkers explode, the men will assault through the opening, sweeping both north and south.

''The group moving to the south will take the Tai hootches. Those heading to the north will take out any VC who happen to be on the north wall.''

Gerber stepped back to the map on the wall. ''Now what we'll want to do is force the VC to retreat to the south. Push them in that direction. We won't block that route of escape but let them have it. There is open ground on the south side of the camp for about five hundred meters. Fast mover support should be on station at dawn and will take out targets of opportunity south of the camp.''

''Since the bunkers are all mined,'' said Kepler, ''when Tony gets the firing controls, why don't we just blow up all the bunkers?''

Gerber smiled. ''A tempting idea, but then we'd have to rebuild everything, not to mention the equipment that we'd destroy. Besides, if the attack works as planned, the VC will abandon most of the bunker line. If we find that we're having to assault too much of it, we'll take them out with the mines.

''Okay, on to specifics. As I've mentioned, Sergeant Fetterman will take one helicopter and one team to assault the command post. Sergeant Bocker will take another and hit the commo bunker. Sam, you'll have to take the men to rescue Miss Morrow.''

''Yes, sir. Shouldn't you do that?''

''No. I'm going to take the team into the redoubt. We'll hit the team house to free the general. T.J., I'll want you with me on that one.''

''Yes, sir. It strikes me that there'll be guards in there and it won't be all that light,'' said Washington.

"Good point. Anyone have a recommendation?"

"Yes, sir," said Kepler. "I've an idea. Comes from one of the Intel reports I just read. We could get one of the weapons men to rig a couple of carbines with flashlights taped to the barrels. Sort of a spotting-type scope."

"That seems a little cumbersome," responded Gerber. "How about a couple of us carrying pistols and flashlights and maybe a backup man with the weapon you recommend?"

"Yes, sir. That would work."

"What about weapons for the guys inside?" asked Fetterman. "The last thing we want to do is leave a bunch of people in the team house protecting them."

"Hell," said Gerber, "they're all soldiers. Granted, most of them are paper pushers who probably haven't touched a weapon in years, but they are soldiers. We'll give them a couple of rifles, let them have anything we pick up off the VC and leave them to their own devices."

Gerber looked around. Then he said, "T.J., once we've taken the team house, you'll have to take the machine gun bunkers covering the entrance to the redoubt. At that time I'll use the tunnel to join Sergeant Fetterman in the command post."

"Sir," said Anderson, "what do I do once Miss Morrow is freed?"

"That we'll have to play by ear. The last thing we'll want is to get a reporter killed. The best course may be for you to hold the hootch and wait for relief."

Gerber turned his attention to Kepler. "Derek, you'll have to bring in the main heliborne assault. Organize the company on the east side of the runway. I'll try to join you there.

"Greg, I'll want you to bring in the Mike Force."

"Captain Gerber," said Henderson, "you're leaving my team out of this."

"Yes, I am. I'm sorry, but this is our camp, and I want us to take it back."

"Seems to me," said Henderson, "that Custer refused an offer of help because he wanted all the glory for the Seventh Cavalry."

Gerber couldn't help smiling. "And he got it, didn't he? Seriously, I think we can handle it. We'll need a reserve here, and if I call for help, then you and your team should bring it in."

"All right," agreed Henderson. "I just wanted to make sure that you had thought this through and weren't excluding us because of some perverse feeling that you had to do it all."

"Not at all," said Gerber. He clapped his hands together once and said, "Anything else?"

"Captain," said one of the Huey pilots, "what's clearance in those areas you want us to land?"

"The only real problem will be in the redoubt, but if you keep to the northern side, you should have sufficient blade clearance. The walls are only five feet high, and there isn't much on top of them. Sitting on the ground, the blades should clear the top of the wall. All other locations should have sufficient distances from the structures that landing will be simple."

"Yes, sir. Is there somewhere we could get an accurate, to scale map of the camp?"

Gerber pointed at Fetterman. "Sergeant Fetterman can answer any questions that you might have of that nature. See him after the briefing."

"Sir," said Kepler, "I hate to bring it up, but in the event the attack fails, what do we do?"

"Sergeant Fetterman will destroy the command bunker on the north wall, along with two or three others, and we will escape and evade to the north. Each man will be on his own at that point. However, I will announce the retreat with a single red star cluster flare."

"Weapons?" asked someone.

"The specific logistics will need to be worked out. Each man will carry his personal weapon. Any special equipment that you need, see the weapons men here." He looked at Henderson.

"Sergeant Brown is my weapons specialist," said Henderson. "And we have a large stock of captured weapons."

"Thank you," said Gerber. "That reminds me. Going in we won't need to take a lot of backup supplies such as C-rations and the like. Each man should carry a canteen of water and a first-aid kit. We don't know what shape the dispensary is going to be in. Of course, you can take anything you feel you need, but we'll either have won or lost quickly, I think, so resupply won't be a problem."

Gerber glanced around the room. The men were grim, sweating and intense. They were professionals who knew their jobs.

Gerber had wanted to know more about the specifics of the helicopter assault but realized that all he had to do was tell the pilots what he wanted and they would arrange anything they felt they needed. All he had to do was tell them where he wanted his force landed and at what time.

It was the same with the other men. Gerber told Bocker that he wanted the commo bunker and Bocker would lead the men to take it back. Gerber didn't have to tell him how to do it. In fact, detailed instructions were of no benefit because, the moment the battle started, the plan would have to change with the fluid nature of the assault.

Fetterman knew how to take the command post and knew that he couldn't drop grenades into it. He wanted the firing controls for the charges planted around the camp intact, and if he started throwing grenades around, he would ruin them.

Novak would be able to handle the parachute jump. Gerber was sure that Henderson had trained his Mike Force well enough that they would follow any American officer. All Novak had to do was get them on the ground and point them in the right direction. Since no one was sure what the direction might be by the time Novak was inbound, he would have to determine it.

All in all, it was a good group of men, well trained and well prepared. They knew their jobs, and the only thing that would prevent them from doing those jobs was a bullet in the head. Gerber wanted to buy each of them a drink but didn't want alcohol clouding anyone's judgment. Besides, when the fighting was over, he would personally buy every man a beer.

Gerber checked his watch. "I make it twelve thirty-five. We'll meet here at three-thirty to discuss anything that might jeopardize the mission. Any specific questions, see the man who will have the answers. That means if it's a flying question, talk to the pilots, and if it's a weapons question, talk to Brown, and so on. Anything else?"

When no one spoke, Gerber said, "Okay, that's it." He watched the men leave the room.

As he moved forward to exit, one of the Huey pilots stepped up to him and said, "Sir, you do understand that we'll have to move the Mike Force to Cu Chi for loading. Runway's too short here for loaded 130s."

"Shit!"

"Yes, sir," said the pilot. "Shouldn't be too big of a problem. We ought to be able to move the Mike Force to Cu Chi in about forty minutes once the Shit hooks arrive."

"That's going to be a real coordination nightmare," said Gerber.

"Yes, sir. Can't be helped."

As the pilot ran off, Fetterman moved in. "Strikes me, Captain, that the VC tried to take the camp with a reinforced regiment once and they failed. We've barely got a battalion here and we're going to take it?"

"Tony, you old pessimist. The VC were trying to take the camp from us. We knew it. We built it. Now they're trying to hold something that they don't know. Besides, we have vertical envelopment. In other words, we can put men into the camp by leaping over the wall. That was something they couldn't do and that gives us the advantage."

"Yes, sir. Advantage."

BY THREE IN THE MORNING, Gerber knew it would work. He had been around talking to each of the men who was organizing the various parts of the mission. Brown had shown him the jury-rigged M-2 carbines. There was a flashlight taped to the left side of the barrel. He had test fired it on the range and found that the bullets struck at the right edge of the light.

"You put the light on the guy's right shoulder if he's facing you, and the rounds should hit him close to dead center," Brown said.

Gerber nodded and moved on. Bocker had been in radio contact with Smith and Tyme and had spent nearly twenty minutes explaining the mission to them using a variety of code words and double-talk. When he was finished, Bocker looked as if he had run a road race, but he thought that Smith and Tyme understood and doubted that anyone else did. The VC, if they had monitored the transmission, should have been thoroughly confused.

Novak appeared at one point. He was wearing his combat gear and carrying his liberated machine gun. "Captain, we're about ready to leave. I'm going with the Mike Force to Cu Chi."

"Okay, Greg. I'll advise you on the radio when we need you. Your TOT will be nine minutes after the assault starts."

"Understood."

Gerber grinned. "See what happens when you disobey orders? I asked you not to lose the camp, and now we have to go through all this nonsense to get it back."

"Yes, sir. I'm sorry," he said in mock seriousness.

"Don't sweat it. Hey, and good luck. I'll buy you a beer in the team house a little later."

"Thanks, Captain. Good luck to you." Novak looked as if he wanted to say more but couldn't think of anything. "Good luck," he repeated and then turned, heading for the runway.

Gerber watched the big man trot off into the night. "Good luck," he mumbled under his breath. "We're all going to need it before the day is over."

AT THREE-THIRTY HE HELD the final briefing in Henderson's team house. They went over the plan one last time, checking the details and talking about problems that they thought would arise, working through them for solutions.

Finally there seemed to be nothing else to say. Everyone understood his job and was prepared to do it. The equipment was assembled and ready, and the Vietnamese strikers were on the airfield waiting to board the choppers. The preflights had been finished, and the crew chiefs and door gunners were standing by.

Gerber looked at the men a final time. From face to face. Then he nodded. "Let's do it. Be careful and good luck."

As the men got to their feet, he called to them, "I'll buy the beer in the team house at noon. Won't be cold, but then neither will we."

That brought a laugh. The apprehension that Gerber felt seemed to vanish for a moment. How could these men fail when they seemed to be worried about how cold the beer was going to be? He knew exactly how they could fail but pushed the thought from his mind. By noon the camp would be his again.

# 18

## THE FLIGHT LINE
## AT MOC HOA

Gerber walked up the line of Huey helicopters sitting there with their engines shut down and the aircrews waiting in the backs. The loads for each of the choppers had been designated, and the men of that load had stacked their equipment, mainly weapons, spare ammo and first-aid kits, by their choppers. This airlift wasn't like a normal one into the field where the enemy might be lurking. This was an actual assault on an enemy-held camp. It was the first time it had been tried, as far as Gerber knew.

Fetterman approached, looming out of the dark. He took off his boonie hat and wiped the sweat from his face using the sleeve of his fatigues. "Everyone's ready, Captain."

"Okay, Tony," said Gerber, consulting his watch. "I make it another fifteen or twenty minutes before the attack on the west wall starts."

Fetterman nodded. "This is going to be a strange one, sir."

"Yeah," said Gerber. "I hope I'm not riding into the Sioux with eighty good men."

"So you know," said Fetterman. "Not many Americans remember the Fetterman massacre."

Gerber felt the urge for a cigarette, a cigar, a cup of coffee, anything. Instead, he leaned against the cargo door of one of the Hueys and put a hand on the M-60 machine gun mounted in the crew chief's well. "You've referred to it occasionally. I always wondered if you were related."

"Yes, sir. I'm afraid so. Captain Fetterman, formerly bevet Lieutenant Colonel of the Eighteenth Infantry, was a great-great grandfather. His eighty men didn't last long against the two thousand Sioux."

"I wonder if he felt like I do now. Like we're about to ride down into that trap." As he said that, Gerber realized that it was the second time that night someone had mentioned a massacre. First Custer and then Fetterman.

Fetterman leaned his weapon against the helicopter next to Gerber. He crouched and looked up. "I doubt it. From everything I have ever read, Captain Fetterman was sure that he was going to beat the Sioux. Never considered the possibility that the Indians might know what they were doing." Fetterman grinned, his teeth nearly glowing in the dark. "Besides, he didn't have artillery support, air support and nearly a thousand reinforcements that would be landing within ten minutes of the first attack."

"No, I guess he didn't." He started as the running lights on the helicopter snapped on. He glanced up the line and saw that the lights were flashing on most of the choppers. "I guess we had better get going."

"Yes, sir. Good luck."

"Same to you, Tony. Buy you a beer when this is over."

Fetterman grinned again. "I think that's what my great-great grandfather told his sergeant major."

"Thanks for the encouragement." He watched Fetterman walk away, disappearing into the dark that wrapped the airstrip. A moment later he heard someone shout "Clear!" and the turbine of the Huey next to him began to whine. He stepped back to the pile of equipment and crouched with the other men, watching the Huey's blades begin to swing as the engine roared to life.

The crew chief, who had been standing to the left and rear of the helicopter, watching the turbine to make sure that nothing burst into flames, stepped close to Gerber. "You can load now."

Gerber stood, grabbed his gear and watched as the strikers with him did the same. Washington loomed out of the darkness carrying his weapon and his medical bag. Gerber watched him approach and climb on board. Gerber got in after him and then tapped the aircraft commander on the shoulder. The man turned, saw Gerber and then stripped off his helmet.

Gerber unfolded the rough map he had drawn of the compound. Over the noise of the Huey, he yelled, "You know where you're supposed to land?"

The man put a gloved finger on the map, in the center of the redoubt.

"Right. Remember, you got the fire control tower here, which is twenty-five feet high. And you got antennae on the commo bunker that you'll want to avoid."

"Got it, Captain," said the pilot.

"Should be plenty of room to land in the redoubt. Stay to the north side."

"Sergeant Fetterman briefed me on this. We know what to do."

"I know," said Gerber. "Just trying to cover all the bases."

The copilot reached over, touched the AC on the shoulder and pointed to one of the radios. The man turned in his seat and slipped his helmet on.

Gerber moved back to the troop seat, grabbed at the ends of the seat belt there, but then let go of them. The last thing he needed to be doing was trying to unbuckle his seat belt in a hot LZ, and the landing at the camp would be hot. He relaxed slightly as the aircraft came to a hover but tensed again as the nose dropped and they raced along the runway. A moment later they shot into the sky.

Next to him was Washington, looking cool, almost bored. Gerber leaned close, his lips next to Washington's ear, and shouted over the sound of the turbine, popping of the rotor blades and the roar of the wind through the cargo compartment, "You get a chance to test fire that contraption?"

Washington nodded and jacked a round into the chamber of his M-2 carbine. He still looked cool.

The crew chief reached around the transmission and touched Gerber on the shoulder. He pushed his boom mike out of the way and shouted. "We're about five out."

Gerber took the mike for his PRC-10 and said, "Zulu Rover, Zulu Rover, this is Six. It's a go. I say again. It's a go."

On the ground Tyme acknowledged the radio call and handed the handset back to the RTO. He looked out over the sea of elephant grass that spread all the way to the west wall of the camp. He could see it, a couple of lights twinkling there. Kepler couldn't tell what they were because of the distance. It just meant that the

VC and NVA had managed to take the generator intact when they captured the camp. Someone on their side knew how to run it.

Tyme got to his feet and motioned his men up. He glanced right and left at the two ragged lines of Vietnamese strikers. He yelled, "Let's do it," and began to run through the grass, a scream bubbling in his throat. He let it erupt into a shout and then fired from the hip.

They crossed nearly two hundred yards of open ground before the VC saw them. A single shot was fired, and everyone with Tyme fell to the ground. They all opened up then, firing as fast as they could, trying to make the bunker line with their M-1s, M-2s, M-14s and a variety of weapons salvaged from the Second World War and Korea.

"Grenades," ordered Smith.

Two dozen of the strikers replied. Tyme rolled to the left, jammed a round into the grenade launcher that he had slung over his shoulder. He adjusted the sights, guessing at the distance, and fired. He watched the round explode short of the bunkers. It landed among the concertina wire, detonating in a fountain of whitish-yellow sparks that hid the command bunker from him.

At that moment it seemed that the bunker line blew up. There were a dozen explosions along it and a sparkling as the VC soldiers began shooting. Tyme tried to push himself deeper into the ground, suddenly feeling naked. He was lying in the elephant grass, the remains of a short paddy field dike in front of him, but he felt exposed. Felt that every VC could see him, and from the evidence in the camp, they were all shooting at him.

The tracers, many of them ruby colored since the VC were using the camp's weapons, lanced outward at him. At first they were points of light that looked like embers burning through black paper, but they grew until it seemed they were glowing baseballs thrown at his face.

Around him the strikers were shooting back. More ruby tracers flashing into the camp and then bouncing high as they ricocheted, tumbling. The bloopers kept spitting, the rounds detonating all along the line, revealing bunkers in their flashes, outlining them.

Then over the sounds of the shooting and the crash of the M-79s, Tyme heard the pop of rotor blades and knew that the helicopters were close. He turned, searching the sky to the north un-

til he saw a single point of flashing red light that was on the last
chopper in the flight. By staring he could see the running lights
on the rest of the flight as they swooped toward the camp. At what
he thought was the last moment, he shouted, "Cease fire! *Cease
fire!*"

GERBER HAD MOVED FORWARD, kneeling near the radio console
so that he could look out the windshield of the helicopter. He
could see the darkened outline of the camp. The west side spar-
kled and flashed as the enemy returned Smith's and Tyme's fire.
From his vantage point, Gerber could see both sides, each marked
by the muzzle flashes of their weapons. A few green tracers flew
from the camp, bright emerald like the rays from a science fiction
weapon. Red ones streaked back. Hundreds of them, bouncing
across the ground in what seemed to be slow motion.

Suddenly it seemed that the bottom dropped out of the helicopter. Gerber felt himself lifted and reached up as if to keep from
hitting the top of the chopper. He scrambled back to the troop
seat, grabbing at it with his left hand, holding on. Through the
cargo doors he could see the camp rush up at him as the helicopter dived for the ground.

The door gunners held their fire until the camp seemed to
erupt, and then they shot back. Gerber watched the six strands
of the concertina wire flash under him. They crossed the north
bunker line with a roar. They seemed to rise slightly and then
dropped so that Gerber had to look up to see the top of the FCT.
At that moment the chopper broke to the right and turned up on
its side so that Gerber was looking down, out of the cargo compartment door. The aircraft was parallel to the ground, and the
pilot sucked in an armload of pitch, forcing Gerber into the floor
in a gravity stop. Just as it seemed as though the chopper was
going to drop onto its side, the pilot righted it so that the skids
touched the red dirt in the center of the redoubt.

"Get out! Get out! Get out!" shouted the crew chief, his hands
locked on the handles of his M-60 machine gun. He stared into
the brightening of the dawn, looking for targets, afraid to shoot.

Gerber leaped to the ground, a .45 in one hand and a flashlight
in the other. A Tai NCO followed him. It was Krung. Washington and another striker grabbed at the straps of a duffel bag loaded
with spare weapons, dropping it in the dirt.

As soon as the helicopter was empty, the pilot took off, lifting straight up for twenty or thirty feet and then dumping the nose. The chopper dived at the ground picking up speed. Firing broke out, and Gerber saw a couple of tracers flash upward at the helicopter.

But then he could no longer worry about it. He ran for the door of the team house, Krung running right next to him, Washington following to provide cover.

Gerber charged down the steps and hit the side of the hootch, reached out and jerked open the door. He glanced at the Tai and jumped through, hitting the floor with a crash. He yelled "Everyone down!" as he snapped on his light. The beam swept through the room, and Gerber saw a VC trying to grab his AK off the table. Gerber fired once, the round catching the man in the shoulder with a wet smack. As he toppled to the right, Gerber shot him again. The round took off part of the man's chin, spraying blood down his chest.

To the right was a burst of fire and a shriek of pain. Gerber fired at the muzzle flash and heard a body collapse.

There was a noise from the rear of the team house near the bar, and Washington opened fire with his M-2 carbine. There were three distinct shots. Gerber used his flashlight and saw a sandaled foot sticking out. He emptied his pistol into the wood of the bar.

As the man behind it fell, Gerber hit the magazine release and dropped the empty to the floor. He clawed at the pouch on his belt, dragging a fresh one clear. He slammed it into the butt of his pistol and turned.

From the outside there was a wild burst of firing, AK-47 against M-14 and M-2 carbine. Gerber used his flashlight inside the team house. He could see two men sitting in chairs, their hands bound behind them. Ropes around their chests held them upright, although both were stained with blood. One of the men had a third eye in the center of his forehead and a fist-sized hole in the back of his skull where the round had blown out. The other was covered with blood from a couple of holes in his chest. His blank eyes stared upward at the ceiling.

The rest of the prisoners had managed to kick their chairs over. As his light touched one of the men, he bellowed, "Get me out of here."

Gerber recognized Brigadier General Billy Joe Crinshaw.

"Room's clear," said Washington.

Gerber holstered his weapon and pulled his knife. He cut the ropes holding Crinshaw to his chair. He handed the blade to Crinshaw and said, "You free the rest of your men. Washington, get the weapons duffel and toss it down here."

"Captain—" began Crinshaw.

"Sorry, General," said Gerber. "I don't have time to socialize. I've got to take my camp back."

He leaped up the stairs and took the duffel from Washington. He opened it, took one of the M-14s, a bandolier of ammo for it and tossed the rest down. "You men will have to defend yourselves." With that Gerber disappeared out the door.

FETTERMAN'S HELICOPTER CROSSED the wire right behind Gerber's but then broke to the right so that it was over the runway. The aircraft flared, the nose popping up so that it seemed as if the helicopter was going to leap into the sky, but then the skids dropped and it settled to the ground. As it touched down, Fetterman jumped clear, racing past the fire control tower to the command post. He stopped by the door, glanced back to see four strikers following close as the helicopter lifted and climbed out to the east.

From the west side of the camp, Fetterman heard the firing begin again as Smith and Tyme started another fake attack there. As Fetterman turned to look back at the command post, a head poked out the door as if someone wanted to see what was going on. Fetterman put the barrel of his weapon against the man and pulled the trigger. The impact slammed the VC against the sandbags. He dropped to the ground without a sound.

With that Fetterman dived to the floor of the command bunker. He rolled once and came up on a knee, his weapon leveled. There was a flash of movement in the opposite corner, and Fetterman fired a three-round burst. There was a grunt of surprise as the man was thrown into the wall, then slipped to the floor. The only VC in the bunker sat in the corner in a spreading pool of his blood.

"Check the radio equipment," said Fetterman. "I'll see if the control panels are still in place."

"Sure, Sergeant Tony," said one of the strikers.

"Okay." He pointed at another of the strikers. "You watch the steps. Nobody comes down here." He looked at the hole in the wall where the sandbags had concealed the entrance to the tunnel that led back into the redoubt. "We'll have to clear that."

"Yes," said one of the strikers. "I look forward to it."

BOCKER'S HELICOPTER LANDED behind the commo bunker. Bocker and his men jumped from it as the skids touched the dirt; the instant they were off, the airship lifted and spun. It climbed out the way it had come in. There was a sporadic rattling of weapons on the east and north as the VC tried to down the chopper, but it was uncoordinated and poorly aimed.

As Bocker started around the corner of the bunker, someone began shooting at him, the rounds smacking into the sandbags near his face. He dropped to the ground and rolled to the left so that he was pressed against the side of the bunker. He looked back where the strikers with him lay. He snapped his fingers to get their attention and then pointed to the rear, making a circling motion. They were supposed to run around the back of the bunker and then along the other side. That might give them a field of fire against the VC pinning him down.

He looked again, poking his head out. There was a burst of fire as he ducked back. He saw the muzzle flashes. He pulled a grenade from his belt, yanked out the pin and threw the best he could. The Army said to throw it like a baseball, but he had never had to throw a baseball lying on the ground, pinned down by an enemy rifleman.

He dropped his face and closed his eyes, trying to protect his night vision. Dawn was beginning to brighten the eastern sky, but it still wasn't light enough to see well. He needed all the help he could get. There was a shattering explosion.

From the other side of the bunker, he heard an M-14 open fire. Bocker looked around then, but no one shot at him. He heard an AK fire once, caught the muzzle flash and fired himself, aiming at the center of the flash. There was a second when nothing happened, and then he saw the VC topple from his perch near the redoubt.

As that happened, Bocker was on his feet. He ran to the entrance of the commo bunker and slid to a halt. On the other side, facing him, were two of the strikers. Bocker pulled a second grenade and nodded, indicating that they were to do the same. Bocker jerked the pin free, let the spoon fly, hesitated for a second and threw the grenade into the bunker. As he flattened himself against the side, the Vietnamese strikers, one leaning around the other, tossed their grenades into the commo bunker.

Bocker heard one of them hit the planking of the floor, bounce and then explode. It was followed by two quick detonations. There was a crash inside as something collapsed, and smoke boiled out the entrance.

Bocker rubbed a hand across his face and wiped it on the front of his fatigues. He stared at the strikers, nodded and then leaped. With his back against the thick planks that formed the entrance leading down, Bocker entered the bunker, his weapon ready. As he reached the floor, he moved to the right, away from the entrance, until his leg banged against the map table. He crouched there and stared into the blackness. He couldn't see a thing but could taste the dust in his mouth and smell it in the air. There was a scrambling on the floor that he couldn't identify. It didn't sound like a man moving, even one trying to be quiet about it.

Bocker heard the strikers enter the bunker. He pulled his flashlight from his belt and held it at arm's length. He flipped it on, but couldn't see much in the dim red light. There were three men lying on the floor, ragged wet stains near them that Bocker assumed was blood. The red light made it look black.

To the right there was a flash of movement, and Bocker fired at it. He didn't hit it, but he saw it. A huge spider, maybe a foot across with the legs extended. It was trying to duck back into a hole in the corner where the sandbags didn't quite fit. Bocker hadn't known that the things lived in the bunker. He thought he would have to do something about them.

As the strikers moved to check the bodies, Bocker got to his feet. The counter was riddled with shrapnel damage. He couldn't see any of the indicator lights on the radios burning. He stepped behind the counter, found another body and knew the man was dead. Most of his head was missing, the brain turned to a jellied mess that had leaked onto the planks. He kicked the man's SKS away from his outstretched hand.

The commo sergeant then examined the radios and saw that someone had cut the power cables and antenna leads. He figured that it would take him twenty or thirty minutes to repair the damage, if that was all that was wrong with them.

"Okay," said Bocker. "Put the map table across the entrance and keep guard."

ANDERSON'S HELICOPTER BROKE from the rear of the small formation and shot its approach to the end of the runway just north of the spot where a Huey sat tied down. Anderson knelt next to the pilot and pointed through the windshield at the end of the hootches near the north edge of the runway. The pilot nodded, dumped the nose and raced to the side of the Vietnamese compound. He hauled back on the cyclic, dropped the collective to kill the lift and set the chopper on the ground.

Anderson leaped from the cargo compartment, took one running step and jumped. As the helicopter lifted and shot for the south end of the camp, Anderson crashed through the screen door of Dung's hootch. He dodged to the left as two Tai strikers followed him. There was a burst of fire from an M-2 carbine.

Anderson didn't turn. In the glare of a Coleman lantern sitting on the floor, he could see Dung. The man's pants were around his ankles. He wore a khaki shirt that was unbuttoned, but even with that it was obvious that Dung was sexually excited. Anderson glanced out of the corner of his eye. Lying on the floor were two VC Main Force soldiers, and from the collar tabs Anderson knew that they had been officers. Both had died as the Tai striker fired. One was lying facedown, a hole in the middle of his back. The other was lying on his side against the wall, his blood staining the floor.

"Cover the door," Anderson ordered them.

There was a quiet moan that drew Anderson's attention. Morrow was tied naked to the desk. She was leaning across it, one hand bound to the right corner and the other to the left. Her feet were roped to the desk legs. There were bloody welts from her waist to the backs of her knees.

Anderson turned his attention back to Dung, who hadn't moved. He slowly raised his hands in surrender. Anderson could see that he wasn't armed.

He glanced back at Morrow. Her blood had splattered the desk drawers and the floor near her feet. He couldn't tell if she was conscious.

"She was most entertaining," said Dung, misunderstanding Anderson's interest in Morrow.

Again he turned and studied Dung. He had been caught with his pants down and was now trying to talk his way out of it. Outside, Anderson could hear sporadic firing in the camp, suggesting that the others were having some success. From the west was a steady roar as Smith and Tyme and the assault force faked another attack.

Dung began to lower his hands, a smile on his face. "I am your prisoner," he said in perfect English as if he had rehearsed the speech for hours.

Morrow moaned again. A quiet sound that was filled with desperation. A sickening sound because of the helplessness in it. Anderson found it hard to keep his eyes off her. There was something fascinating about the horror of the scene. Something that seemed unreal. Anderson just couldn't believe a man could do that to a woman.

"I quit now," said Dung. "I *chieu hoi.* I become Kit Carson scout. I help you."

The horror of the situation finally got to him. He aimed his M-3 submachine gun at Dung and pulled the trigger. The three rounds caught Dung in the center of his chest, lifted him off his feet and tossed him against the wall. His head punched through the screen, and his back splintered a couple of the boards of the wall. Dung was frozen there for an instant and then fell to the floor. His blood bubbled in his lungs as Dung tried to take a final breath. Anderson fired again, putting half a dozen rounds into Dung's chest and stomach. One of Dung's feet kicked out spasmodically, and he died.

Anderson moved to Morrow. He set his weapon on the floor, jerked his knife from its scabbard and sliced through the rope, holding her left hand in place. He moved around and cut the other, but Morrow didn't react. He leaned close and raised one of her eyelids. Her pupil constricted immediately.

He walked around the desk and cut the rope around her ankles and then gently lifted her shoulders so that she was standing upright. Her eyes opened and she stared at him, but she didn't seem to recognize him. There was a large black bruise on her stomach where it was obvious that she had been punched.

She allowed him to walk her to the rear of the hootch where there was a bamboo sleeping mat on an elevated platform. He helped her kneel, letting her lie facedown. Then he examined the welts. She had been whipped with something that broke the skin easily. There were going to be scars from the beating.

She moaned again and turned her head. "It hurts, Sam," she said.

He was surprised because he hadn't realized that she was conscious enough to recognize him. He leaned close, touching her shoulder, and asked, "Are you badly hurt? Anything vital?"

"I'm sick," she said quietly. "I'm real sick."

Anderson stripped his fatigue jacket off and draped it over her, covering the worst of her wounds. He wasn't sure that it was a good idea, but he couldn't stand the thought of her lying there naked.

"Robin," he said. "Robin. I've got to leave you here. I have to help with the rest of the mission. I'll leave one of the strikers."

She reached out with a hand, groped for him, but gave up. It was too great an effort. "Please," she whispered. "Please."

Outside, he heard the firing die on the west wall. From far away he could hear the heavy beat of helicopter rotors indicating that the CH-47s were inbound with their loads.

# 19

## INSIDE SPECIAL FORCES
## CAMP A-555

Gerber raced from the team house to his own hootch. He found the trapdoor open. He crouched near it and then shone his flashlight down it but saw nothing and heard nothing. He sat on the edge of it and dropped down, landing carefully, but still heard nothing. He began scrambling forward, his weapon probing the darkness ahead of him. Seconds later he came to the command post, the sandbagged wall already collapsed.

As he entered, he heard a muffled explosion from outside, and then he saw Fetterman staring at him.

"Choppers inbound, Captain."

"Good. Team house secured. It wasn't Westmoreland, it was Crinshaw. I didn't take time to find out how he managed to get himself captured."

Fetterman shook his head in disbelief. "You had to rescue him?"

"Sorry. It was too late by the time I realized who it was."

"Guess it couldn't be helped," he said. "I've got the firing controls. We could take out the whole bunker line, Captain. Blow them all."

"I know. There is some merit to the idea, but we wouldn't get all the VC."

"We hold the redoubt?" asked Fetterman.

"Washington and the strikers took the machine gun bunkers without firing a shot. Doesn't seem to be any VC inside it now."

Fetterman nodded gravely.

"Okay, Tony, you stay here with the firing controls." He checked his watch. They had been on the ground for just under five minutes. "I'll go join the strikers coming in by helicopter and direct the assault on the west wall."

"Yes, sir. Once I blow the bunkers, I'll link up with the Mike Force. The firing controls still work. I just used them to knock down the fire control tower."

Gerber took the steps two at a time and crouched in the doorway, looking at the runway. The camp was brightening and the ground was now a dark gray, but he could pick out details. He could see a body lying near the helipad and could hear shooting in the west. It would only be a few minutes now.

As he stared to the north, Gerber could barely make out the shapes of the CH-47 helicopters that were inbound. Lying in front of him was the remains of the fire control tower, dumped by the explosives that Fetterman had triggered. At the northern end of the runway was a single Huey helicopter, probably one of those used by Crinshaw. The other sat in the middle of the helipad. Across the runway and beyond the Vietnamese striker quarters, Gerber could see the flickering light of fires and the hint of smoke. The shooting over there began to taper off as Smith and Tyme again halted their attack.

There was a noise to the right, and Gerber turned, aiming into it. He saw Bocker working his way toward him from the entrance of the commo bunker. Bocker slid to a stop and crouched.

"Radios are out. It'll take thirty minutes to fix them."

"Okay," said Gerber. "Let's help the strikers get on the ground."

The Chinook helicopters were now on their final approach, the roar of the twin turbines filling the air. As Gerber watched, a single line of tracers reached out for them. It was answered by a burst from the lead ship. Then it seemed that the entire west side of the camp erupted. Dozens, hundreds, of tracers lanced upward at the helicopters. The door gunners returned fire.

Gerber watched helplessly because there was nothing he could do about it. He couldn't see where the VC were hiding. They were screened by the hootches on the opposite side of the runway.

"Captain," shouted Bocker, standing.

Gerber waved him down. "Take it easy. Relax. Let the choppers touch down before you move."

As Bocker dropped back, there was a loud popping near the rear of one of the choppers, and it began to pour smoke. The controlled descent ended as the chopper swung back and forth like a pendulum gone wild. It vibrated in the air and then suddenly plunged the last fifty feet to the ground. It hit, left side low, and the tires exploded like detonating grenades. The Chinook bounced, rocked up on the right side and slowly toppled over like a drunken ox. The rotor blades hit the ground and disintegrated into a cloud of splinters.

The second aircraft landed farther down the runway, and as the wheels touched the PSP, the doors opened and the troops boiled out, sprinting for cover. Firing erupted all around them, some of it from the Vietnamese hootches.

Gerber slapped at Bocker. "That's it! Let's go." He was on his feet then, running around the side of the redoubt and out onto the runway.

Fuel began to bubble from the ruptured tanks on the downed chopper. A door, now on the top of the fuselage, opened, and a man climbed out. He stood and reached down to grab a hand, but before he could do anything for the people inside, a bullet smashed into him, flipping him to the ground.

The third and last of the Chinooks diverted to the left and landed on the open ground on the east side of the runway, using the other two helicopters for protection. Firing increased then, the tracers slamming into the aircraft. Flames began to lick at the downed craft as the ramp opened and the men trapped inside fought to get out.

Gerber slid to a halt, reversed himself and ran back. He pointed at the east side of the runway and shouted, "Rally there! Rally there!"

The two Chinooks lifted as one, leaving the men scrambling for cover. As one of them crossed the wires to the south, it was hit by an RPG-7. There was an explosion in the rear, high near the engines, and the aircraft dropped like a bird that had been shot. It hit the ground and exploded into a mushroom of orange flame and black smoke.

"Jesus," said someone.

At that moment the Chinook on the runway burst into flames. Fire raced along the bottom, spreading on the JP-4 that had spilled on the PSP. The fire continued to the north until the Huey burst into flames from the spilled JP-4. From inside the aircraft there were screams from the trapped men, but there was nothing that could be done for them.

Gerber found Kepler crouched with a group of strikers on the east side of the runway, using the bunkers and hootches there for protection as they fired into the west side of the camp. Gerber waved his men in that direction, trying to get them away from the burning aircraft.

As he neared Kepler and his men, Gerber turned, sprinting across the runway, attacking the Vietnamese quarters. He ordered, "Follow me! Follow me!" He fired from the hip, shooting as fast as he could pull the trigger.

Across the runway, he dived for cover, rolling close to the sandbags around a hootch. He could hear movement inside, but no one seemed to be shooting. Gerber grabbed a grenade, but before he pulled the pin, he realized that he couldn't use it. He had no idea who was in the hootch. It could be strikers taken prisoner by the VC.

Instead, he got to his feet, crouching so that his head wouldn't be visible over the tops of the boards on the hootch. In the growing light of day, he could see shapes in the hootch but couldn't identify them. He reached up, touched the handle on the screen door and jerked it open. In one fluid motion Gerber was through the door and rolling across the floor until he was up against the wall. He spun, his back protected now, and aimed. There were two strikers in the room, tied hand and foot, but no one to guard them.

Gerber used his knife to free them. He leaned close and whispered, "Where are the others?"

One of the men pointed at the rear of the hootch.

"Guards?"

"They run when helicopters land."

Gerber pulled his pistol and handed it to the striker. He gave his knife to the other. "You clear this hootch and then get out to the runway. You move to the east then, but keep down."

He worked his way through the hootch and kicked open the rear door. Outside, he could see a couple of his men pinned down by a deadly fire coming from a hootch. Gerber ducked back, pulled a grenade and then leaped out. He took two running steps and then dived for the sandbags around the hootch, rolling up against them. He shot a glance at his men, who ducked back, waiting for Gerber to act.

Gerber jerked the pin from the grenade and looked up at the door. It was hanging by the top hinge. Gerber let the spoon fly, counted to three and threw the grenade in the door. He could hear men scrambling around, and someone screamed. A moment later the grenade detonated. As the smoke and dust boiled out of the hootch, the men who had been pinned down were up and running. They disappeared inside; there was a flurry of shots and then a momentary silence.

As that happened, Gerber heard the roar of C-130 engines and looked up to see the Mike Force tumbling into the air, hundreds of parachutes blossoming in the morning sky. Tracers began to weave up, spreading through the formation. At that instant it seemed that the eastern bunker line exploded as Fetterman triggered the charges hidden there.

As soon as he had received word that the C-130s were inbound, Fetterman had dragged his control panel to the doorway of the bunker. The machine gun in the command bunker on the east wall opened fire, a line of ruby-colored tracers aimed at the men swinging under the chutes. Fetterman touched a switch, and the bunker exploded into a cloud of dust and debris.

He hit the controls and blew up the bunkers flanking it to provide a huge gap in the defenses for the men of the Mike Force. As he watched, someone began shooting from another of the bunkers. Fetterman smiled, touched the control and watched as the bunker disappeared and the firing died away.

Each time firing began, Fetterman stopped it. Finally he gave up and hit the controls that destroyed the whole east side of the camp. Flaming debris rained down, setting hootches, bunkers and equipment on fire.

Fetterman watched as dazed VC scrambled from the ruined bunkers. One of them, finally clear of the rubble, stood upright, a rifle clutched in one hand. Blood ran from his ears, nose, mouth and eyes. Finally he fell backward and didn't move.

As NOVAK TOUCHED the ground, he hit the quick release on his chest and felt the parachute harness drop away. He crouched, watching as the Mike Force landed all around him. He had seen the bunker line blow up—an inspiring sight as the lines of tracers reached out and then ended in a flash of orange light quickly obscured by dust and smoke. Novak lifted his M-60 over his head so that the strikers could see him. Then, on his feet, he ran forward, through gaps in the wire caused by the explosions. Behind him the Mike Force rallied and ran, firing at the remains of the bunkers, but there seemed to be nothing in return.

Novak ran through the pungi moat and leaped up onto the smoking remains of the command bunker. As the strikers joined him, he shouted, "Half you men head north. The rest follow me."

Novak dropped into the compound and turned south, running past the entrance to the redoubt, past an ammo bunker that was burning and past a couple of mortar pits. He fell to the ground behind a low wall of sandbags and surveyed the camp near him. He saw people moving among the Tai hootches, many of them carrying AK-47s and SKSs. Novak aimed and fired, dropping two of the VC. Others began shooting at him, and he ducked, forcing his face into the dirt as the rounds whined over his head.

Firing erupted behind him. He turned and looked. The Mike Force had formed a skirmish line that was anchored by the bunker line on the east and the mortar pits on the west. The men crouched behind the available cover: sandbagged walls, overturned fifty-five-gallon drums and wreckage of destroyed jeeps and trucks.

The few VC who had been in the open were cut down, their bodies sprawling in the dirt. Firing came from the hootches. It was uncoordinated and ill planned.

Novak returned fire, moved to get up, but firing became heavier. Rounds tore into the ground around him, ripping into the sandbags and lancing overhead. Novak dropped flat again, struggled to grab a grenade. He rolled on his back and then tossed the grenade at the Tai hootches. He heard it explode, but the firing from the enemy didn't taper.

Suddenly there was a roar like a demon right from hell, and a stream of fire engulfed the VC position. Novak looked to the left and saw Fetterman standing in the middle of the skirmish line, a flamethrower strapped to his back. When someone shot at him from another of the hootches, he turned the weapon on that target, sending flames nearly fifty feet into the air.

There was a scramble from the hootches as the VC tried to get clear. In the growing light, they became easy targets for the Mike Force strikers. The firing increased until it was a steady roar. Very little of it was incoming.

Novak got to his feet and ran over to Fetterman.

"Thought you could use a little help, sir," said Fetterman.

"How was that?"

"Goddamned near perfect," said Novak happily.

"Think maybe you better clear the hootches?" asked Fetterman.

Novak nodded and waved his men forward. They avoided the burning structures, kicking in the doors of those behind them. They used grenades and rifles as they entered, sweeping the VC in front of them, driving them back to the south as the plan called for. Around them they could hear the crackling and popping of the fires as they slowly spread from hootch to hootch, helped by a breeze that had sprung up.

ON THE WEST SIDE of the camp, Gerber led a group of strikers in an assault on the command bunker there. They rushed over the open ground, the bullets of the VC defenders whipping around them. Gerber jumped to the rear of the bunker, pulled a grenade and jerked the pin. He leaned around and threw the grenade into the bunker, ducking back as it detonated.

Before he could move, a group of the enemy rushed him. Gerber leaped to his feet, his weapon out in front of him as if there was a bayonet on the end. Two of the strikers tried to shoot into the enemy, but they were there too quickly. Both were pushed to the ground. Gerber heard the grunts and screams of the men, and then he was busy fighting for his life.

He stepped forward to meet the thrust of a Vietcong weapon. With his own rifle he pushed the enemy's to the side and then pulled the trigger. The VC took three rounds in the stomach.

Gerber stepped back, turning to the left so that he could meet the threat there. He shot three of the VC, clubbed a fourth and whirled to the right. He watched one of the strikers smash the butt of his rifle into the face of an enemy, continuing the motion so that he could hit the man next to him.

Gerber dropped to one knee, firing at the VC he could see around him. Some were fleeing for the protection of bunkers on the south wall. Others were trying to gain the hootches that had already been cleared. As they ran toward them, firing erupted, cutting them down.

Now it was the enemy's turn. They had been fighting a defensive action, trying to hold on to what they had captured. Now they were on the offensive, trying to get out before they were killed.

Two dozen Vietcong realized that they would soon die if they didn't get away. They fled from bunkers, running straight for Gerber and his strikers. One of the striker NCOs leaped to the top of a bunker, shouting at his men, and then fell as he was shot again and again. Suddenly all the strikers rushed the VC and became mixed with them, wading in swinging their rifles as if they were baseball bats. There was some shooting, sporadic shots that toppled one of the men.

Gerber followed them, wishing he still had his knife and pistol. He watched a couple of the strikers go down, the VC attacking them. He used his rifle, shooting rapidly, killing the enemy soldiers.

One of the strikers was screaming, the words unintelligible, lost in the sound of the hammering machine guns, the bursting of grenades and the cries of the wounded and dying. Gerber retreated toward one of the hootches and opened fire on another group of running Vietcong.

He emptied his weapon, dropped the magazine clear and slammed another one home. He fired a couple of shots, but the VC had disappeared. Gerber lowered his weapon and looked at the damage. A half-dozen hootches around him were on fire. Most of the bunker line was a smoking ruin. There were weapons and bodies scattered everywhere. But the firing was tapering, slowing as the enemy's coordination disintegrated.

He saw a dozen, maybe more, VC leap from a bunker on the southern side of the west wall and scramble for safety in the rice fields and elephant grass. Gerber knew that Smith and Tyme and the blocking force were there. He waited, listening, and heard no shooting. He stood up and looked just as the blockers opened up. The VC died in a hail of bullets.

Gerber saw that the VC defense of the west had collapsed and the enemy had fled. There were a couple of holdouts, men trapped in the ruins of bunkers or hootches, shooting at anything that moved. The strikers could handle the mop-up.

Gerber turned to the north and ran along the side of a smoking hootch. He came to the body of a striker, felt the throat but could find no pulse. He glanced at the man and saw a massive wound on his right side. There were glints of white bone showing through the holes in the fatigue shirt, and Gerber thought that he could see a bit of the lung.

He stepped around the dead man and kept going until he reached Dung's hootch. He worked his way around it until he could look through the damaged door.

"Coming in," he called.

"Come ahead," said Anderson.

Gerber stepped up and in. He glanced to the right and saw Dung's body lying in a pool of blood. He noticed the two other men and then saw Morrow's form in the corner where she would have the best protection from the shooting and shrapnel.

"How is she?" asked Gerber.

"Little worse for wear. Alive."

"Let's get her to the dispensary," said Gerber.

Anderson got up. "I was waiting for the fighting to die down before I tried to move her." He leaned close to Gerber so that Morrow couldn't hear. "She's been badly beaten. I don't think she's been permanently injured, but she's not going to feel well for a week or so. Captain, she's been raped, too, I think."

Gerber crouched next to her and took one of her hands. He squeezed it. "How you doing, Robin?"

She turned her head and looked at him. She tried to smile but failed. "They hurt me."

"Yeah," said Gerber. "I'm sorry about that. We'll get you over to the dispensary and have Washington give you something."

Anderson jerked a blanket away from the foot of the bamboo mat, folded it lengthwise, and spread it out next to Morrow. He reached down, touched her shoulders and said, "Please shift over."

She tried to move but collapsed onto the bunk. Anderson stepped around and lifted her feet. Gerber, on his knees, moved close and slid his hands under her. On Anderson's word he lifted and pushed. With Morrow's help they got her onto the blanket, lying facedown.

"One of you men help," said Gerber.

As Anderson picked up one end of the blanket, another man grabbed the other end. Gerber held the left side and the last striker took the opposite side. Anderson kicked the door open, and the men hurried out.

They skirted the runway, staying away from the burning aircraft there. They cut across the helipad, dodged between the downed fire control tower and the command bunker. Some of the rubberized sandbags had caught fire from the flaming debris and had spilled their contents to the ground. The wooden frame around the doorway was pouring smoke.

They worked their way around the side of the redoubt toward one of the machine gun bunkers. From inside Washington shouted, "Better hold it, Captain."

The four men moved as one, setting Morrow on the ground next to the redoubt wall. Anderson rolled a fifty-five-gallon drum next to her so that she was somewhat protected.

Washington appeared, crawling around the edge of the bunker. "Sorry to stop you, sir, but we've got a bunch of VC holed up in the dispensary. Don't know where they came from, but we've been taking periodic fire from them."

"Shit!" said Gerber. "I thought we had the redoubt cleared."

"Yes, sir. So did I. But they're in there."

"Any of our people in there with them?"

"No, sir. I think our people are all in the team house. I haven't seen Crinshaw or any of his boys stick their faces out of there."

"Okay," said Gerber. "Get the machine guns turned, and hose down the dispensary. I'll take Anderson to the other bunker, and once we're in place, we'll use grenades."

"But, sir, that'll destroy it. Ruin the medical supplies."

"I don't give a shit. We've got more coming in as soon as we secure the camp, and I'm tired of fucking around." He looked over his shoulder. He could barely see Morrow. "You got one of your medical bags with you?"

"Always, Captain."

"Okay. I want you to take a look at Robin and see if there is anything you can do for her. Dung or one of his cronies whipped her, and her backside is a mess."

"I'll see what I can do." Washington scrambled up the side of the redoubt, leaving deep footprints in the soft earth. He disappeared into the bunker. He reappeared a moment later and worked his way to Morrow. As he crouched over her, the M-60 in the bunker opened fire, riddling the dispensary.

There were a couple of return bursts, the rounds burying themselves in the sandbags of the bunker or the earth of the redoubt. As the hammering from the M-60 continued, joined by M-14s and M-2 carbines, Gerber and Anderson dodged across the entrance of the redoubt. They moved up and over, dropping to the rear of the machine gun bunker there. They entered it and found it empty except for the body of a VC soldier who wore only black shorts. It looked as if all his equipment had been taken from him as he died.

"Shit!" said Gerber. "I hadn't expected them to strip the bunker. How many grenades you got, Cat?"

"Six or seven."

"Here's what we'll do. Try to blow the end off the dispensary, and then use the grenades that we have left to force Charlie out."

"Yes, sir."

"It's going to be tricky, trying to land the grenades so that the sandbags don't absorb the shrapnel and force of the explosion."

A voice from outside called, "Need some help?"

Gerber recognized Fetterman and called back, "What you got?"

"Flamethrower."

"Good Christ, Tony, get up here."

Fetterman slid into view and then dropped into the bunker. He eased his way around because of the tanks strapped to his back. "What's the problem?"

"Just burn the back off the dispensary. The Cat and I'll take care of the rest of it."

"Yes, sir. It'll only take a second." Fetterman moved back to the entrance, braced himself so that he was looking at the rear of the dispensary. The bunkers had been positioned with the assumption that the Americans would hold both the bunkers and the redoubt so that Fetterman had an excellent view of the dispensary.

He pulled the trigger, and the compressed gases forced the napalm stream out. It covered the back of the dispensary. Fetterman shifted and hosed down the side as well. A couple of shots were directed at him from the dispensary, but they missed.

Then a volley slammed into the bunker. It came from Gerber's quarters. Fetterman didn't hesitate. He whirled and pulled the trigger, setting the Captain's hootch on fire. A man sprinted from the door, and the machine gunner in the other bunker cut him down.

A second burst came from Gerber's hootch and then a piercing scream as the flames engulfed the whole building. Apparently a second man had not run.

Gerber remembered the tunnel that connected his hootch with the command post where the firing controls had been. He turned and said, "Tony?"

Fetterman understood the question. "No problem, Captain. I collapsed the tunnel before I vacated that position. If there is anyone in your hootch, they won't get out that way."

At that moment six men burst from the dispensary, their weapons firing. Gerber jammed his rifle out the firing port, against the edge so that he could see back into the redoubt. He fired rapidly. The M-60 in the other bunker opened up, spitting ruby tracers at the men. One by one they fell, sprawling into the dirt.

Gerber then dodged around Fetterman and out the rear of the bunker. He slid down the outside of the redoubt and moved across the entrance to where Washington crouched with Morrow.

"How is she?"

"She'll be okay, Captain. Her injuries, while extremely painful, are not life threatening. I gave her a shot."

"Good." He looked up as Novak appeared beside him.

"Most of the camp is secure, sir," he reported. "Damage has been held to the maximum."

Gerber rubbed a hand over his face. He noticed suddenly that there was very little shooting going on—an occasional round fired, or the explosion of a round cooking off in one of the burning bunkers. Now that the sun was up, he could see the damage to the east side of the camp. It didn't seem that there was a structure left standing that wasn't burning. Black smoke billowed everywhere.

Inside the redoubt the fires in the dispensary and his hootch had spread so that the Americans' quarters were burning, too. The top of the team house was beginning to smoke, indicating that it would go up soon.

"Cat," called Gerber, "get those people out of the team house before they fry."

There was no response, but Gerber saw the big man appear and sprint for the team house. Gerber turned his attention back to Novak. "You got a casualty list yet?"

"No, sir."

"Okay. We're going to have to see if any of Minh's LLDB team survived. Any who might be on our side. They can help sort this out. Minh should be in on the first chopper. Bates arranged to get him recalled from Saigon." Gerber looked around and yelled, "Bocker?"

The commo sergeant appeared. He was carrying an M-2 carbine. The sleeve of his uniform was torn, and there was dirt smeared across his face. There was a ragged stain of blood on the front of his shirt.

"You hurt?"

Bocker looked at the blood and smiled. "Not mine."

"Good. We got any working radios?"

"Take a few minutes more, but I think I can get the uniform up. Providing the antenna isn't down."

"Do what you can. Don't waste a lot of time on it. Worse comes to worst, you can use one of the Prick-10s and see about getting assistance in here."

"Yes, sir."

"Tony?"

"Yes, sir."

"Get on the radio as soon as we find one that's working and get the Air Force to hit the open area south of the camp. They might get someone. And see if you can get Justin and Sully's people in. They don't need to stay out now."

"Yes, sir."

Gerber looked down at Morrow. Then he glanced around the camp and realized that it was gone. Burned. Everything was either burned or in the process of burning. There was no firefighting equipment on the camp. There were some fire extinguishers but nothing to deal with the problem that he had now. All he could do was watch Camp A-555 burn and hope that no one was killed in the fires.

He saw Crinshaw and his men coming across the open area of the redoubt and wanted to duck away but knew it wouldn't work. Crinshaw would find him sooner or later.

As he got close, Crinshaw shouted, "I want my aircraft to get off this camp. I want it now."

Gerber shook his head. He was tempted to tell Crinshaw to take one of those that was burning on the runway but said instead, "Transport will be arranged as soon as the wounded are evacuated." He didn't tell Crinshaw that one of his Hueys had survived the assault. Gerber was going to pull one of the pilots aside and talk to him about flying the most seriously wounded out.

"You just hurry it up, boy," said Crinshaw. "Now where can I wait?"

Gerber looked past the general at the destruction around him. The commo bunker seemed to be in about the best shape. He could see that one of the walls had fallen in and that some of the sandbags were smoking where flaming debris had landed.

Gerber shrugged, "I don't know, General. Take your pick of locations. Now, if you don't mind, I have a camp to worry about."

"Looks like you ain't got shit," said Crinshaw.

"You might be right about that," agreed Gerber, "but there are some things I've got to do." He turned his back on Crinshaw and headed toward the remains of the Tai area. There was a large group of men standing around there in a dazed state, and Gerber wanted to get them spread out. No sense in giving a Charlie with a suicide complex a chance to take a bunch of them with him.

He felt Crinshaw's eyes on his back but didn't care. Too much had happened during the past few hours, and there was too much to do. In an hour or two he would worry about Crinshaw, but right then all he wanted to do was survey the camp, see if he could get a count of the dead and a muster list. Then he would worry about Crinshaw and his staff. But not until then.

# 20

## SPECIAL FORCES
## CAMP A-555

In the hours since the last VC had fled into the elephant grass and fields south of the camp, many of the fires had burned themselves out. The aircraft that had crashed onto the runway were smoking debris no longer recognizable as aircraft. Almost every hootch in the Vietnamese and the Tai sections of the camp had burned. There were walls of sandbags where the hootches had been and piles of black smoking rubble inside them. The bunkers had been destroyed; most of them now resembled craters. The fire control tower lay on its side, the platform on top shattered.

Inside the redoubt the destruction continued. The dispensary was gone. Gerber's hootch and the quarters of the other Americans had burned to the ground. The team house had finally collapsed in on itself. The only thing that had survived was the refrigerator. It was blackened by the fire and the door handle had melted away, but the kerosene engine still ran.

Washington had set up shop on the helipad, figuring he was going to have to evac everyone who was hurt, after the Huey that Crinshaw's staff had arrived in took off for Saigon with wounded. He had used everything that he had carried in his medical bag, everything that he had scrounged from the first-aid kits, and was reduced to giving the wounded water. Dust-Off ships had been in four times, taking the badly wounded out. Morrow had refused to go on any of those ships, claiming that men shot in combat deserved first priority.

Gerber had been by to talk to her once, laughing when she had reminded him that it was his fault. He had told her to stay in the camp where she would be safe. He had laughed because her words cut to the bone. She was absolutely right. It had been his fault. But then the decision had been the correct one. He just didn't argue the point with her.

From there he had split the men into teams to get the camp into some kind of shape. He included the strikers and LLDB members who had come in with Smith and Tyme about an hour earlier. They were working to restring the concertina wire outside the camp and were attempting to get a couple of the key bunkers ready for nightfall.

That finished, Gerber strolled the camp again, surveying the damage. There were bodies lined along the runway. The ones covered by poncho liners belonged to the strikers killed in the attack. Those tumbled into heaps at the south end of the runway belonged to the enemy.

Gerber stopped and stared at the long line of covered bodies. Somehow that made them seem more dead. Lying in the dirt where they fell was one thing, but when the graves registration people came through and picked up the bodies, it somehow made the death more real. More final. Gerber wouldn't have been able to explain it to anyone who asked. It was just something that he felt.

Bocker approached and announced, "Choppers are inbound. I think this is General Hull's party. Asked for permission to land and made it clear that, if it's inconvenient, they'll divert."

"No," said Gerber. "Tell Hull he's welcome. Advise him to shoot to the south end of the runway. I'll get Crinshaw and we'll go meet the aircraft."

Bocker smiled. "Old Billy Joe is hopping mad. Was screaming at me for not getting the radios working sooner so that he could get out. Threatened to have us all sent home or to LBJ."

"I might remind you that Crinshaw is a general officer."

"Yes, sir. There's no accounting for some things."

Now Gerber smiled. "I try to chew you out diplomatically and you turn it around on me."

"Yes, sir. I'll tell General Hull that you're expecting him."

Gerber watched Bocker walk back to the commo bunker. He had set up the radios on the outside of the bunker, using the PRC-10s to complement the single UHF radio he had managed to fix.

Moments later the captain heard the sound of helicopters in the distance and turned to look. He raised a hand to shade his eyes. He hadn't noticed how hot or how bright it was until now. He watched the helicopters approach. He saw Crinshaw leave the commo bunker, three of his flunkies in tow. Crinshaw stopped near the ruin of the fire control tower, glanced into the sky and then pointed out the helicopters. Crinshaw changed direction then, moving rapidly toward Gerber.

"Captain," he shouted. "I'll want to catch a ride back on those choppers. You arrange it."

Gerber looked away and then back at the general. "Not my choppers, sir. You'll have to make your own arrangements." He turned to walk away.

"Captain Gerber," snapped Crinshaw, "I have had about enough of your attitude. I want you to think about that."

Gerber stopped and spun. Behind Crinshaw Gerber could see the smoking ruins that had been his camp. Flanking him were the bodies of the men killed. Crinshaw had swooped in without coordination, had violated a dozen regulations with his actions and now was demanding that he be put on the first available transport. Gerber just couldn't see it.

Before he could speak, the lead aircraft crossed the wire on the northern side of the camp and hovered down the runway, over the wreckage of the crashed helicopters and the remains of Crinshaw's Huey. The rotor wash caught the edges of some of the poncho-wrapped bodies, flipping the covering back, revealing the dead. Gerber looked at them and then at Crinshaw but didn't speak.

The lead ship touched down, and as the pilot rolled off his throttle, General Hull stepped out. Hull, wearing a helmet, clean fatigues and a holstered pistol, surveyed the ruins and then stepped to Gerber.

"What's the situation?"

"Well, General," Gerber began, "as you can see—"

Crinshaw forced himself between Gerber and Hull. "We managed to hold the camp, General," said Crinshaw. "I directed the

fighting in the redoubt and would now like to get back to Saigon.
I have important duties to perform.''

"Yes," said Hull coldly. "I imagine you do. Now why don't you
just shut up and let me talk to Captain Gerber."

"General Hull," protested Crinshaw, "I might remind you that
I, too, am a general officer and I demand—"

"You demand nothing, Brigadier," said Hull, emphasizing the
fact that he outranked Crinshaw. "Now, Captain, what's the
story?"

"If you can spare your helicopters," said Gerber, "I could use
them to take wounded to Dau Tieng and Cu Chi."

"Of course," said Hull. "How's Sergeant Fetterman?"

"Tony is fine. I believe he's working on the east wall right now,
if you care to speak to him."

Hull nodded. "Listen, Mack, I'm here only to learn what you
need to get this camp reestablished. You did a hell of a job taking
it away from the VC with the limited forces you had." He smiled.
"You may have rewritten a couple of pages of military history. I
don't think a combined heliborne-airborne assault has been
tried."

"We did our best."

"Yes. Oh, what happened to the reporter?" asked Hull.

"She'll be okay, I hope. It wasn't very pretty, but Sergeant
Washington tells me there's nothing that won't heal in time. I'd
like to use one of your choppers to get her to Saigon."

Hull noticed that Gerber was glancing around as if looking for
something. Hull said, "I know you have things to do. Go and arrange to get your wounded out. I'll get everything I need from
Tony." He patted Gerber on the shoulder. "Good job. Well
done."

As Hull moved off, Crinshaw fell in beside him, talking rapidly. Hull shot a single glance at Crinshaw and continued to walk,
trying to ignore him.

Gerber grinned at that and then headed back up the runway.
At the helipad he stopped to ask Washington, "How are your patients doing?"

"They'll all be happy to get out of here. What's the word on
that?"

Gerber hitchhiked a thumb over his shoulder. "General Hull
has given us permission to use his. Make the arrangements with

the pilots there. And make sure you tell them which hospital to use."

"Yes, sir. I'll coordinate that."

Gerber moved across the pad to where Morrow lay on her stomach. She was wearing a fatigue shirt, the tails pulled away from her waist, which had been wrapped in loose gauze. There were bloodstains on it. Her lower body was wrapped in the gauze, too, and covered with a towel.

Gerber knelt beside her and took her hand.

"Hi, Mack," she said, turning her head to look at him.

"Hi. We'll have you out of here in a few minutes."

"Oh, that's okay," she said slowly in a singsong voice. "I'm fine now. Sergeant Washington gave me something."

Gerber glanced down at her bloodstained bandages. He felt something grab his stomach and massage it with an icy hand. "Robin, I'm sorry about this. I really am."

"Not your fault. Not your fault."

Gerber rubbed his eyes and tried to think of something to say. Something that could take away the pain she had to feel but didn't know what it would be. Words were just that—words. They couldn't bring back the dead strikers who lined the runway waiting a graves registration party, and they wouldn't help the wounded. He knelt there, looking at her, wondering what he could say.

"I'm coming back," she told him. "In a couple of days, as soon as the danger of infection has passed, I'm coming back."

"Robin, don't take this wrong, but maybe it would be best if you waited a while before you returned. You said that you had a job to do. Maybe you should spend some of your time doing it."

"You let me worry about my job, Gerber."

He smiled. "Yeah, I really should do that. Let me put it this way. We'll need time to rebuild the camp before we'll let tourists, even pretty tourists with a job to do, back in. How's that?"

"Pretty shitty, Gerber," she said. "But you're probably right. I'll look into a couple of the other aspects of the war on a single condition."

"You name it and you got it."

Even through her drug-induced haze, she saw that comment for what it was. "I could ask for the moon."

"You could, but I trust your judgment."

"Then I'll just ask for permission to come back out here when you're ready."

"You got it," said Gerber.

"And maybe a dinner," she added. "A night in Saigon, like the one we had once before."

Washington appeared beside him. "Chopper's ready, Captain. We should load Miss Morrow."

"Come with me, Mack?" she asked.

Washington grabbed one end of the stretcher, and a Vietnamese picked up the other. They began walking toward the helicopter. Gerber was beside them, holding one of Morrow's hands. They reached the chopper and shoved the stretcher in.

Morrow looked up long enough to say, "Just like the last one. Our last night in Saigon."

"Okay," said Gerber.

He, Washington and the striker moved away from the helicopter as the pilot started the engine. At first it was a quiet hum that built quickly to a high-pitched scream. Over that noise Washington shouted, "Sounds like you've got a date in Saigon, Captain."

As the helicopter lifted to a hover and then took off to the south, Gerber said, "Yeah. I guess I do. But not for a while. Not until we get the camp rebuilt."

"So we're going to rebuild it, then?" asked Washington.

Gerber turned and stared at the medical NCO. "Of course we are. If we don't, then the VC have won. They've been trying to throw us out of here for a year. They couldn't do it when we first arrived, and they couldn't do it now. We can't give them the victory in the end."

"But we've rebuilt the camp once already," Washington pointed out, "and repaired damage a dozen times."

"Makes no difference. Besides," said Gerber, "now we can make it better."

"Yes, sir. Better."

He clapped Washington on the shoulder. "Of course, better. And Charlie will think twice about attacking us again."

"But is it really worth it?" asked Washington. "When all is said and done, is it worth the price?"

Gerber caught sight of the men who had died in the fight. At the bodies lined up and waiting. "Yes," he said. "Otherwise, we've betrayed their trust. That makes it worth it."

# GLOSSARY

AC—Aircraft commander. The pilot in charge of an aircraft.

ACTUAL—Actual unit commander, as opposed to the radiotelephone operator (RTO) for that unit.

AFVN—Armed Forces radio and television network in Vietnam. Army PFC Pat Sajak was probably the most memorable of AFVN's DJs with his loud and long, "GOOOOOOOOOOD MORNing, Vietnam!" The spinning Wheel of Fortune gives no clues to his whereabouts today.

AIT—Advanced Individual Training.

AK-47—Selective fire assault rifle used by the NVA and VC. It fired the same ammunition as the SKS carbine, which was used early in the war. The AK-47 replaced it.

AO—Area of Operations.

AO DAI—Long dresslike garment, split up the sides and worn over pants. Rarely seen in the countryside.

APC—Armored personnel carrier.

AP ROUNDS—Armor-piercing ammunition.

ARVN—Army of the Republic of Vietnam. A South Vietnamese Army soldier. Sometimes disparagingly called Marvin Arvin.

ASH AND TRASH—Single ship flights by helicopters taking care of a variety of missions, such as, flying cargo, supplies, mail and people among the various small camps in Vietnam, for anyone who needed aviation support.

BAR—.30-caliber Browning Automatic Rifle. A sort of Second World War vintage squad automatic weapon.

BEAUCOUP—Many. Term derived from the French presence in Vietnam prior to the war.

BISCUIT—C-rations. Combat rations.

BLOOPER—See *M-79.*

BLOWER—See *Horn.*

BODY COUNT—Number of enemy killed, wounded or captured during an operation. Used by Saigon and Washington as a means of measuring the progress of the war.

BOOM-BOOM—Term used by the Vietnamese prostitutes to sell their product.

BOONDOGGLE—Any military operation that hasn't been completely thought out. An operation or idea that is ridiculous.

BOONIE HAT—Soft cap worn by the grunts in the field when they were not wearing a steel pot.

BURP GUN—Any compact submachine gun, especially the 7.62 x 25 mm Soviet PPSh-41 or any of its variants, such as the Yugoslavian M49 and M49/57, the Hungarian M48 and the Chinese Communist Type 50, which was sometimes called a K-50.

BUSHMASTER—Jungle warfare expert or soldier highly skilled in jungle navigation and combat. Also a large deadly snake not common to Vietnam but mighty tasty.

C AND C—Command and Control aircraft that circled overhead to direct combined air and ground operations.

CARIBOU—U.S. Army twin-engine cargo transport plane.

CHINOOK—Army Aviation twin-engine helicopter. A CH-47. Also known to the troops as a Shit hook. Depending upon the model, it could carry thirty to forty-five troops, or up to eight tons of cargo in an external sling.

CHURCH KEY—Beer-can opener used in the days before pop tops.

CLAYMORE—Antipersonnel mine that fires seven hundred and fifty steel balls with a lethal range of fifty meters. It can either be command detonated by electricity or manually detonated by a trip wire or pull device. It was a directional mine, designed to throw its fragments outward in fan-shaped pattern rather than indiscriminately.

CLOSE AIR SUPPORT—Use of airplanes and helicopter gunships to fire on enemy units near friendly troops.

CO—Young unmarried Vietnamese woman. Cô is roughly equivalent to Miss.

CO CONG—Female Vietcong soldier.

DAI UY—ARVN rank equivalent to a U.S. Captain.

DCI—Director, Central Intelligence. The head of the CIA.

DEAD ZONE—Radio dead spot. A location where, because of the geographic or atmospheric conditions, radio communication is difficult or impossible.

DEROS—Date of Estimated Return from Overseas Service. It came to mean going home.

DING—To shoot someone was to ding him.

DINK—Slang applied initially to any Vietnamese. Later it was used for any person of Southeast Asian extraction; usually it was uncomplimentary.

DINKY DAU—Crazy. From the Vietnamese *Dien cai dau*, literally, off the wall.

DONG—Unit of North Vietnamese money, about equal to a U.S. penny.

E and E—Evasion and Escape.

EOD—Explosive Ordnance Disposal. This aspect of demolitions deals with booby-trapping and the disarming of explosive devices.

FAC—Forward Air Controller. U.S. Air Force pilots who flew tiny O-1 and O-2 light observation aircraft, later OV-10, and directed artillery fires and close air support strikes, served as scouts and as aerial radio relay links and conducted psychological warfare operations.

FAST MOVER—Jet aircraft. Also called oil burners. Usually referred to a tactical support aircraft, such as the F-100 or F-4 fighter bombers.

FCT—Fire Control Tower. An elevated structure protected by sandbags, used within a camp to direct mortar, artillery and machine gun fire when the camp was under attack.

FIFTY—Browning .50-caliber heavy machine gun.

FIIGMO—Fuck It, I've Got My Orders. Pronounced fig-mo.

FIRE ARROW—Large wooden arrow with burning gasoline cans affixed to it used in Special Forces camps to mark the direction of enemy troops for close air support at night.

FIVE—Radio call sign for the Executive Officer of a unit.

FNG—Fucking New Guy. Any replacement that had recently joined a unit.

FREEDOM BIRD—Name given to any aircraft that took troops out of Vietnam. Usually referred to the commercial jet flights that took men back to The World after they had completed their tour of duty and were eligible to DEROS.

FRENCH FORT—Distinctive, triangular-shaped fortification built by the hundreds throughout Vietnam by the French.

FUBAR—Fucked Up Beyond All Recognition (or repair).

GARAND—Second World War vintage U.S. rifle, .30-caliber M-1. It was replaced in U.S. services by the M-14. The Garand was issued to Vietnamese troops and Special Forces advisors early in the Vietnam War.

GOOK—Derogatory term used by U.S. troops chiefly to describe the Vietcong enemy. Later it became a racial slur by the American media, although to grunts it remained a generic term for the enemy without any particular prejudice attached to it, much as calling a German a Jerry during the Second World War. See also *Dink*.

GO-TO-HELL RAG—Towel or any large cloth worn around the neck by grunts to absorb perspiration, clean their weapons and dry their hands.

GUARD THE RADIO—Term meaning to stand by in the commo bunker and listen for incoming messages.

GUNSHIP—Armed helicopter or cargo plane equipped with miniguns, used in the close air support role.

HE—High-Explosive ammunition or bombs.

HOOTCH—Almost any shelter, from temporary to long-term.

HORN—Specific radio communications network in Vietnam that used satellites to rebroadcast messages.

HORSE—See *Biscuit.*

HOTEL THREE—Helicopter landing area at Saigon's Tan Son Nhut Airport.

HUEY—UH-1 helicopter.

IN-COUNTRY—American troops operating in South Vietnam were all said to be in-country.

INDIAN COUNTRY—Bush slang for enemy-controlled territory.

INTELLIGENCE—Any information about the enemy's operations, including troop movements, weapons' capabilities, biographies of enemy commanders and general information about terrain features in a specific area of operations that would be useful in planning a mission. Also refers to the branch of the military specifically dealing with the gathering and dissemination of such information. Often abbreviated to Intel.

JP-4—Enhanced kerosene fuel used in military jet aircraft and jet turbine helicopters.

KABAR—Generic term for a type of military combat knife.

KEMCHI—Foul-smelling Korean delicacy made of fermented cabbage.

KHMER SEREI—Cambodian underground political group similar to the KKK (which see) but more reliable and trustworthy.

KIA—Killed In Action. Since the U.S. was not engaged in a declared war in Vietnam, the use of the term KIA was not authorized to refer to U.S. troops. Americans were referred to as KHA, or Killed in Hostile Action, while KIA came to mean enemy dead.

KKK—Khmer Kampuchea Kron, a nominally pro-U.S. Cambodian exile group, which operated as guerrillas against the VC in Cambodia. It was often difficult to manage, sometimes being little more than a group of border bandits.

KLICK—One thousand meters. A kilometer.

LBE—Load-Bearing Equipment. Web gear. A pistol belt and attached shoulder harness assembly for carrying a soldier's individual equipment and ammunition.

LBJ—Long Binh Jail. A military stockade near Saigon.

LEGS—Derogatory term for regular infantry soldiers used by airborne qualified troops. Also known as grunts.

LIMA LIMA—Land line. Refers to telephone communications between two points on the ground.

LLDB—Luc Luong Dac Biet. The South Vietnamese Special Forces. Sometimes disparagingly referred to as the Look Long, Duck Back.

LP—Listening Post. A position outside the perimeter of a camp manned by a few men up to a squad to warn of the approach of enemy troops.

LZ—Landing Zone. An area designated for helicopters to land.

M-14—Standard rifle of the U.S. Army and Marine Corps during the late 1950s and early 1960s. A replacement for the Garand M-1 rifle, it was itself eventually replaced by the M-16. The M-14 fired the 7.62 x 59 mm NATO cartridge, known to civilians as the .308 Winchester.

M-16—Became the standard infantry weapon of the latter part of the Vietnam War. Derived from the excellent AR-15 assault rifle designed by Eugene Stoner of the Armalite Corporation. The rifle underwent a series of modifications by the U.S. Army, which made it both fire at an excessively high rate and prone to both fouling and jamming. This version, properly known as the M-16A1, is the weapon most grunts carried in Vietnam after late 1966, and accounts for the weapon's poor reputation as a combat rifle. The original AR-15 design was an excellent weapon, and the few examples of it that found their way into Vietnam frequently brought high prices on the Little Black Market in Saigon.

M-79—Short-barreled, shoulder-fired weapon launching a 40 mm grenade. The grenades could be high explosive, white phosphorus or canister (sometimes called buckshot rounds). The M-79 was also known as a blooper, bloop tube and elephant gun, the former deriving from the sound made as the grenade left the barrel, the latter because of the diameter of the weapon's bore. It could effectively launch grenades up to about three hundred and fifty meters, and the bursting radius of the grenades was about fifteen meters.

MACV—Military Assistance Command, Vietnam. The headquarters of the U.S. Advisory and assistance effort in Vietnam. MACV (pronounced Mack-Vee) replaced MAAG, the Miliary Assistance Advisory Group, in 1964.

MARS—Military Affiliate Radio System. A link through Signal Corps and Stateside volunteer amateur radio operators allowing a soldier to send messages to The World.

MEDEVAC—Medical Evacuation. Also called Dust-Off. A helicopter used to take the wounded to medical facilities.

MG—Machine gun.

MIA—Missing In Action. Someone who has vanished while in contact with enemy forces.

MOST RICKY TICK—At once. Immediately.

MP—Military Police. They enforced order and escorted convoys.

NCO—Noncommissioned officer. A noncom. A sergeant.

NCOIC—NCO In Charge. The senior NCO in a unit, detachment or patrol.

NDP—Night Defensive Perimeter (or Position). A secure or defensible position for troops to laager in overnight.

NEXT—The man who said it was his turn next to be rotated home. See *Short*.

NHA TRANG—SFHQ was located in this city about halfway up the seacoast of South Vietnam. The term was used interchangeably by Special Forces troopers to mean their headquarters.

NINETEEN—Average age of the U.S. combat soldier in Vietnam, as opposed to twenty-six during the Second World War.

NOUC MAM—Foul-smelling fermented fish sauce used by the Vietnamese.

NVA—North Vietnamese Army. Also any soldier of the NVA.

OD—Olive Drab. A dark brownish-green color.

OP—Observation Post. A location for observing the enemy.

OP—Operation. Any military mission.

OPERATION BOOTSTRAP—Program in the U.S. Army to help men on active duty complete a college education. Men in the program were considered to be still on active duty while attending a college.

P-38—U.S. Army designation for a small, two-piece, hinged can opener supplied with C-rations. One of the few really good items of equipment the Army came up with.

PBR—Pabst Blue Ribbon beer.

PETA-PRIME—Black tarlike substance used to hold down dust during the dry season, applied to roads and runways alike. It had a tendency to melt in the extreme heat of day in Vietnam, turning into a sticky black nightmare that clung to boots, clothing and equipment and frequently ruined them. Pilots considered the stuff to be almost useless.

PETER PILOT—Copilot of a helicopter.

PF STRIKERS—Popular Forces. Similar to RFs but used on a more local level.

POL—Petroleum, Oil and Lubricants. Frequently used to indicate a refueling point for aircraft.

POON TANG—See *Boom-Boom*. The product.

PRC-10—U.S. Army portable radio transceiver used from the Second World War through Vietnam. Eventually replaced by the PRC-25. Both were backpack-type units with a telephone-like handset.

POGUES—Derogatory term used to describe the fat, lazy soldiers who inhabited the rear areas, taking all the best supplies for themselves and leaving the leftovers for the grunts in the field.

PSP—Perforated Steel Plate used instead of concrete paving for runways and roadways.

PULL PITCH—Term used by helicopter pilots that means they are going to take off.

PUNGI STAKE—Sharpened bamboo stake hidden as a booby-trap to penetrate the foot. Sometimes dipped in feces or water buffalo urine to increase the likelihood of infection.

QT—Quick Time. It referred originally to the rate of march of foot soldiers, but came to mean talking to someone on the side in order to expedite matters, rather than going through channels.

R and R—Rest and Relaxation. It came to mean a one-week vacation outside Vietnam, where the soldier was supposed to be able to forget about the war. Shorter, in-country R and R's were also sometimes granted to soldiers who had done a particularly good job. R and R was also known as I and I (Intoxication and Intercourse) by the troops, since these were the two activities most often engaged in when one went on R and R.

RF STRIKERS—Local military forces recruited and employed within a province. Regional Forces were usually used to guard key locations, such as power plants and bridges, and to protect the province political chief.

RINGKNOCKER—Graduate of a military academy, such as West Point. It refers to the ring worn by all graduates.

RON—Remain Overnight.

RP—Rally Point or Rendezvous Point.

RPD—Soviet 7.62 x 39 mm light machine gun.

RTO—Radiotelephone operator. The radioman of a unit.

RULES OF ENGAGEMENT—Rules that told the American troops when they could shoot and when they couldn't. Full Suppression meant they could fire at will. Normal Rules meant they could return fire only when fired upon first by the enemy. Negative Suppression meant they could not fire back even if fired upon.

SAPPER—Soldier trained in the use of explosives. Especially a VC soldier whose primary job was to blow up bunkers and barbed wire entanglements during an attack on a camp.

SCRAMBLED EGGS—Distinctive design on the visor of the cap of a Field Grade or General Officer.

SFHQ—Special Forces Headquarters. In Vietnam, SFHQ was located in Nha Trang.

SHIT HOOK—Another name for the CH-47 Chinook helicopter, so called by troops and pilots because of all the "shit" stirred up by the massive rotors during a landing.

SHORT—Term used by everyone in Vietnam to tell all who would listen to him that his tour was almost over.

SHORT-TIMER—GI who had been in Vietnam for approximately the duration of his tour (usually about a year), and who would be DEROSed or rotated back to The World soon. When the Short-timer's DEROS time was the shortest in the unit, that man was said to be next.

SIX—Radio call sign for the unit commander.

SIX-BY—U.S. Army six-by-six-wheel drive, two-and-a-half ton truck. Also called a deuce and a half.

SIXTY—M-60 General Purpose Machine Gun, caliber 7.62 x 59 mm NATO. Feeding from a disintegrating metal link belt, it had a bipod fixed to the barrel for use as a squad automatic weapon (SAW) and could also be mounted on a tripod, co-axially in a tank turret or on a vehicle pintle mount.

SIXTY—U.S. M-60 Main Battle Tank.

SKS—Soviet-made semiautomatic carbine firing the same round as the AK-47 and eventually replaced by it. It was also used as a generic term to refer to any of the Com-Block or Chicom copies of it.

SMG—Submachine gun.

SOI—Signal Operating Instructions. The booklet that contained the call signs and radio frequencies of the units in Vietnam.

SOP—Standard Operating Procedure.

STEEL POT—Standard U.S. Army helmet used in Vietnam. It consisted of a fiber helmet liner with an outer steel cover.

STRAC—Strategic Army Command or Soldier Trained and Ready Around the Clock.

STORMY WEATHER—Code name for the Cambodian border.

TAI—Ethnic minority group composed of several differing tribes found throughout Southeast Asia and inhabiting chiefly the mountainous regions and the Mekong River delta.

TDY—Temporary Duty.

THREE—Radio call sign of the Operations Officer.

THREE CORPS—Military region around Saigon. Vietnam was divided principally into four Corps areas and a few Special Zones.

TOC—Tactical Operations Center.

TOT—Time On Target or Time Over Target. The former referred to a concentrated artillery bombardment, the latter to the time that an aircraft is supposed to be over a drop zone or bombing target.

TRACK—Any tracked military vehicle. Especially the M-113 APC (Armored Personnel Carrier).

TRUNG SI NHAT—Vietnamese rank equivalent to a U.S. Staff Sergeant.

TWELVE-SEVEN—The Soviet made Degtyarev 12.7 mm heavy machine gun. Also sometimes called a .51-caliber machine gun.

TWO—Radio call sign of the Intelligence Officer.

TWO-OH-ONE (201) FILE—Military records file listing all the qualifications, training, experience and abilities of a soldier. It was passed from unit to unit so that the new commander would have some idea about the capabilities of an incoming soldier.

UHF—Ultra High Frequency long-range radio. Sometimes referred to as the Uniform, short for its phonetic alphabet abbreviation, Uniform Hotel Fox.

VC—The Vietcong. Often called Victor Charlie (from the phonetic alphabet for the letters) or just Charlie.

VIETCONG—Contraction of Vietnam Cong San (Vietnamese Communist Party, established in 1956).

VNAF—South Vietnamese Air Force.

WIA—Wounded In Action.

WILLIE PETE—Also called WP, Willie Peter or smoke rounds. White phosphorus shells or bombs used for marking targets and as antipersonnel weapons. They were very effective due to their psychological effect.

WORLD—The World. Term used to refer to the United States, where supposedly sanity was still in force, unlike Vietnam, which to the grunts (foot soldiers) was clearly dinky dau. Also sometimes called Stateside, or just the States.

XO—Executive Officer of a unit. The assistant commander.

ZAP—To ding, pop caps at or shoot. To kill someone. Also called grease.

ZIPPO—Slang for a flamethrower, derived from the cigarette lighter popular with the troops. Sometimes refers to a search-and-destroy mission.